Stone of Faith
by
Margaret Izard

Stones of Iona

Copyright Notice
This is a work of fiction. Names, characters, places, and incidents are either the product of the author's imagination or are used fictitiously, and any resemblance to actual persons living or dead, business establishments, events, or locales, is entirely coincidental.

Stone of Faith

COPYRIGHT © 2025 by Margaret Izard

All rights reserved. No part of this book may be used or reproduced in any manner whatsoever including the purpose of training artificial intelligence technologies in accordance with Article 4(3) of the Digital Single Market Directive 2019/790, The Wild Rose Press expressly reserves this work from the text and data mining exception. Only brief quotations embodied in critical articles or reviews may be allowed.
Contact Information: info@thewildrosepress.com

Cover Art by *Lisa Dawn MacDonald*

The Wild Rose Press, Inc.
PO Box 708
Adams Basin, NY 14410-0708
Visit us at www.thewildrosepress.com

Publishing History
First Edition, 2025
Trade Paperback ISBN 978-1-5092-6275-5
Digital ISBN 978-1-5092-6276-2

Stones of Iona
Published in the United States of America

Dedication

Thank you to my husband for all his love and support. Thank you to my kids for allowing Mom the time to tell her crazy stories. For the creatives whose minds wander differently, follow your heart and live the dream!

Chapter 1

Of all the jewels in the sea, none shine brighter than the rarest treasure of all—true love.

"The sea fairy swam fast away, safely over the wave and sea. Gave her heart to her human love. Will she ne'er come back to me?" Ewan whispered as dusk's sea breeze ruffled his hair across his face. The poem from Doug's parents was something John MacArthur wrote for his wife, Marie. The phrases haunted Ewan MacDougall, captain of *The Faithful*, his replica galleon ship he used to travel between times, privateering for the good of those in the past.

Ewan grasped the wheel as the familiar tug from the southern wind comforted him. Would he ever find his siren? His true love?

A seagull flew overhead, crying into the wind, a sign they'd just left a port.

The bird's echoing call rang through Ewan's heart when he spoke the last of the first verse of the familiar poem. *Will ye come back to me? Will ye come back to me? Better loved ye canna be. Will ye come back to me?*

Doug MacArthur, his quartermaster and best friend, stepped beside him on the bridge. "Careful, Ewan, that poem always gave me nightmares after my ma told me of the legend of Lorelei."

His friend shivered as his gaze roamed the horizon. "The fairytale of an *alluring enchantress* comes from a legend about a siren who lived on a rock in the Rhine River, Germany. According to the legend, Lorelei would sing a beautiful song to lure sailors to their deaths. The name Lorelei is a combination of two German words—*lore*, meaning to *lure*, and *lei*, meaning *rock*." Doug glanced back at him, "I always feared if ye call out to her, she'd come to take ye away."

Ewan kept his eyes on the horizon. "I always felt connected to the ocean, like I'd find my love at sea." He turned to his longtime friend. "Like a promise of my destiny."

Doug shook himself. "That's it, Captain. The slaves we freed are offloaded with papers in hand, each with a fair share of the prize." He turned and exhaled in the wind. "Back home now, the twentieth century."

Ewan huffed. "Aye, I suppose." When they'd started their time hops to the past, at first, the trips were a game. He literally played pirate, like his sister Evie joked. But after a time, he noticed something shift inside. He could do more than play the part—he could *become* something greater. Traveling to the past wasn't just an adventure. It was an opportunity, a test, a proving ground.

He had always wrestled with what it meant to be a man. Not just in the sense of strength, skill, or daring but in the weight of responsibility, in his depth of purpose. He'd never known where he fit in his own time—too young to be taken seriously, too restless to stay within the lines others had drawn for him. But here, in the past, he carved out his own legacy. The choices he made had consequences, and for the first time, he felt *needed*.

When they kept running into the same captain

hauling slaves for sale and profit, Ewan seized his first real chance to make a difference. He attacked, took the ship hostage, offloaded the enslaved people, and freed them. That moment was more than an act of rebellion—it was his declaration to himself, to the world, that he *could* shape history.

What started as an impulse became a mission. What drifted his way became resolve. He turned opportunity into purpose, then purpose into action. He *would* be the kind of man who made life better for those in need.

And yet…

Though the victories filled him with pride, an emptiness lingered he couldn't name. He had fought, won, and saved lives—but in the quiet moments when there were no battles to fight, no ships to raid, he felt something missing. Was it the thrill of the chase that drove him? The need to prove himself again and again? Or was it because he had never stopped to ask what he truly looked for in all his efforts to become something more? For all his triumphs, the question lingered, unanswered.

His good friend nudged him. "A great haul. From the looks of it, Captain Low planned on targeting more than slaves. There was a large cache of jewels."

Ewan shrugged off the nagging feeling of doubt. "Aye, he mentioned hell would come our way from his sponsor, whomever that may be."

Doug nodded. "Aye, best we get on about it before Low finds us."

"Ship starboard, coming in fast." Both men glanced to the lookout on the crow's nest.

Billy lowered his looking glass and yelled in his teenage squeaking voice. "It's Low! His gun's 'r out,

Cap'n!"

Ewan yelled, "To arms, mates!" He handed off the steering to his first mate, One-eyed Joe. Everyone joked, since he only had one eye, how could he steer the boat? But his tactics in battle were legendary. The entirety of his crew were ghosts, conjured from the past to serve Ewan in his endeavors. They were all spirits his spell called, and the men were happy to serve a MacDougall captain again. All ghosts but he and Doug. They had started a movement to free slaves, and Ewan intended to finish the job.

Doug checked the guns. "Too late, damn it. Why can't we just slip away like the other times."

As Ewan paced toward the railing, he raised his spyglass. "We've plundered him one too many a time, but his thirst for slaves made him a target I could not refuse."

"Come on, man, shift us now. Let's disappear before the fighting begins."

Ewan shrugged off the grip Doug had on his arm. "No, there is something to Low's aggression, and I must know what it is."

He turned, addressing One-eyed Joe. "Play chicken, Joe."

A smirk cracked the sailor's weathered face. "Aye, bring us close, head-on. At the last minute, bring ye alongside, starboard so Fireman Flint can let 'em have it."

Doug jumped from the bridge, heading to the gunners, calling over his shoulder, "One day, Ewan, yer luck will run out, and we'll find ourselves stuck in the past."

He shook his head as he turned, yelling at the lead

gunner. "Fireman, ready the guns, starboard. We're playing chicken again!" The gunners called back, cheering. All made chicken noises, the sounds of *bawk, bawk* brought a smile to Ewan's face.

Flint replied, "Hit the guns! Aye!"

Ewan lifted his spyglass and grinned when Low appeared in the circle. "Too long? Maybe, Doug, but today's not that day."

Low ran up and down the side of his ship, shouting orders. He stopped and lifted a spyglass, eyeing Ewan through the glass. Ewan lifted his left hand and flipped the offending man his middle finger. The British fop yanked his spyglass down and marched away.

Ewan chuckled, muttering to himself, "Good. I've got the prize, and I'll damage him before we hop through the portal." The bloated fool had recently captured a new ship, naming her *The Fancy*. Ewan barked a laugh. *The Fancy* won't be so fancy when he's finished with her.

The ships came head-on at each other. Ewan stood at the bridge, confident in the game he played. The closer the vessels sailed, Low's crew ran around, yelling and pointing at Ewan's craft.

Ewan's crew cheered. His guns sat at the ready but not out to give away which side he planned to pass the other boat. The closer they came, he noticed Low's guns were out on the starboard side, the wrong side to hit *The Faithful* if he intended to pass on Low's port side. The greedy man made this all too easy.

Doug shouted, "She comes!"

When they came closer, Low shouted, "Hard to port!"

Ewan flicked his wrist, signaling One-eyed Joe, who pulled hard on the wheel. *The Faithful* swung wider to their starboard. Ewan's replica galleon, outfitted with a more modern steering system and a wider rudder, turned quicker than the eighteenth-century frigate barreling at them.

When the jibbooms crossed as the ships began to pass each other, Doug yelled, "Guns at the ready!" Their gunner ports opened, and the roar of rolling cannon racks rattled *The Faithful*.

Fireman Flint yelled, "Fire!" *The Faithful*'s guns rumbled when the vessels came side by side. Both ships seemed to pause at the midpoint of battle as multiple booms rocked Ewan's eardrums, suppressing his mind for a millisecond. As splinters of wood flew off Low's ship, both ships crashed into action. The roar of Low's men's howls rang through the air. The ships continued passing while sailors' top side, shot at one another.

Low shouted, and his gun ports opened on his port side. Damn, that was a fast turnaround.

The other captain's voice carried, "Fire." The roar of cannons boomed again, taking out sections of Ewan's ship.

Flint rallied with another answer to the volley. Low's precious ship, *The Fancy*, took another brutal hit.

Through the smoke, Ewan spotted Low, who raised his fist, yelling, "You will regret this! Blackbeard's ghost? Not! I see you clear as day! The warlock will find you!"

Ewan saluted him. "I do hope he does. Tell him his jewels will make a perfect addition to my collection!"

Low followed Ewan's passing with a sharp eye.

Ewan called back, "Why so many? Does yer sponsor need extra adornment to look pretty?"

The cannons drowned out Low's response as Ewan

spied the woman again, standing on the bow alone—the same as she had every time he'd robbed Low. No one else seemed to see her, and the battle raged on without hitting her once.

As the wind tossed her bright red hair, the mane spread around her head. That scent—fresh seaweed and sun-warmed air—washed over him, just as it did every time he saw her. Her cream-colored skin glowed. When their eyes connected, a blush rose on her cheeks. She possessed Fae eyes, a brilliant white-blue that shone on their own. A siren she was, a woman from his dreams. Someone no one else saw but Ewan. She took his breath away each time, touching his soul and making his heart beat harder. Butterflies erupted in his belly.

He whispered, *"Tha thu bòidheach."* *You're beautiful.*

Doug shifted in front of him, breaking the spell. The sounds of the battle rushed back like a freight train.

His friend yelled, "Ewan, ye must shift us before the ship breaks up! We've taken the plunder and already freed the slaves. It's time for Blackbeard's ghost to disappear."

Cannon fire broke apart pieces of his prized ship. Doug was right. It was past time to disappear.

Ewan gathered energy, concentrating on the Chapel in the Woods at Dunstaffnage Castle in the future. He thrust his hand out, opening the portal, and sent a ball of energy through. He called the ship, and all within forward in time.

The world swirled, and the ship tilted as Doug's cheer rang in Ewan's ears, drowning out all sound when the vessel flew through space and time, popping out of the chapel door and landing in the loch beyond

Dunstaffnage Castle, rocking a bit from the force. He and Doug tumbled on the chapel floor, coming to rest, lying on their backs. The crew Ewan knew faded—spirits brought back to serve him who dissipated with his spell. Ewan lay there for a moment, allowing his body and mind to rest. Doug did too, their breaths echoing in the empty nave.

Boot steps sounded, and before Ewan could rise, his da's angry face appeared over him, upside down. "About damn time ye returned! I've waited half a day for ye to get yer pirate ass home!"

His da strode away, calling out when he neared the chapel door, "Both ye sorry mongrels get yer asses into the study! And, Ewan, make that scraggly beard disappear!"

Ewan sat up, waving at his chin, the long hair fading as Doug stood. "Mr. Mac, it's just a bit of fun, that's all!"

Colin Roderick MacDougall stopped, straightened his back, and turned slowly.

His angry countenance was one Ewan rarely witnessed. "Just a bit of fun, Douglas MacArthur? Just a bit of fun?"

His da fisted his hands. "Yer pirate games have gone too far!" He slashed his hand to the side. "The study, now!" The last he bellowed, echoing beyond the chapel.

Ewan stood, knowing his da's wrath did not easily rise to the surface. Even when disciplining his children, except when..."Wait, Da, what has happened?" He and his sister Evie had gotten away with so much as kids and on into adulthood. Most of the time, his da had grunted while applauding their Fae skills. But when a Fae fable showed and a magic Iona Stone needed hunting for the Fae…

His sire pointed a finger at him. "A Fae fable has appeared. That's what's happened!" He strode to Ewan and aimed the finger, hitting Ewan's chest, jabbing when he yelled, "The Stone of Faith!"

Ewan blinked. The Stone of Faith fable had two stories they knew of—both including the Stone of Lust. The one in the *Fae Fable Book* from the Stone of Lust story told of a greedy man and an island sinking with his ma on the land representing *the maiden* and no ending. Then there was his Auntie Ainslie's version told to her by his grandma—the story of a female Viking warrior, like Auntie Ainslie. As children, when Brigid the MacDougall Fae had him and his sister learn all the fables, the Faith stone didn't have a tale of its own.

Ewan tilted his head. "Ainslie's story or the other one of the island and treasure?"

His da folded his arms, then growled his answer. "The island of treasure." He leaned forward till their noses nearly touched. "And the tale is not about yer ma. The fable's one of its own, and the damn thing has an ending!" He turned and strode out of the chapel.

Ewan blinked. "The Stone of Faith has a fable?"

****

The last cannon shot hit true to home. Gunpowder erupted from the hold, forcing her to jump overboard. She'd stayed as long as possible to see her dream man, the captain with the black beard and the haunting sky-blue eyes. Each time she sought him out, her body hummed.

In her human form, swimming at first was a challenge, but now she had little difficulty. As the ship's debris floated past, she dove deeper to avoid the wreckage. Her lungs burned for air and she fought the reflex to suck in water to gain oxygen like her true shape. She pushed upward for the air she so badly needed. Her body shifted and twisted at the madman's calling as she burst to the surface. No, not now!

Sucked through space in a blink, she landed on the cold stone floor before the maniac, the plantation owner with powers beyond her and her people's knowledge. Dripping wet, she eyed him from between her tresses as hate flowed through her.

The day he'd caught her on the docks trying to get closer to the humans flashed in her memory. In the same breath, she cherished and detested that day. Scrambling on the dock, she dragged her tail, but managed to hide behind some sacks, grain if her nose didn't betray her. She had to get closer to the humans. Just once more, to see what they were like.

A force gripped her body, squeezed her till she couldn't draw breath. Above the water, she only had a few moments each time before her lungs needed seawater. Blackness teased the edges of her vision.

Someone whispered in her ear, evil twisted within the sound's cadence. "What have we here?" The invisible force brought her closer till they came nose to nose. His eyes, darker than night, almost hypnotized her. Her father had powers beyond any Selkie Fae, but this man? No, this Fae possessed deeper powers.

The Fae's gaze roamed her body. "A Fae for certain, but one I've never seen."

He didn't know of her people. No one did. Her father said they'd use them all. Abuse their powers and drain each one until none of her kind were left.

She had to keep her people and her kingdom a secret. "I'm one…lost. I search the humans for help."

That was no lie. She loved humans and desired, above all else, to be one.

The Fae's eyes glittered. "So, ye desire to be human. Tell me, fish, if I give ye all ye desire, all ye want in the world, what will ye do for me?"

She closed her eyes, shaking her head as memories flashed of men who followed her deep into the ocean when she sang her song, leading them to their deaths. Her magic only hurt. She'd vowed never to use the power ever again.

His deep chuckle came to her. "I see how it is, sweet one. Such a wonderful ability for one so beautiful." Had he read her mind? She must be careful.

Closing off her mind, she cleared all other thoughts. "I only desire to be with the humans, not to hurt them."

The Fae brought her close again, the invisible grip tightening. "Ye wish to be human?" He leered as he waved a hand, and her legs tingled. They heated and burned. With an open mouth, she tried to scream, but nothing came out. Her body stretched beyond the natural shape, then snapped back when she landed hard on the wooden deck. When she flipped her fin, she tried to find the deck's edge and the water beyond, but her bottom half moved in two pieces. Her eyes traveled fast to her tail; there on the decking were legs—stunningly, pale human legs. She reached down, her fingers gently brushing the skin, then her hands rubbed the burning sensations away. Legs, real human legs! They were so magnificent! She wiggled her toes, marveling at them.

His stern voice spoke over her. "Ye will sing when I tell ye. Distract." He chuckled. "Even kill when I demand it."

The Fae waved his hand, and her legs burned, then

snapped back into a tail. "Ye will do this when I want, and a human ye will be, permanently."

She shivered as the memory faded but took joy that she'd be human one day. How this man possessed so much power was a mystery. His cruelty knew no bounds. She had to keep her people a secret, focusing on him only to keep her knowledge away from his probing mind.

The madman's voice came out gravelly. "My siren from the sea. Ye have done yer service. Deterred the men of the British frigate *The Intrepid* allowing Captain Low to secure the prize." He tsked. "But ye permitted the sailors to live instead of the death promised by the magic of yer voice."

The memory of her song echoed as the music lifted in harmony. The sailors aboard the targeted ship all craved her for the beauty she promised. As commanded, her song tilted into the siren's scream, only promising death to men diving overboard seeking her solace. She'd halted, letting the men rise to the surface while Captain Low ransacked the ship, taking everything his crew could carry. The poor, imprisoned, dark humans were so sad as they moved onto another boat, knowing they would only meet the same miserable fate—slavery. That's why she'd helped her dream man but couldn't think of him in the madman's presence. No, she had to keep him safe too.

She tossed her hair aside as she struggled to sit up, her human legs still something of a challenge. "I will not kill for you or anyone."

The evil Fae slammed his fist on a grand wooden chair resembling a throne he'd set in the main room before the fireplace. The only light in the room now that night settled on the land. "Ye rob me of part of the prize, men writhing in death's grip!" Not even the moonlight sought to brighten the room—a testament to the evil lurking in the one who called this place home.

The madman heaved and shook himself. "Actually, ye gift me with their capture, plunder, and death on the next shipment."

A servant shuffled into the room—a large ebony-skinned man in uniform—another of his slaves. "We've spotted Captain Low's ship. He heads to your port, Master."

The madman stilled, took a deep breath, and let the air out.

She sensed the evil man's mind crawling through Low's and shivered when he spoke. "He's returned empty-handed." His head turned as a frown marred his face. "And his ship is heavily damaged by the ghost again."

The tall black servant bowed. "It will be a while before he makes berth."

The madman rose, tipping his chair over, roaring, "Blackbeard again! The bastard's dead!" His breaths heaved, and he stood staring at the fire. The firelight cast him in red and black shadows as a multitude of expressions crossed his face, all fierce. The servant stood still while she froze on the ground. If he noticed her, a naked, wet woman on the floor, he made no comment.

The evil one hissed over his shoulder, "Have him brought to me as soon as possible."

The servant bowed. "Yes, Milord." The uniformed man turned and stepped from the room. The door's click echoed.

She rose shakily to her knees and stood, hoping this interview was over.

The madman turned to her—his sneer visible. "Just where are ye going?" He flicked his wrist, and power encircled her, pulling her from the floor. "My pet ye must return to yer place." An energy, of the like she'd not seen since he threw her in there the first time, pulled her over to the large glass box. The seawater's scent tickled her nose in invitation making her body tingle in anticipation of returning to her true form. The madman called the container a tank. She called the box a prison.

He breathed, and the energy released her, dumping her into the welcomed seawater. Her form flexed, and her actual shape sprung forth as her body sighed in relief. She took in a deep pull of water, then another while the madman approached the tank, his frame wavering from the water's density.

His voice came to her clearly in her mind, *The Stone of Faith is close. I feel it. Ye will bring it to me.*

Flicking her tail fin she slipped into the small rock cave that served as her temporary home. The hideaway was a gift for completing her first dirty deed for the madman. Holding out was the only option. An entire kingdom depended on secrecy—their location hidden from the madman. If knowledge of their power fell into the wrong hands, the magic would be twisted, the people enslaved or worse—destroyed.

Chapter 2

Ewan strode into Dunstaffnage Castle study only to be brought up short by his ma as she rushed forward, taking him into her arms. "Honey, are you all right?" She rocked back, licking her thumb and rubbing a smudge of dirt from his cheek like when he was a child.

He brushed her off. "Aye, Ma. Just fine." Mid-twenties and she still treated him like a babe.

His da spoke from his desk. "Leave the boy be, Bree. He has a lot to answer for."

Doug snuck in behind Ewan while his da bent over the *Fae Fable Book*. The book that told the fate of each magical Iona Stone. Love, Fear, Hope, and Lust were all retrieved by various family members. The missions seemed to land each MacDougall with their fated love. The most recent, Stone of Doubt, his sister, Evie rescued the gem and found her dream Fae boy, Aodhán.

Doug's arrival did not go unnoticed, and Ewan's da's voice carried when he spoke. "Doug, ye and Ewan…" The last he bellowed. "Sit!" Not one to tempt *Laird Mac's* wrath, Doug picked up his coattails, relocated swiftly to a chair before the desk, and sat obediently like a loyal hound.

Ewan was less eager to please. Regardless of his da's fury, he was more concerned over the *Fae Fable Book*. As children, when he and Evie learned of their Fae powers from the MacDougall Fae, Brigid, she had them memorize each fable. Claiming that the knowledge gave them a fighting chance since their father hadn't known the stones even existed or of his duty as the guardian and all that entailed until forced to by Ewan's grandda's death. His da hadn't learned all the fables—he'd never needed to. But Ewan sensed there was more to this new one than even his sage father could grasp.

He crossed his arms. "Ye mentioned there's a separate Fae fable, Da. What's it say?"

"Oh, Ewan, the story's a tale of loss and love, pirates and a…"

His da growled from behind the desk, "Bree…"

She came up beside Ewan as he gaped at his da.

His ma turned, patting his cheek. "Best listen to your father, son." She stepped toward the couch, leaning on the back. "At least we know what this stone looks like. I've held the jewel once, a blue gem shaped like a diamond."

Ewan continued to stare at his da, waiting.

They stood there, the older, glaring at the younger. Ewan figured this was what he'd look like dealing with his own wayward son. He snorted. His son would likely end up more of a bother than Ewan was to his da, just to curse him.

His sire spoke lowly. "I asked ye once before, and I ask again. Ye will tell me the truth. Have ye seen any Fae in yer pirating adventures…" His da's eyes roamed his outfit and returned to his face with a raised eyebrow. "In the sixteenth century, if yer clothing is correct?"

His ma spoke from the couch. "Eighteenth darling, the coattails and lapels give the date away."

His da's eyes flickered to his ma, but his tone

softened when he spoke. "Eighteenth."

Ewan stood taller. "No, Fae, Da." Evie was the one who'd seen a Fae, and now married to one, her daughter Annie already showed budding Fae powers.

His da's growl brought him out of his musings. "Doug, any Fae?"

Doug shook his head. "No, Laird Mac, just the ghosts manning *The Faithful* brought on by Ewan's spell."

His sire tapped the *Fae Fable Book* as he sat. "An interesting name for yer ship, son."

Ewan stood still. His da said the story was the Stone of Faith. Interesting just turned eerie.

His da always said Grandma Emily told him, *The Fae fables are our bedtime stories. Some tales haunt, and some make ye laugh. Ye'll never understand them until ye are fully grown, and then, my son, they will become yer sole existence.* A chill swept down his spine.

"The fable is nearly identical to the one shown for the Stone of Lust. A man searching for riches and in his greed takes on too much, sinking the island, creating his own demise."

His ma crossed to the desk, resting her hand on his da's shoulder. "But the story has this wonderful, sad part about a Selkie Fae kingdom." She bent over his da's shoulder, reading, "The great Fae race lay hidden for many centuries from the realm of humans, deep beneath the sea. Long ago, the Fae and humans co-existed, living together in harmony. Eventually, as with many of the Fae realm, the greed and selfishness of humans caused the relationship to falter, and the Fae took to their realm in hiding."

His da tried to move the book, but his ma's hand

stopped him while she read on. "One female, Selkie Fae, grew restless. She felt there was more to the human world and often snuck out seeking the humans."

"Once, she came upon a horrific battle between two pirate ships. From the clear ocean depths, she spied the most gorgeous man. He spotted her in the ocean and stopped fighting." The vision hit him as the redheaded woman's face swam before him—her beauty making his breath leave.

He took a deep breath, focusing on what his ma said, "Someone struck him, and he fell into the ocean, sinking toward her. She came to him, and they locked gazes. He captivated her and stole her heart. Soon, the water depths became too much for his human body to take, and he began to choke. The Selkie Fae breathed life into him, saving and returning him to his floundering ship."

She sighed. "Each new moon, his ship would pass over her hidden realm. The female Fae would swim up to see her love."

His ma leaned on his da as his da placed his hands over the text. "Must ye romanticize everything?"

She stood, placing her hands on her hips, mimicking his Scottish accent perfectly. "Must ye romanticize everything?" She barked, "Yes, you brute," using her normal American voice, she continued. "Are you going to tell him about the greedy madman and how he captured the Fae and used her to betray the sailor for revenge?"

His da grunted. "Well, now I don't have to."

Ewan froze. A Selkie Fae, a siren from the sea—the redhead's face flashed again, smiling at him, bringing a flutter in his chest. She was in the fable. Nothing good ever came of the maiden in each tale. The commotion in his chest dropped like a rock to his belly. What was her ending?

He grasped the chair's back. "The ending, what's the ending?" His ma folded her arms and glanced away.

His da took her in his arms. "He'll have to know whether ye believe this to be the boy's fate or not." As she blinked back tears, his ma hiccupped. Ewan's worry for the girl in the past grew.

Ewan gripped the chair harder. "The ending?"

His da's voice came flat. "Same as yer ma's but not. The gods, angry with the greedy man for taking too many riches, destroyed the island. They cast a spell upon her true love, but it went awry."

His ma spoke up, her voice wavering. "The female Fae stepped before the bolt, taking the spell meant for her true love. Much as in my fable," she whispered, "the stone demands its maiden's sacrifice. I cheated the fable, and now fate will take Ewan's love." The room sat suspended in silence.

Doug grumbled from his seat. "Well, that fable is flawed. Ewan has too many women for one love." Ewan glared at his friend, dreaming of all the ways he'd enjoy torturing him.

His sire cleared his throat. "I don't need to hear of yer exploits on the high seas."

Doug sniggered. "It's not in the seas but the taverns in port."

Ewan fisted his hands. "Enough, Doug! We could discuss yer plundering of the maids, but we won't bore them."

His da chuckled while Ewan spoke. "Each fable has an ending and a quote, usually two. What are they?"

As his sire bent over, he read from the book. "The

spell intended for the greedy merchant hit the Selkie Fae and turned her into a seal, thus launching her into purgatory. Leaving her forever separated from her true love."

His ma took up the story. "The human watched in horror as the woman from the sea who'd saved him turned into a seal and slid into the ocean. He cursed the gods and all men, cutting off the head of the merchant, and vowed never to stop sailing the seas till he found his true love."

She took a deep breath. "To this day, his ghost haunts the seas, searching for his true love. No one found the Stone of Faith. Faith is confidence in what we hope for and assurance about what we do not see. Everything is possible for one who believes." His da took her on his lap and she wiped a tear from her eye.

Doug sat forward. "Wait, that's the Selkie seal story ye tell about the seals on Dunstaffnage Point." He turned to Ewan. "The seals on the point are people separated from their true love for doing a bad deed. The fable fits."

Ewan growled. "It does *not* fit. The female Fae in this fable did a good deed, not a bad one."

Doug lifted his finger. "But the ghost…"

He glared at him, sending a mind message. *Shut yer gob!*

Sitting back, Doug folded his arms. Ewan's message clearly delivered. His parents didn't need to know Ewan played at being Blackbeard's ghost, making part of the fable match.

He gripped the back of the chair. "The quotes. Ye haven't gotten to the quotes."

His da spoke as he shifted his ma in his lap. "They are in the story marked separate from the rest of the text."

His finger ran down the left side. "The first is about the greedy merchant. The love of money is the root of all evil: which while some coveted after, they have erred from faith and pierced themselves through with many sorrows."

He skimmed to the right side while his ma sat forward reading. "The second, I recall easily from the story's last line. 'Faith is confidence in what we hope for and assurance about what we do not see. Everything is possible for one who believes.' "

Ewan roared his response, "That's it? No direction? Evie got waves at sea." He paced behind the chair, damn fickle Fae. "Da, ye had the clue of the heart necklace to find the Stone of Love." He gripped his hair. "Shit! Dagda, King of the good Fae, even gave ye the Brooch of Lorne filled with magic Iona Stones to fight the Fae. All I get is faith?"

His da stood, almost dumping his ma on the floor. "Language, Ewan! The brooch was to send Balor, King of the evil Fae, away." Both son and father stood glaring at each other.

Doug spoke from his seat. "Balor's now dead, and his son, Manix, exiled. Good riddance to both. But what do we deal with now?" He glanced between Ewan and his da. "Who's the greedy merchant? Fae or human?"

Ewan stood taller while he spoke to the room but more so to himself. "No matter, this is my fable, my stone to find even if I have nothing to go on."

His ma stood, crossed to Ewan, hugged him, and then held him by the shoulders. "Ewan, you don't have nothing, son. You have faith."

Chapter 3

Manix sat at the long formal dining table with a servant who stood by fanning him. In exile and stuck in the eighteenth century, what he wouldn't give for electricity and air conditioning. While he could provide modern comforts, that would gain too much attention, hidden away on his private island, Waitukura, in the Caribbean—his little paradise. The islanders dubbed this place, *jewel beneath the tall waves*, a literal translation of the native word. He snorted, *jewel* was what this place had, and he wanted, no needed—now.

A servant in a white uniform strode into the room, carrying a platter on her shoulder with a silver dome. She set the plate before him and removed the cover, revealing a large, rare steak. The smell of the barely cooked bloody meat made his stomach growl. He cut into the juicy morsel and took a large bite, savoring the fresh flavor as the servant turned and left the room.

As he chewed, he mulled over his little heaven. He'd done his research before choosing his hideaway from the Fae realm. Waitukura—his little island—had become Manix's prize. He'd landed in port and bought up most of it, claiming all he could by bending the governor's will with mind control, sweetened by bribes of coin and a steady flow of rum to distract the man from Manix's zealous trade in privateering. The sugarcane plantation, a coverup, was very profitable. He smiled after he swallowed.

Time was not on his side—the completion of his task stood between Manix and departure. Finding the Stone of Faith was his final obstacle. He took another large bite of steak as determination settled in. Manix had to finish this soon.

As he chewed, he stared out the window at the mountainous area of the island sporting an active volcano. A natural hot spring flowed through the valley of tropical rainforests, and in the valley's center sat a volcanically heated, steam-covered water mass called Boiling Lake. To the west was a village with colorful timber houses and botanic gardens. Waitukura was truly a beautiful place.

The volcano rumbled in the distance. Manix watched smoke rise from the top. The locals believed the volcanic disruptions was God telling them they had done wrong. He snorted and took another bite of his breakfast. The locals were naive, which suited his purpose. They spoke of great creatures from the depths, the water that surrounded the island. Some claimed these sea beasts protected them, calling them a gift from the gods, while others feared them. Manix chewed and swallowed, wondering if a shark was as tasty as beef. Fish were certainly more plentiful than cows on the island, yet he loved meat.

He yawned, still dragging from his sleepless night after the encounter with his critter. Her legendary powers drew on a man, draining his resolve while he fought her allure. And that was without her song. When she let loose her voice enhanced with her powers, the pull became nearly irresistible, a force both intoxicating and perilous.

Caution was necessary. His pet's abilities had to be wielded to his advantage, yet distance remained crucial. Why she didn't just sing her spell luring him to the deep sea, to what she would assume as his death, was a mystery to him but so be it. Being immortal, he'd not die. Maybe she knew that. Her fear drove his possession of her, and her powers served his purpose, to search the world's gems for a magic Iona Stone, the Stone of Faith.

Manix's head house servant, Monroe, slipped into the room and bowed. He loved owning enslaved humans. Their obedience came under a hard hand, and their fear fed his soul. He smiled as he ate another bite of steak.

Monroe raised his head. "Master, Captain Low has arrived."

Manix chewed and nodded, not bothering with a verbal response when Monroe turned to exit.

The ship captain stumbled past the exiting Monroe. "Lord Skene! What is the meaning of hauling me up here? I spent all night sailing into port on a damaged ship. Then had to secure the vessel and assess the repairs needed." The captain's British accent was something Manix had a hard time getting used to.

After swallowing his steak, he eyed his knife as the captain continued his tirade. "We were set upon. Just after pillaging *The Intrepid*. Blackbeard's ghost ship sailed in, attacked, and took the prize!" The whine in the Brit's voice gave away his weaknesses, yet he had a greedy soul that suited Manix's needs.

Manix flipped the knife, catching the blade by the handle, wondering if his aim was still good. While in exile he kept his Fae abilities hidden, not using them often in front of the humans, trying not to draw attention.

The captain, unaware he tempted fate, continued his

rant. "The damn man took it all."

Flipping the knife again he caught the sharp end perfectly. "My jewels?" He'd learned what had happened when he'd read the man's mind last night. Yet, assuring everyone's complete obedience to himself was something Manix enjoyed.

Captain Low adjusted his coat and repeated, "Gone."

Too easy. Too calm. Manix's lip curled. No tension in the man's voice, no tremble in his spine. This situation reeked of safety—and safety bred defiance. With a flick of his wrist, the knife shot forward, slicing the captain's ear and embedding itself in the painting behind him. The female servant fanning Manix froze. The captain flinched—his fingers grasped his ear. When he pulled them back, they were covered in blood.

"You cut me, drew my blood."

Manix stood and then sauntered past the captain, retrieving his blade. "Be glad that's all I cut." He eyed the painting. "Too bad, I liked that one." Even forced to use manual torture and not magic, he still got a rush of pleasure.

As he strode past the offending captain, he flipped the blade again. "Was there a large gemstone in the cache about the size of yer palm?" He also knew the answer but pressed the captain in case he hid something. The man had a strong desire for money and success. Also hints of a strong will and mind that if asserted might hide details from Manix's mind-reading abilities. He exhaled. Evie MacDougall had proven that theory. He sighed. Manix hadn't thought of her for a day. His heart bled even as his blood boiled. She was his soul mate, stolen by her Fae boy. Anger seethed beneath the surface whenever he thought of her.

The captain pulled out a handkerchief dotting his ear. "No, all small. Smaller than your smallest fingernail." A mental reach slipped into the captain's thoughts, uncovering the truth. The gems had passed through his hands—small yet tempting. The urge to pocket a few without notice pulsed clearly in the man's mind.

As he glanced at his perfectly kept nails, Manix shifted his attention when Monroe, the ever-loyal servant, entered and bowed. "Master, the overseer has the escaped slaves. Begs you to come for the…" He took a deep breath. "Punishment." Monroe's gaze connected with the servant girl fanning him, and they both turned away. *Good, fear feeds obedience.*

He strode past the captain and then stopped so they were face to face. "With me, Captain Low. Come see what happens to people who fail me." People who disappointed him made Manix think of her—Evie. He shook himself. A slave beating was just the diversion he needed.

Captain Low wiped the blood from his hand with his handkerchief as he replied. "I rather think I'll focus on repairing my ship."

Manix stopped holding the knife before the captain's face. "Ye mean *my ship*."

He used mind control, emphasizing his desire when he spoke the following words. "Oh, captain, ye *will come* and *now*."

The captain's eyes bulged, but he nodded. "Yes, Master." Following his command, as he should.

Manix smiled. "I thought so."

He strode out of his house. A castle by standards at

this time, but a large hut more or less compared to twentieth-century homes. As he moved to the yard, a stable boy held two mounts. The captain who lumbered behind him, groaned when he eyed the horses.

Manix chuckled. The captain was a seafaring man, not much for living on solid land. He mounted and held the animal tight, his mind taking control of the beast.

Captain Low easily mounted, but his horse sidestepped, pulling on the reins and giving him some trouble. Manix sighed—he could have flown in his other form. Hell, he could easily shift with the flick of a wrist. But to use Fae powers left a mark, a trail for another Fae to find—not a good idea for a creature hiding. With Captain Low's mount under control, Manix led them toward the slave's jail—a requirement for his wayward, wandering property.

Upon arriving, his overseer, Skully, already had one large male hung by his hands from a tree. Skully sat on his horse, chewing his tobacco. His scarred face spoke of the harsh life he lived and the abuse he took that turned him into the evil, twisted excuse of the human he was today. Manix enjoyed being around a man who understood—torture.

Manix dismounted with ease as Captain Low slid from his horse. The animal shifted only to be stopped by a slave boy set to hold their mounts. Skully chuckled when they approached. The captain kept even with Manix until they stopped. Skully spit at the captain's boots when the captain sneered at the overseer.

His manager nodded to the slave. "Master, the leader of the escapees. I waited for your arrival before I began." Skully turned to the other prisoners gathered in the yard, eyeing each, delivering his implication. The beating was as much a message for them as the punishment was for the one tied to the tree.

Skully's sneer returned to Manix, who only nodded. That was all the permission the man needed. He dismounted by swinging his leg over the front of the saddle, and grabbing his whip, he strode to the slave, delivering a lash so quickly he even impressed Manix. The prisoner screamed. Captain Low tensed and stepped back.

Manix turned, glaring at him. "Ye will attend me *by my side*." The last he delivered with a mind command.

The captain jerked upright, stepping beside him. "Yes, Master."

Skully delivered a series of lashes with a grin. While Manix watched the spectacle, he felt a tiny bit of pity for the man. Reminders of his captivity flashed in his mind—being chained in his cell—the hunger. Another clap of the lash echoed, reminding him of the beatings he endured. Manix shook himself as he focused on the task at hand. He had a message to deliver as well.

As Skully took a break for a drink from his flask, Manix leaned over toward Captain Low. "Those who betray me find only punishment."

The overseer stuffed his flask into his belt, wiped his hand over his mouth, and delivered another hit. The prisoner bellowed in a long howl.

Manix whispered. "Those who fail me will only find pain and suffering."

Captain Low breathed when he turned away. "Blackbeard's ghost is behind every failure." He heaved again. "But he's merely a man. I've seen him up close. Not a ghost at all."

Manix paused—seen him? Who was this man

parading as a ghost?

Extending his power, Manix's mind crawled through the captain's, searching for the memory. The mental picture was, on the surface, easily seen. The face, covered in a black beard, seemed slightly familiar to Manix. He tilted his view one way and back, but he couldn't place who the man was. He had to question his pet. Had she seen the man as well?

Manix stood taller, addressing Captain Low. "Ye will remember my message." He nodded toward the horses. "Leave me. Fix the ship. Report when yer ready to sail."

Captain Low shoved back without looking at the beaten slave. While known for his brutality as a pirate captain, Low was particular in his dealings. His crew followed him anywhere, but he needed to understand. The man in question stopped on his trek down the trails toward the dock. He nodded once, then turned onward to his duty.

Good, he understood Manix's message.

Chapter 4

Low pivoted toward the docks, focused on returning the ship to the open sea, ready for another round of plundering. A brief pause on the trail, then a single nod toward the madman, met with the same in return. No words were needed—failure brought consequences. The message was clear.

Punishment held weight, a principle well understood. Discipline ran deep among the crew, enforced with unwavering consistency. Loyalty thrived under strict adherence to the pirate's articles—prizes divided as promised. That balance of trust and duty forged an unbreakable bond, a code ensuring survival.

Low turned onward to his duty—his ship and his crew.

Soon he came upon his docked prize, *The Fancy*. He admired her long lines and intricate detail when he approached his latest acquisition. She truly was a ship to envy. Holes were blown out on her side, exposing the inner cargo area and a gunner's deck. Low's anger grew, but it eased as his crew hustled about making repairs. He boarded his ship, running his hand along the smooth railing, stopping at the jagged portion. Fury rose again, all centered on the man with the black beard.

His quartermaster, Gibson, approached. "Ship repairs underway, captain."

Low harshly replied, "Good. Estimated time to complete them?"

Gibson sighed. "Hard to say, captain." His gaze traveled the vessel. "We took a hard beating this last time. Blackbeard's ghost, he's a canny one."

Low slammed his hand on the railing. "He's a flesh and blood man, just like the rest of us." He turned, looking out over the bay. "There's no need to fear him."

Gibson cleared his throat. "It's not the ghost the men are afraid of, captain. It's *her*."

Low glared over his shoulder at his quartermaster. He'd been with him since they both stole *The Titleist*, a ship they served on under the royal navy. They'd stranded all who refused to pirate with them on a small island in the main shipping lanes, knowing another ship would rescue the men within a day. Some sought him out after, wanting a share of their profits. Pirating would pay better instead of low British wages. Yet, the men were all superstitious, something Low typically used to his advantage.

"Her?" Low faced his quartermaster, who scanned the area before leading him to the bridge, away from prying ears.

Gibson bent, whispering. "It's her they're all afeared of."

Low sighed, "Her who?" Low knew who his quartermaster spoke of, but he'd tried to keep her presence more of an apparition than the real, live woman she was—great powers and all.

Gibson spit in his hands, clapped them together, turned around three times, and then rubbed his hands on his shirt.

Low groaned—not another superstitious fairy tale.

There were too many Scots on his ship for his liking.

Once finished, his quartermaster whispered, "The Fae from the sea, the siren, come to call for our souls." He sputtered. "Ye didn't see her? Come to sing her song, luring the men to her with her appeal."

The man gripped Low's arms, tightening his grasp as he spoke. "Pulls at a man. She takes ye to the sea promising to meet all yer manly desires, everything ye ever wanted." Gibson yanked on his arm. "After she's hooked ye well, her song changes."

Low pulled back, but his quartermaster's grip was firm. "Her melody, the haunting sound blinds ye, makes yer mind crazy. In yer daze, she takes ye deeper till yer breath runs out, and ye die in the depths of the sea taken by Lorelei, the alluring enchantress from the Rhine River." The last was whispered while he waved his free hand to some imaginary place only he saw.

Low gripped his quartermaster's hand hard as the man's eyes rose fast, meeting his. "No fairy tale will stop my men from taking what is rightfully mine, the prize."

As Low removed the hand from his arm, he shoved his crewmember back, forcing him to almost stumble from the bridge. "You will impart my message to the crew. There is no siren, and Blackbeard is a man, flesh and blood. The next encounter will see him bleed." He straightened his coat. "Ensure the crew understands any more talk of ghosts or sea sirens, and the offender will be dealt with swiftly."

Gibson nodded. "Aye, captain, but ye have more to deal with than that ghost."

Low raised an eyebrow. "And what is that?"

His quartermaster stepped close, whispering. "The men speak of ye breaking the agreement."

Low stepped back. "Unheard of, I've stuck to the articles."

His crewman shook his head. "They saw the cache of jewels. Ye didn't list them as part of the prize. Plunder due to be distributed fairly."

Damn Blackbeard for finding them, thus exposing Low's real assignment. Locate all the jewels on every ship and deliver them to Lord Skene. Low had no clue what jewel the maniac searched for, but the gem was obviously important—significant enough that Lord Skene forsook his part of the prize, giving a share to the crew and taking the larger gems alone. However, as Gibson mentioned in the pirate articles, their fair portion of the prize should be distributed to the crew, including all gemstones found. He needed a way to placate the crew, even if he broke the articles.

Low's eyes met Gibson's when the man spoke. "They threaten mutiny, sir."

He stepped closer to his crewmember, his only confidant. "You will ensure their obedience and distribute what prize I have as the code states. Anyone who doesn't...appreciate their position may find themselves abandoned like the last crew we plundered."

Gibson nodded. "But captain..."

Low put his hand up. "Extra rum rations for the crew. A gold piece for each and tomorrow off for work well done." Low knew how to appease his crew. Reward them now for the hard work to come. An alluring siren from the sea, he huffed. They'd soon forget her after a night and day drunk and wenching in the town tavern. They'd return, forgetting about some illusion seen in the heat of battle.

As for Blackbeard's ghost, he'd get what's coming

to him soon enough.

****

Manix stood a moment longer as his overseer coiled the whip and nodded to the others. They dispersed silently, steps crunching against the packed earth, none daring to meet his eye. Stillness settled, but not peace. It never did.

He should've felt satisfied—discipline delivered, order restored. But instead, his mind drifted again to *her*. Evie MacDougall. That cursed name.

The heat of her presence never left him, even when she wasn't near. It curled under his skin, sharp and unrelenting, a fever he couldn't shake. She haunted him like smoke—never quite within reach, never dissipating.

He clenched his fists, jaw tight. Every time he broke another man, it should've been her watching. It should've been her understanding of what power meant—*his* power, forged from blood and shadow.

She defied *him.*

Yet the fury that stirred when he imagined her resisting. Her denial laced with something darker. Need. Hunger. A claiming far older than his logic could reason with, yet stolen by her damned Fae boy. She didn't just belong to him—*she was his*. The way his soul had snapped to hers the first time he saw her, like two halves forced apart by the cruelty of fate and now magnetized by something ancient and relentless.

That thought—*she is mine*—coiled inside him more surely than any dragon oath. Not because he wanted her but because he *needed* her. Because in a world that defied him, she made sense. Evie MacDougall was the fire that both scorched and soothed his monster. And one day—soon—she would see it. She would bow, not in submission, but in recognition. Not even the gods would stop him from making her understand.

He drifted behind the trees, thinking maybe exposing a magic trail was worth the risk. He had to know if the ghost was a man. He flicked his wrist, called upon his Fae powers, and shifted into his great room in the main house.

The fire burned low. Someone had opened the floor-to-ceiling curtains, allowing light into the room. Manix faced the life-sized tank of seawater. Various sea plants waved within, yet his little critter wasn't visible.

Manix roared. "Show yerself." He couldn't mentally grab her if he couldn't see her and using magic to call her to him drained his energy. The density of the water dulled his powers, and hers prevented much. She was a formidable prisoner. A challenge that teased his senses, his powers.

His pet swam from her cave in the bottom corner of the dwelling. She was a beautiful creature. As her red hair captured the sun's rays, little golden glimmers flickered with the light. Her naked breasts sat perky in the chilled water. The green-purple tail glistened with a fluorescent glow. His gaze rose to hers, and her white-blue eyes captured his. She was purely exquisite.

Manix closed his eyes, shutting off her allure. "The captain of the ship who seized my prize. Ye will show him to me." Denial radiated from her when a barrier slammed shut even as Manix forced his mind forward. A door locked against the intrusion when he snapped his eyes open. Power surged outward, reaching for control. His little fish's lips parted, releasing a sound—rich, melodic, irresistible. Vibrations lured him in, teasing, drawing on the undeniable pull between them. He let loose a roar while another surge of force clamped over her mouth, yet the song persisted, slipping through as her eyes glowed with defiance.

Gripping her with his power, Manix yanked her from her watery sanctuary, dumping her on the floor. The music stopped as she sputtered, breathing air. Her tail morphed into human legs while she panted for breath.

He strode to her, towering over her prone form. "The man?" His critter shook her head. Pushing his power he probed her mind. In her human form, forcing his way into her memories was easier as her powers diminished when not in her given shape.

The capture of *The Intrepid* flashed. The crew offloaded the slaves. Her focus shifted when another ship approached in the distance. Then her spying *him*. The captain with the black beard.

His pet rose on shaky legs. "Don't hurt him." She grasped his shirt, her wet hands sticking to the cloth. Her breasts pressed against his chest, the wet soaking him, her peaks bringing a rise in him.

A voice roared in his mind. *Focus, boy! To the caves now! We must speak.*

Manix ignored his father as his arms came around his little creature. He hadn't had a woman in some time. What would sex with the sea Fae be like? Having the alluring woman who tempted men beyond their sanity excited him. Her song echoed in his mind while he bent to kiss her.

Must all my sons disappoint me? She tempts ye to yer grave.

He stepped back and gripped his little rodent with his powers and flung her into the tank—the splash reaching his face. He wiped off the water as he glared while her form changed back to half fish, half woman, a smirk on her face. Given the opportunity, she would send him to a watery grave. It was good that he held over her what she desperately desired—the promise to make her human forever.

He shook himself, turned to the fireplace, lifted a scone, and the bookshelf swung open to a set of rocky stairs. He'd deal with his pet later.

Manix took the steps two at a time, needing to reach the bottom faster to confront his sire. His father's last statement echoed in his head. *Must all my sons disappoint me? She tempts ye to your grave.*

Growling as he hit the bottom, his feet landed softly in the sand, the impact swallowed by the vastness around him. Waves echoed through the immense cave—a space large enough to shelter a dragon—their rhythmic laps whispering against the ancient stone walls. At the far end, a narrow opening framed the glimmer of sunrise, the golden light threading through it like a secret. It would widen only at low tide, just enough to slip in unnoticed. The entrance would vanish beneath the sea by high tide, cloaking the cave in perfect concealment.

"I'm here ye old man. Come out!"

His father's laughter filled his head. *So short-tempered, much like yer oldest brother, Dameon.* His old man grunted. *Ye have more to worry over than yer play thing tempting ye.*

Manix nodded. "Aye, I figured as much. The man with the black beard is a mystery." He fisted his hands as his voice rose. "He's plundered my ship again. Taken my slaves! I want revenge!"

The yell echoed as Balor roared in his head. *Enough*

ye fool! The stone is close. His father's mind dove into Manix's while he mumbled, "I want his head."

His sire spoke lowly. *It's the stone ye want, boy. The rest will come after, but the Stone of Faith is what ye seek.* His father's sigh echoed, and his voice continued melodically. *I've seen it. Held it once. Ye need to know what ye seek.*

The image of his hand holding a blue gemstone, glittering in dusk's light, came to him—a bright blue stone shaped like a diamond. The points pierced his hand when he gripped the hard gem. An overpowering sense of faith in all overcame Manix. A power strong enough to achieve all his goals and attain all he desired. Riches, notoriety, and her—Evie. He grew hard, remembering her naked form.

Balor's voice roared, *Focus!* Then whispered, *The stone, boy. The sea is the path to finding the magic Iona Stone. Through the stone, ye will find yer reward.*

The vision faded, but Manix's feelings for revenge grew. His shoulders pulled tight, and a shudder ran through his body as his form stretched and shifted. Dark scales that glittered iridescent off the sun's rays rippled over his skin. Bones reshaped with a low, grinding snap, hands twisting into talons and wings unfurled in a sharp snap. In a breath, he was no longer human—his black dragon form towered, powerful and ready. Strength grew inside him—the stone, he had to find the stone. Blackbeard would give him all with his blood.

****

Left in her prison, Lorelei swam, resting before her cave as the image of the madman wavered, then disappeared into the wall. What was the kind man with the dark beard to him? Why did they fight, and how could she save her mystery man with a black beard and a soft heart?

Chapter 5

Ewan sat at the bar in the kitchen. Delightful scents of eggs, bacon, beans, and haggis filled the air, and a hint of coffee assailed his nostrils. His mouth watered as Mrs. A made breakfast. His da stood opposite him, glaring.

His ma and sister, Evie, sat at the breakfast table with Aodhán. Evie's husband, whose nearly white hair glowed in the sunlight, matching his toddler daughter, Annie, held by his ma.

"She's such a lovely baby, unlike you both, who squirmed till I had to release you, allowing you to do God knows what." His ma spoke while holding the baby in her arms.

Evie brushed the girl's hair aside while the child smiled and cooed. Mrs. A set a full plate of scrambled eggs, sliced tomatoes, beans, bacon, toast, and haggis before Ewan as his stomach growled loudly. He dug into the eggs, then picked up the toast, using the bread as a shovel for the beans, and shoved it all into his mouth.

Mrs. A laughed. "Aye. I could tell ye was hungry."

The housekeeper he'd known since coming into the world turned and filled another plate as his da sipped his coffee.

"None for me, Mrs. A."

She turned, smirking at him. "It's not for ye, Laird."

The housekeeper stood there holding the plate, tapping her foot. His da took another sip of his coffee as his ma wiggled Annie, who giggled.

Doug shuffled in, pulling on his shirt and buttoning the top lopsidedly, taking the place next to Ewan.

He yawned loudly while Mrs. A set down the full plate. "There ye are, dearie. Life's problems will seem much smaller on a full belly."

She turned, grabbing a cup and pouring in coffee as Doug shoveled food into his mouth.

His da stood taller. "Mrs. A, ye may leave us. We have family business to discuss."

She set the cup before Doug and placed her hands on her hips. "Family business—as if I am not a member of this family! The stones are what ye'll be discussing." The woman kept speaking over his da's gasp. "Ye think I don't see what goes on here. For years, yer parents traveled the portal, and now ye all do." Mrs. A pointed her finger around at each person in the room when she spoke. "Ye'll need me, I tell ye." Then snorted, "Ewan, I see yer ship come and go, yet ye come back starved. Yer cook must not be that good."

Doug's words were muffled around his mouthful of food. "He's awful! Except for rolls."

Ewan kept eating, keeping his head down, and out of the argument Mrs. A seemed intent on having. He knew when not to cross her. If he did, she'd hide her afternoon cookies from him—something she still did even into his adulthood.

Mrs. A turned, picked up the coffee press, and poured some into his da's cup without spilling a drop, as he eyed her. "Fine, now to the fables."

The housekeeper set the press next to the floral

ceramic teapot on a silver tray that she lifted, and strode to the breakfast table, serving each person there before seating herself. After pouring a cup of tea, she spoke again. "Ach, is it the one about the maiden with the Bible quote or the one about the arguing teens over candy?" Her question was delivered as if she spoke of what type of weather the day would bring.

His ma choked on her coffee. "How did you know about the stories?"

Mrs. A sipped her tea. "Ewan and Evie had to recite them to me. Helped them remember them I did."

Colin growled from the end of the bar. "If we can get on with it?"

Ewan sat rubbing his full belly now that he'd finished his meal. "Aye, the Stone of Faith has its own fable."

Mrs. A set her cup down. "Faith is the story Emily, yer ma, told Ainslie at bedtime, the Viking tale."

His da set his cup down, wrapping his hands around the small vessel as he leaned on the counter. "Aye, and *this* tale is apparently new. The story combines the Lust fable with Ainslie's, about a greedy man and his riches sinking him to the depths of the sea."

Evie sat forward. "But the fable also combines elements of the Love fable with the maiden's sacrifice and the seals on the point. The maiden sacrifices herself for her sweetheart, but she's become a seal forever separated from her true love."

Mrs. A hummed. "A sad tale ye have on yer hands, Ewan."

Ewan sat back, contemplating all the tales revealed, wondering how this all came down to him. His and his sister's gazes found each other as she poured her preferred coffee drink from the press on the tray.

She shrugged, using her mind speak. *It's ye now, brother. Any ideas?*

Ewan shrugged back while his da stepped between them. "Stop it, ye two. It's rude to speak without us hearing." He pointed between his two offspring. "Ye will not keep information from us like ye both did the last time." He picked up his coffee cup. "Plus, it's annoying that I can only hear yer whispers and not make sense of what ye speak in yer heads."

Mrs. A sat back. "I knew it! I always felt ye kids had some secret language."

Aodhán sighed as he filled his cup with tea. *They worry over the fables and what they mean.*

His brother-in-law's mind speak came to Ewan while he sipped his tea. *A warning, brother, when ye travel the portals back and forth, ye cannot spend too long in another time. There are...consequences.*

Doug nudged Ewan, who he suspected had heard the mind speak between Ewan, Evie, and Aodhán but couldn't reply in his head. Ewan batted him away. He couldn't answer questions by mind or out loud right now. He had no answers.

Evie snorted. *Answers, aye, brother, ye need answers.*

Ewan folded his arms. *Stop reading my mind.*

His sister replied with a lifted eyebrow. *Stop leaving it open.*

Aodhán exhaled. *Both, stop. The rule in the Fae realm states ye will be stuck there if ye stay too long.*

Doug spoke out loud. "Would that be so bad?"

Mrs. A picked up the spoken conversation. "I'd love to be able to speak that way."

Aodhán continued his mind speak. *Ewan, using the portal to move back and forward too close, there are consequences. Yer grandparents know what they are. That's why the Fae haven't explained to any of ye how to work the portals into the future without our help. That's why the council forbids that now.*

Doug spoke aloud. "Bad, aye, Mrs. A. Consequences there are to this."

Evie sat up. *But Ewan travels forward.*

Aodhán replied, *Aye, he figured the spell out on his own.* Aodhán's gaze connected with Ewan's. *It was yer grandparents, Ron and Emily's undoing. Through Constance, Balor saw them in the past and in future times. He came after them in the present, after an Iona Stone. Be wary.*

Ewan shivered as his da spoke. "Bad, aye. What the fable means is Ewan and Doug travel back in time to find the Stone of Faith."

Doug gasped. "But that means we must travel forward to come home!"

Ewan elbowed Doug. "Enough, we will be fine if we stick to the time limit. Aodhán said there was a threshold to being in the past."

Ewan's ma cuddled the babe and turned to his da. "Must they time travel? Can't we just solve the mystery from our own time?"

His da shook his head as he sighed. "The fables are never that easy, Bree. My ma always said the Fae fables are our bedtime stories. Some tales haunt, and some make ye laugh. Ye'll never understand them until ye are full grown, and then, my son, they will become yer sole existence."

Aodhán nodded. *There's more...*

He nudged Evie. *Tell him, or I will, Evie.*

Evie reached over, taking her daughter from their ma's arms. *It's nothing.*

Her husband eyed her while she tucked their daughter into her embrace. Her concern for her family came clearly to Ewan as Aodhán's voice drifted to him. *She's had dreams of Manix coming for her.*

Evie kissed her daughter's head. *They're not that bad. What I feel is my fear that he's still out there. His magic has an undertone of...goodness that makes me. I don't know.*

Aodhán growled. *I don't like it.*

His da eyed his empty coffee cup and then set the mug on the counter. "The stone is with a greedy man on an island. Ewan's pirating in the past. That's where ye'll find the greedy man."

Aodhán stood crossing to him. *For yer ears only.*

Ewan choked on his tea. *Ye can do that? Can I?*

Only if ye focus right. Aodhán waved his hand. *I've sensed good and evil but can't be certain. I fear ye face more than just one Fae's powers.*

His brother-in-law leveled his eyes on Ewan. *I also sense a Fae seeking ye Ewan.*

His da slammed his hand on the bar, rattling his cup. "Ye keep talking with yer minds. I hear the whispers. Out with it! No more secrets!"

Aodhán grumbled. "The fable—they must focus on the new faith fable. Only through that will they find the Stone of Faith."

Mrs. A rapped the table. "Och, a new tale. Tell me the tale."

Ewan stared at his cup while he spoke lowly. "It's about a Selkie Fae seeking her true love as a greedy man searches for a stone, his greed sinking his island. The gods, angered by his greed, cast a spell, aiming for her fated love. She stepped into the spell, sacrificing herself for their love. In the end, fate rewarded her good deed with her being cast into a seal—forever separated from the one she loves."

His ma gasped. "The maiden's sacrifice. The unfulfilled part haunts me."

His da crossed to her, taking her hand. When she stood, he slid into the chair, sitting her on his lap. "Shhh, *mo chridhe*. Ye'll not worry about it." My heart, that's what his da always called his ma. Ewan wondered if he'd ever have one to call his heart as the redheaded woman flashed in his mind.

Aodhán patted Evie's shoulders. "The quotes lead ye to the stone. What are they?"

Ewan's head came up. "Ye don't know them?"

His brother-in-law shook his head. "I haven't read this fable before. This one's new." Ewan glanced at his parents, his da comforting his ma. They'd been through so much for the stones. This time, the task was up to him—a new fable, a new task, a new time. He had to do this one on his own.

He sat taller while he recited them. "The first is about the greedy merchant. The love of money is the root of all evil: which while some coveted after, they have erred from faith and pierced themselves through with many sorrows."

Aodhán folded his arms as Doug spoke from beside Ewan. "The second is the last line of the story. 'Faith is confidence in what we hope for and assurance about what we do not see. Everything is possible for one who believes.' "

Evie chuckled. "Dash Ewan, not even a direction or place like the others leaving ye with nothing."

"I have faith, Evie." He spoke to his sister but nodded at his ma, who rose and crossed to him.

Patting his cheek, she said, "Yes, faith, son."

His da stood. "Ye go back, search for the stone."

Ewan turned to Aodhán. "Ye mentioned a time limit?"

Aodhán scratched his head. "There's never been a set limit, only a warning. When ye travel back and forth too close, the magic compounds yer period in time, but time that's not yers. If ye stay too long, ye become part of that period that's not yours."

His da nodded. "I stayed back in time for a few weeks and didn't have an issue."

His ma placed her hands on her hips. "Only ending up in purgatory."

Aodhán held his hands up. "Ye will feel a sensation. When ye sense time's gone, ye must come back."

Doug stood. "Aye, I've felt that before, our times out. I know."

His da stood patting his arm. "Ye and Doug gather yer things. Yer time has come to search for an Iona Stone."

Chapter 6

Ewan, dressed in pirate garb, his beard already in place, gathered the energy needed to send him, Doug, and the ship to the Caribbean in the year seventeen eighty-seven. As power built within his body, he focused on Captain Low. There had to be a reason they kept running into the privateer. Did this mean the Stone of Faith was somewhere near the man? Before having the Fae jewel drop into his personal life, he thought the reason he and Low's encounters were so numerous was due to good versus evil. The capture of humans and turning them into slaves was a horror Ewan detested. The idea Captain Low thought it was okay to do so only ignited all the honorable genes his ancestors had given him. Slavery was not humane, and if he could help put a stop to just one evil ship's captain's intentions, then he would at least be doing something.

As the ship lifted into the air, each of Ewan's crew members appeared cast into a misty view. Billy scampered up to the crow's nest. Carter, his first mate, strode past with One-eyed Joe following, taking his place at the wheel. Each was happy to resurrect themselves for the service of the descendant of their beloved Captain MacDougall, one of Ewan's grandfathers.

Doug nudged Ewan. "Time to go, Captain, give her all ye got."

In one last push of energy, Ewan tossed the mental mass toward Captain Low, wherever the man may be, and hoped they landed in the ocean and not on land. Explaining a beached ship on the mountainside in the eighteenth century would be difficult. Ewan's mental eye found Low on his boat in Caribbean waters—Ewan held onto the orb of energy, thrust through the portal, and called his ship, crew, and all to him in one burst of power.

Ewan's ship exploded through the realms, landing in the sea in a splash while cannons erupted around them. One-eyed Joe held the wheel as the mortar fell short of the ship, tilting the vessel and rocking them from the ball's arrival. Ewan's gaze found *The Fancy*, poised and ready for battle. Its guns aimed for Ewan's boat. How had Low known when and where they would arrive?

Billy screamed in a youthful, high-pitched voice, ringing Ewan's ears. "Ship port side, Captain!"

Carter called from his right. "*The Fancy*'s on the starboard side, captain, guns firing on us!"

Doug grabbed Ewan's arm. "They aren't firing at us!" He turned them to the left, pointing. "It's that ship! Ewan, ye landed us smack damn in the middle of a battle!"

Damn it all if he had. Well, he wanted Captain Low, and he'd found him all right. Now for the offensive and to get closer.

Ewan called out. "Guns starboard, ready to fire!"

He turned to One-eyed Joe. "Bring me alongside *The Fancy*'s port side."

Doug yelled, "Port side? His guns are out on that side! Ye'll get us all killed!"

One-eyed Joe chuckled. "My pleasure, Captain."

Ewan turned to Doug. "Tell Flint to aim low,

warning shots only as we approach. Send our message in intervals."

Doug's eyebrows went into his hairline. "Ye approach without a full attack. Then what? Board her? He'll blow us out of the sea when we get in range!"

Ewan eyed his nemesis as they drew closer with his cannons loaded, readying for the next volley. "I have a plan."

Doug barked out, "What plan? Invite him over for tea? We stole his prize out from under him and blew his ship apart, then fled, disappearing in the middle of the day."

He grinned. "We haunt his crew." He bellowed at the crew. "Men, when we're near, ghost them!" His crew roared when they faded into wisps, glowing gray.

Flint let loose a cannon volley. When the shot landed short of *The Fancy*, the splash came loudly to them. Good, Flint kept the volleys close. A sign of truce as his ship approached.

The Fancy's reply whistled while the ball sailed, then crashed short of the vessel. Ewan nodded. Low's response was an under aim, missing his ship. Good, Low agreed to sail close to…converse. They'd agreed to come close with no harm. Ewan took off for the galley, hoping his cook, Ralph, had a ton of flour on board. He bent into the hold on his way down to the lower levels of the ship.

Doug groaned, "Good lord, Ewan, that last time we did that, the other ship's crew jumped from the ship. Some died in fright, others drowning. We agreed not to scare anyone again."

Ewan stopped at the galley's doorway and slashed his hand to the side. "I must board her, question Low. As a man, *I* can't, but as Blackbeard's ghost, well, he'll talk to him." When he turned, a pile of flour fell over his head, covering his face. He sputtered while he tried to breathe. "Ralph, ye could have warned me before ye doused me!" The cook laughed and handed Doug the small sack of flour, who sighed as he dumped the powder over his head. Both men, now a pasty-ghostlike, returned to the bridge.

Ewan now sailed behind *The Fancy*. Another round from his ship fell short, and all held their breaths, waiting to see if their adversary would answer, stay silent, or blast them out of the sea.

Both ships rode silently as they pursued Low's intended capture. A Spanish frigate that Ewan couldn't make out the name from this distance. No matter, Ewan's target was Low, always Low. The only sounds were the waves splashing beside the hulls while the vessels broke through the surf. The wind shifted a little, making the rigging creak. They gained on *The Fancy*, who had her guns out, primed and ready. If Low's ship even gave a hint, they'd attack; Flint had their ship's guns ready as well.

All seemed to hold their breath when the ships came alongside. The men from *The Fancy* stared as Ewan's ghostlike crew stood silent. An entire crew frozen in time had a remarkable effect, the ghost crew staring down the live one. The moment seemed to leave the other shipmen wondering whether they saw ghosts or just imagined them. Ewan's focus found Low on the bridge. He eyed Ewan, then turned, signaling someone on his ship's bow.

Ewan blinked when the most glorious sound filled the air. Beauty, like nothing he knew, came to his ears, rising and falling like a breath. Her voice, raised in song, called to him. The hypnotic sound echoed in his mind and pulled at his heart.

All the men from both ships turned as one. On the bow of *The Fancy* stood the redheaded woman, the one he'd seen before on Low's ships—then as she haunted his dreams. Her voice filled the world with joy and beauty, wrapping around his heart and then his soul. She waved her arms overhead, and the sound carried, then swirled around them like energy from a Fae. Ewan blinked. Wait, energy gathered around him like when Brigid traveled the portal, causing him to throw up his mental defenses to ward off any Fae powers. He blinked again, and his eyes rested on her, his redheaded beauty, his siren.

Low yelled, "Fire." But before he finished the *er*, Flint let loose with his guns. Both ships erupted in splinters, rocking them away and back toward each other.

The redhead's song stopped.

Low yelled, "Keep at it! We take Blackbeard's ship, the men alive!"

Her gaze flew to Ewan's. Her mouth opened, poised to raise her voice again. She let her song out, but the tone came eerily this time, grating on the nerves. Men on *The Fancy* bent over, covering their ears. Those on his ship stared while she sang—no reaction from dead men. Weird as the tone sounded, the music drew Ewan, pulling at his heart. Her eyes found him again, and everything snapped into slow motion.

Low cried, "Fire on them!"

Flint hollered, "Fire!" Their ship sailed closer, the guns' aim mainly on the bow of *The Fancy*. If the cannons fired on Low, the beautiful woman would be blown away.

Ewan grabbed a line, loosening the rope as he swung off his ship. Gunfire erupted from both sides. Between the volleys, he swooped in, grabbed her around the waist, and swung back toward the safety of his ship when the cannonballs struck true to the bow she'd just stood on, breaking the wood into pieces. Another shot clipped Ewan's ship on the stern, rocking them into the sea.

Spinning in air, Ewan and the woman landed hard on the deck. He yelled to One-eyed Joe, "Hard to starboard, get us outta here!" That scent, fresh seaweed mixed with sun-warmed air, came strong to him. Before, he thought her aroma was part of her spellcasting. Close to her, the intoxicating scent was the woman herself. As Ewan turned, Joe slid to the deck, pulling the wheel an entire quarter. He'd already tugged on the helm before Ewan called the order. The ship responded with a groan when it took a sharp turn to the right and away from *The Fancy*.

Captain Low yelled, but the crashing of the waves against Ewan's ship's hull muffled what he said. Another volley of shots rang out from *The Fancy*, but they splashed into the ocean.

As they lay on the deck, a hand touched his beard. "You aren't a ghost?" Her whitened fingers came to her mouth, and then she licked them. "Flour?" The sight of her tongue flicking over her digits had Ewan biting back a groan. His gaze found her—electric blue eyes. Up close, white rings glowed around the edges as silver flecks sparkled in the middle. He coughed, and a puff of flour hit her face, making her scrunch her nose and then sneeze.

Ewan's hand brushed her hair from her eyes, leaving a trail of white. "Bless ye." He chuckled when more dust puffed at her. The flour was an old trick from his and Doug's childhood. A prank they played on Mrs. A using her fright of Dunstaffnage Castle's ghost to terrify her. When she discovered the missing flour and its usage, they both had to help her in the kitchen for a week. The chore wasn't all bad. Mrs. A would take pity on them and feed them chocolate chip cookies, their favorite.

Doug's boots appeared beside him. "And what do we have here? A siren washed up on our deck?"

Ewan sat up, pulling the redhead with him. She followed, clinging to him as she shook.

His eyes roamed her body and found a gash on her leg. "A damsel in distress, Doug."

****

She shifted, trying to stand, and stumbled.

The nice, bearded man caught her in a cloud of white. "Easy lass, I've got ye."

His friend, Doug, murmured. "Rather she has ye. Caught up in her spell ye are."

As they stood, he held her to his warm chest. Flour covered Lorelei, but she didn't care. Blood dripped down her leg. Her pretty human leg hurt from the blast. The cut stung, and she reached down to touch the afflicted limb.

He caught her hand. "I saw yer injury. Don't touch the cut, ye'll infect the wound." He lifted her into his arms as she grabbed his neck. When he turned, she gripped him tighter, worried that he'd dump her overboard. He strode toward the bridge, ducked under and through a doorway held by a ghostly crew member. Was his glow a trick of the light, or were they Fae, too?

Doug called out. "Back to yerselfs men, excitement's over." He turned to the captain. "The cove?" The bearded man nodded as he gripped her tighter.

In a blink, the crewman faded into regular coloring, looking normal. Doug tipped his bent tricorn hat, and flour floated in a puff while the bearded man carried her into the ship. They didn't travel far. Near the back, he elbowed into a cabin. Windows lined the ship's back wall, greeting her with bright sunshine that lit the room nicely. Two on the end were broken, likely from the blast. A desk dominated the room, and the view swung as the man turned, setting her gently on the bed.

He called over his shoulder. "Have Ralph send up hot water, enough for two."

Doug stuck his head in the doorway. "Aye, Ewan." His eyes met Lorelei's, and he winked. "My best friend and ye are the one who gets to have all the fun."

Ewan, his name was Ewan.

His friend's head disappeared, and the door closed with a click. The sound of Ewan rummaging in the cabinet brought her focus back to him. Flour still covered the top part of his body. He piled a few items on a counter as he stripped off his coat. With the coat gone and his back to her, she could admire his form. The flour faded at his waist. He had britches tucked into his well-worn, sturdy boots. His broad shoulders quickly narrowed to a trim waist. Even with his shirt on, his muscles undulated when he disarmed himself. First, the straps filled with knives and guns came off with one fluid motion as he laid them on the chair. His belt swung with his sword attached when he placed the strap on a chair's back. Next, he grabbed a thick fabric and rubbed off as much flour as possible from his beard and hair. The puffs coming from him made her giggle. He looked like bread dough, similar to some she'd spied once on an excursion above the water. That was before…she shook herself.

Setting the material aside, he picked up the collection from the cabinet and turned to her. He held a small bowl, a bottle filled with clear liquid, and some cloth. A leather pouch sat on top. When their eyes connected, he stopped, and she held her breath. Did Ewan like what he saw? She hoped he did. Her simple skirt and blouse were not her usual attire but required when with humans. She wiggled her toes since the boots pinched her feet. When she shifted, the cut burned, bringing out a whimper.

Ewan knelt beside the bed. "We must clean the wound. Yer cut could fester if not treated right away."

A knock on the door came before a young boy poked his head in. "Water for ye, Captain." At Ewan's nod, he stumbled into the cabin carrying two buckets filled with water.

An older, heavy-set man followed with a tray filled with a teapot and cups. "Hot water and yer special healing brew steeping." Shifting scrolls aside, the man set the tray on the desk. He stood and beamed at her.

Ewan placed his hand on her leg, making her jolt. "Shh, I only tend ye, lass." The youth and the large man shuffled out of the room, each staring and smiling when they passed her. The door clicked shut again.

Her gaze met Ewan's when he spoke. "Nothing to fear here, lass, just sailors. Ye are under my protection." She nodded, knowing she was much safer here than elsewhere in the human realm.

Her host rose, poured the tea, and handed her the cup. "Drink it all. The blend is a healing brew. Can't have ye in pain while I stitch ye up."

She took a sip. The drink had a soothing, sweet taste

with a bite of sour leaves near the end, like rotten seaweed. Ewan nodded, and she drained the warm liquid. He took the cup, placed the item on the tray, and knelt again. As he lifted her skirt, he peeked at her leg, probed the wound a bit, then folded her skirt upon her knee. She thought of healing herself. Minor injuries were not complex. It'd be much easier. But the idea of him caring for her—well, that was worth a little pain. She laid back and blinked when the cabin tilted a little.

Cold water hit her leg—the sting was not so bad this time.

Ewan's soft voice came to her. "Aw, there now. Rinsed out. Yer cut is not so bad, maybe no stitches, eh?" He turned, winking at her. "Maybe the wound will leave a little scar. I'll wrap it up."

She leaned forward, trying to see, and nearly fell off the bed.

He caught her. "Easy, lass, the brew has started to work."

Lorelei blinked dreamily. The room spun, so she closed her eyes. The previous vision of his smile meeting hers caused her to relax fully. He shifted, and something covered the wound. Something like cloth wrapped around her leg, and she hummed in relief.

His chuckle came to her. "What's yer name, lassie?"

She whispered. "Lorelei. You are my dream man, my savior." As she opened her eyes, his form wavered—far then close.

His lips brushed her forehead. "Rest, Lorelei."

Safe in her dream man's presence, she gave in to much needed rest and closed her eyes while his voice washed over her. "Sleep, my siren, my beauty from the sea."

Chapter 7

Lorelei came awake with a jolt, gulping for water, yet only the dryness of air filled her chest.

As she tilted over, warm arms encircled her. "Whoa, there dear, I have ye." Ewan pulled her against his chest, bare now, the hair tickling her cheek. She clung to him as she tried to adjust her breathing now slower, less energy needed to draw in air than water.

He shifted till he sat on the bed, adjusting her in his arms till her head rested on his shoulder. Ewan's embrace created a safe cocoon. "Yer rest was fitful. Are ye still in pain?"

Lorelei shook her head and sighed while he swung his legs onto the bed, lying alongside her. She'd dreamed of this moment, with him in the human realm. Her stomach fluttered and she took a deep breath. Ewan's fingers trailed up and down her arm lightly, hypnotic in touch as they soothed. They lay there for a moment in the stillness. Wait, stillness?

She sat up. "We don't sail?"

Ewan shook his head while he stared at her, his sky-blue eyes wide. "No, we lay in at a cove. A place to rest overnight, make repairs." Her focus traveled to the windows lit with warm hues of the dusk light. How much time had passed? Would the madman call for her?

A knock rapped at the door. Ewan released her and

stood, slipping on his shirt as the door opened.

His friend Doug carried the same tray as before, but the platter held more items. "Yer best friend, and now I must be yer maid too?"

Ewan took the tray and set the platter on his empty desk. "The repairs?"

Doug stared at her, and she shrunk into the bed's corner against the wall.

His expression seemed friendly when he replied. "Almost done. I told the men to take extra rations of rum with supper." His grinning vestige returned to Ewan, whose eyes ran over the tray as if taking inventory. Doug blew out a laugh before speaking again. "Flint cracked a joke they can't eat since they're ghosts but I took my extra share anyway."

Ewan looked up, meeting his friend's expression with one of his own. He patted Doug's shoulder. "Aye, good call." He shoved his friend to the exit, who chuckled at her when he passed the doorway. "Enjoy yer meal." Ewan shut the door and leaned against the wood, a sigh escaping.

She sat forward, swinging her legs over the side. "I hope I am not intruding." She flinched at the pinch to her leg.

Ewan was beside her in a step. "No, ye are not. Actually, ye are an honored guest." He helped her stand. "Let me help ye to the chair." When she stood, she wobbled and gasped at the pain in her leg.

His arms came around her while he led her to the chair before the desk. "I know yer leg pains ye, but walking will help get ye up and about quicker." As he helped her sit, he brushed his hand over her shoulder, a caress that made her heart race. Ewan sat opposite

Lorelie and picked up a bowl. He ladled soup, and the scents of spices with a rich fish broth filled the air. She eyed a stack of freshly baked rounds and licked her lips. She loved bread.

Ewan's chuckle had her lifting her gaze as he grabbed a roll, handing the bread to her. "Ralph isn't the best of cooks. But somehow, he can bake fresh bread in a pot over a flame."

She gripped the offering while he set the bowl before her. Bread was her weakness. In her realm, baked goods weren't something they had. Puffy coral was a poor match to the flaky softness of bread. She bit into the morsel, savoring the spongy texture. There was even a hint of butter, making her moan while she chewed.

Ewan smiled as he set his filled bowl down and took his first spoonful. She set her roll aside and tried the soup. Using the spoon like she'd seen humans do, whitefish with brown broth and herbs met her tongue. A little seaweed gave the meal a salty taste. She liked raw whitefish, but this dish had a hearty, filling flavor.

Lorelei's gaze lingered on Ewan while he tore a piece of bread from the loaf, his fingers strong and sure. He dipped it into the steaming soup, letting it soften, then lifted it to his lips with a quiet ease that made her ache. Something about how he moved—calm, grounded, entirely unaware of the storm he'd walked into—made her chest tighten. *Had he known Captain Low's plan and, more importantly, her part?*

She sat frozen, watching him as if the answer might flicker across his face. *What would Ewan do if he knew the truth? That the woman sitting across from him, whose hands itched to reach for him, was not only a liar but a weapon Low had sharpened for someone else's war? Would he still look at her the way he did, with that quiet steadiness that made her feel almost safe? Or would the light in his eyes vanish, just like it had with everyone else who ever saw what she really was?*

A direct gaze studied her as he ate the wet bread, a dribble wetting his beard that he tapped with a napkin. "Yer thoughts read clear on ye face, lass." He reached for her hand, brushing the back softly. "Whatever yer issue is, I will help. Ye have my word."

"Meal first, then we deal with yer dilemma." Ewan smiled. "Mrs. A always said life's problems seem much smaller on a full belly." His eyes moved to his bowl, and he ate quietly. Not confronting her again with his focus or voice. Her belly rumbled, and he grinned as he kept his gaze on his meal.

He was right. She was hungry—starved. Lorelei picked at her bread, eating little bits, savoring each one. Soon, her hunger won over, and she scooped some soup, enjoying the warm meal. She tried dipping her bread like he had and stuck the morsel in her mouth. The savory broth in the rich bread burst into her mouth. As she rolled the bite around, she smacked the morsel. His chuckle came to her, and she glanced up.

Ewan sat staring at her. "Better now that ye have a full belly?"

Lorelei smiled back and nodded. "Yes." She picked up her mug and took a sip. Sweet, honeyed ale flowed down her throat, cool and soothing.

Ewan sat back, steepling his fingers while he settled his intense gaze upon her. "So, Lorelei, what were ye doing on Captain Low's ship?" Choking, she glared at him.

He sat forward, setting his elbows on the table and

folding his hands tightly. "Ye spoke yer name as ye passed out." When she set her mug down and stared out the windows, the dusk lit them with a red-orange light that faded quickly. Too quickly. What was she to say to Ewan? She wanted to tell him everything but couldn't without risking so much.

The pat on her hand had her jolting. He'd come closer without her notice.

When she pulled away, he gripped her hand, then loosened the hold. "Whatever it is, Lorelei, I will help ye. A damsel in distress is what ye are. This I know." He released her and sat back, his eyes softening. "Ye can trust me with yer life. I promise, lass." Ewan gripped his hands before him as he tilted his head. "Unburden yer soul. I can tell ye need help."

Her father's soft yet firm voice echoed—*the truth, always the truth, daughter.*

She sat staring at him, her supper souring a little in her stomach. "I'm trapped. A prisoner."

Ewan grinned. "Well, good it is that I came along." His hands opened wide as if welcoming her. "Now ye are free."

Tears gathered. "It's not that simple." One spilled over, then another. Why were human emotions so much more powerful than a Fae's? In her human form, they overwhelmed her at times.

He breathed. "Lass, do not fret so. We'll make a plan that will keep ye free."

Ewan stood and handed her a piece of fabric, soft and pure white. "Dry yer eyes, lass. They are too pretty to have tears fill them." She dotted her eyes and handed the soft fabric back.

He shook his head. "I have many handkerchiefs.

Keep it."

Lorelei stared at the material, and the letters ERM was on the corner embroidered in blue swirly lettering. What do the *R and M* stand for? The humans all had multiple names—she had only one. She tucked the handkerchief inside her skirt, happy to keep something of his.

His fingers grazed her cheek. As she gazed up at him, another tear fell. He pulled her hand, and she stood swaying on her injured leg.

"Come, lass, let me hold ye." Ewan sat and settled her onto his lap. He took her in his arms, and she rested her head on his shoulder like she had when they lay side by side before. She hummed without magic as he rocked her a bit, content in his care.

"My da holds my ma this way when she's sad." He squeezed her once. "My ma says his care chases her tears away." Lorelei exhaled, thinking of home and her people.

The humans were so different. "What is your family like?"

Ewan chuckled. "A pain in the ass sometimes." She sensed a teasing manner in his response. He took a deep breath and let it out. "Loving, caring, kind people they are." He chortled. "I have a sister, a twin. We got into so much trouble when we were young." A whisper tickled her ear. "Still do." She smirked, thinking of her eleven sisters and all the antics they pulled in their youth.

The teasing reminded her that Ewan had mentioned someone earlier. "Who's Mrs. A? Your mother?"

Ewan grunted. "She acts like it, but no. She's the housekeeper, but more than that. She's family."

The way he said that word *family* seemed to resonate

in his soul. His feelings reached her, what the meaning that the word was to him. Sure, in her realm, she had her sisters and her father. But the way Ewan spoke of his. The way his emotions vibrated, spoke of so much more. She craved that—wanted more than anything to have someone feel that way about her and her about him.

Ewan sat back till their gazes came even. "Ah, see, lass." His thumb skimmed her cheek. "No more tears. That's how I like to see yer face, Lorelei, tearless."

He bent, brushing his lips against hers softly. The beard tickled a bit. A tingling grew to consume her body. Her first kiss ever. As his lips touched hers again, she returned the caress. His arms encircled her, bringing her flush against him.

Her hand slid into his unbuttoned shirt. His chest hair was springy to her touch, like his beard. He deepened the kiss, drawing a soft sigh from her. The moment her lips parted, his tongue slipped in, teasing, tasting, claiming. She wiggled and squeaked at the contact, so new and foreign to her. He lifted his head, and then his eyebrow raised in question.

She whispered, "Didn't you mention making a plan?"

He smiled. "Making plans is for tomorrow. Tonight is for kisses."

Lorelei opened her mouth with the intent of replying, and he covered hers with his. His tongue worked havoc on her senses. His hand trailed from her back to her front, molding her breast. The tip peeked, and his thumb brushed the nub. She wiggled as sparks shot over her body. What he did to her, she could hardly catch her breath, but he seemed to breathe more into her with his kisses. He kissed his way to her ear, and she moaned.

Ewan stood carrying her and turned to the bed, laying her upon the covers.

He stared at her with a tilted grin on his face. "I like ye there, lass." He stripped his shirt off and came over her, crushing her with his weight, but the firmness was welcome. Ewan kissed her again and again till she felt senseless. He unbuttoned her top till her breasts were freed.

In her kingdom, all women went uncovered, but here, with him, she felt exposed. When he sat back and gazed upon her naked chest, warmth spread through her.

He whispered, "Devine," and he gripped one then the other. He dipped his head, capturing one peak between his lips before moving to the other, drawing a gasp from her while she arched into him, desperate for more. Lorelei's fingers tangled in his hair, holding him close as he worshipped her with his mouth and hands, loving her the way humans do. Her hand traveled to his pants. She wanted to love him the right way, like humans. When her hand skimmed the front, he jolted back. She sat back. Had she done the act wrong?

His hand came to hers and brought her palm to his lips, kissing a fingertip. "Lass, while I enjoy yer attentions, I only meant to kiss tonight."

He kissed each finger as he spoke. "Tonight."

Then, the second one. "I plan to enjoy our kisses."

He kissed another. "Yer charms."

Ewan's eyes went to her bare chest, and a smile formed on his face as he kissed another fingertip. "Tomorrow, we can explore our kisses more."

He kissed her fourth and last finger, her thumb. "But tonight, let's enjoy being together."

As he settled her in his arms, they lay there, bare

chest to bare chest. His fingers drew the lazy lines they had before that seemed to hypnotize her into a dreamy haze. She enjoyed being in a man's arms. Her first, and she prayed, the only man to hold her this way. After a time, Ewan's arms relaxed as his breathing became deeper, and a light snoring escaped his mouth.

She shifted, and his arms tightened. "Shh, ye are safe when ye are with me." The last faded into a mumble, but she understood his words. When she was with him, she felt alive, human, and more.

She whispered, "When I am with you…My body hums with energy. I sing to the gods. My love shines in my smile for you. My soul burns with the hope of our souls united."

Ewan sighed while his arms tightened again. "United, aye."

Now relaxed for the first time in so long, exhaustion overcame her. Ewan's heartbeat thumped against her ear, steady and comforting. She drifted off, praying this was how she would live her life, as his human match.

****

My pet, come to me! The madman screamed her name into the night. His summons was one she couldn't ignore. In her dream, her feet tingled and then twitched. Lorelei fell and hit something hard. Her eyes opened, and she stared at the wood plank flooring. She'd fallen from the bed, the impact jolting her awake. Her legs twitched again, shaking.

Not now! No, please, not now!

Lorelei glanced at Ewan, who had rolled over in the bed, mumbling something. She prayed he didn't wake, prayed with all her might.

Now ye fishy bitch! The madman's summons came

stronger, too strong for her to ignore. She tried to stand, but her legs gave way, the tingling signaling her transformation was soon upon her, whether she willed it so or not.

Lorelei stood and ran for the broken window. Her legs came together, stinging with the effect. Crawling up onto the sill, she bent over the edge and held on as she flung her legs over. She gripped the window's edge and glanced back at Ewan, asleep safely in bed—vowing she would do everything to keep her human love safe, even if she had to sacrifice herself.

In one last jolt, her body's shake forced her to release her grip. Hitting the surface of the sea hard, the water consumed her while pain engulfed her soul. She gripped Ewan's handkerchief.

Jolting into her natural form, Lorelei drew in a deep pull of water, rejuvenating her body as she took another form. When her human clothing faded away, she held the fabric tightly. She swam away, running from the madman's call and herself.

Lorelei pulled up, stopped in the water, turned, and stared at the vessel's hull at the water's edge—Ewan's ship. She gripped the handkerchief harder, desperately wanting to keep something of his—anything to prove her encounter with Ewan was real and not a dream.

With the fabric to her cheek, she spoke. "I promise, Ewan, with all my love, we will reunite." She hid the item in her hair, allowing the masses to secure her treasure as she reluctantly swam away to keep her people safe.

Chapter 8

Ewan came awake swinging. He clipped someone who groaned. "Oww, Ewan, yer right hook hurts!" Ewan stumbled from the bed, a little disoriented. Still fighting the remnant of his dream, he fought for Lorelei, keeping pirates away.

He wrestled against his friend as he righted himself. "Shit, Doug. Don't scare me like that!"

Doug gripped his arms. "Ye must shift us now! The feeling is strong. We have to go to the future." Ewan dropped his hands while he searched the cabin. Where was she? He checked the bedding, then under the desk.

He raised his head to see Doug's frantic expression. "Lorelei! Where is she?"

Doug pulled on his arm. "Not here. Now, Ewan!"

He yanked free. "Not without her. She's in trouble."

"We will be stuck. Now, Ewan!" Doug slammed his hand on the desk.

Angered and frustrated, Ewan used those emotions to build an energy force quickly. He closed his eyes, intent on the Dunstaffnage Chapel door, the portal. In his mind, the portal opened, and he threw himself and Doug through space and time. When they landed on the chapel floor, his hand reached back, and he pulled *The Faithful* through. The ship flew through the opening, and the crew faded as the vessel landed in the loch beyond

Dunstaffnage Castle, its wooden structure rocking from the force. The wave unsettled the many sailboats and larger boats near the marina, but he couldn't stop the spell's power. He needed to move fast.

Ewan stood. "Damnit, Doug, she's in trouble. We must go back." As he twisted his hands in a circle, he gathered more energy.

Doug jumped up, grabbing them. "Ye can't, Ewan. The rules. We must stay here for a while." Ewan tried to yank back, but Doug gripped harder. "While I like pirating, I don't want to be stuck in the eighteenth century."

Ewan pulled again, and his friend released his hands. "Shit, Doug. I failed to save the enslaved people and stop Captain Low." He paced as he ran his hands through his hair. "She's out there, a captive."

Doug stretched and sat on a pew. "Prisoner? Is that why she was on Low's ship? But the singing, what was that?"

He stopped and fluttered his fingers, removing the long beard. When the scraggly mess disappeared, he scratched his chin. "We didn't get that far into it." He chuckled. "I got a little distracted."

His friend smirked. "So, she's a good kisser?"

Ewan paced, racking his brain, trying to recall their discussion as her kisses consumed his mind. "She said she was a prisoner, but I freed her." He stopped and turned to Doug. "Why leave?"

Doug rested his hands behind his head and closed his eyes. "That's obvious. Her capture might have something to do with her leaving. She had to go back to keep something or someone safe."

Ewan huffed. "But what and why?" He paced again.

"I must find her. I've lost the girl I rescued."

Doug stood and chuckled. "Ye haven't found the stone either."

****

When she neared Waitukura Island, meaning jewel beneath the tall waves, she started for the surface and her inevitable interview with the madman, dreading what was to come.

Two Telkhines guards swam toward her, their jagged spears glittering in the sunlight from above. She stopped waiting for them as she recognized Murus and Razos, members of her father's personal guard.

Murus pulled up before her. "Your father has summoned you."

Lorelei swam around him. "He knows I cannot come." Razos grabbed her arm, stopping her. She yanked free. "And he knows the reason why."

Murus floated before her again. "Our people can fight the madman. The gem from the gods protects us. You do not need to sacrifice yourself this way."

She shook her head when Murus took her arm, bringing her close. "I do not want you to be *his* prisoner." It figured Murus wanted her for her position like he always had.

She yanked back. "Yes, well, where would your goal to seek the throne of the Telkhines fall? Each of my older sisters has a mate. The younger ones are too young for you. Each male mate has failed the trial for king."

He floated past her, passing close. "This obsession with the humans will be your end. The madman promises the impossible. Something he will never deliver."

Lorelei swam away, calling over her shoulder. "I will be human in full. One day, you will see."

Razos swam beside her. "Your father truly worries."

As she sped up, she called over her shoulder. "Tell him I do this for all." She kept swimming toward the sunshine, the top, and the madman.

She whispered as she headed for the human realm. "The madman will bring on his own death. The greedy always do."

Lorelei broke the surface beside the dock. On the other side, *The Fancy* floated while the crew made repairs. If anyone noted her appearance, no one commented—except him.

The madman stood on the dock, peering down at her. "What took ye so long? I've summoned ye since late last night when *The Fancy* docked without ye."

She ducked beneath the dock, but his energy wrapped around her and pulled her out toward him. Heaving for water, she choked up what was inside. His grin widened when the world tilted, and her vision swam before her eyes. Pain radiated when her true form hit the cold stone floor of his main house—still gasping for air. Her form shivered as her legs tingled. Lorelei breathed in the air again, and her shape shifted into human. She hated how he could teleport himself and whomever he wanted. Shaking the dizziness off, she peered at him between the strains of her hair, imagining they were bars of a human prison. In a way, she resided in a human jail.

The maniac paced before her as she lay on the cold floor naked, wet, and cold. "Ye have failed me again."

She shoved the hair aside. "Captain Low failed you, not me." When she sat up, she caught his roaming eye and methodically used her hair to cover her female areas.

He hissed. "Ye were to sing the sailors of *The San Miguel* to their death. Low was to bring me the slaves and the gems. The ship had a large chest of jewels! The rest of the prize was for the crew as payment."

She sat staring at him, hating him from the core of her being. "Your *captain* failed to sail close to *The San Miguel*. Another ship attacked, and *your captain* lost. I had to jump into the sea to survive."

She exhaled, glancing away, sarcasm dripping in her tone. "And where would your little search be without your secret weapon?"

The madman advanced on her, shouting, "Ye serve me!" He stopped, "The other ship, Blackbeard, again?" The maniac crawled through her mind so fast she gasped from the intrusion. The images of her and the man with the black beard flashed. She didn't have time to block him. Damn, she needed to watch herself in his presence.

Her sailor's face swam before her. Dark hair, sky-blue eyes. He smiled as he caressed her cheek. Her lips tingled and he kissed her, and butterflies fluttered in her belly while their time together appeared in her mind.

The madman's voice came low and threatening. "Ye were with him this whole time. My treasure, ravished by another. I don't know whether to be angry or toast yer ingenuity."

She stood. "Please don't hurt him." She stumbled, falling to her knees, opting to stay there. Tired, dizzy. She felt so worn down.

****

The pleading in her voice almost undid him. His little critter was hopelessly falling for this Blackbeard guy. But her weakness would be his strength. This pirate was certainly no ghost. Low was right on that account. But who was this man?

Manix brought back the vision of him up close.

She'd been so close when they kissed. Saw the sky blue of his eyes, the silver flecks near the pupil. When she pulled away, there was care and softness in the man's eyes.

Those eyes, he'd seen that sky blue before. But where? He searched his mind, and his time with his soul mate came to him. He'd kissed her, pulled back, and stared into her eyes.

Evie MacDougall's eyes! She had a twin brother. Could it be? In his own mind's eye, Manix stripped the beard away, roaring at the face staring back at him.

It can't be! The very man robbing him in the eighteenth century was none other than Ewan MacDougall—Evie's twin brother from the future.

He roared, "Ewan!"

A female gasp rose to him. "You know him? Blackbeard?"

Manix glared down, wondering what Ewan was to her. His pet had spent the night with him, had she? He searched her mind. No, still a virgin and powerful. An idea clicked into place, the perfect plan. Through Ewan, he'd get the stone, then *his* Evie. Blackbeard's ghost, Ewan, was not. But the man would give him all with his blood.

He growled. "The man with the black beard is Ewan MacDougall, who came from the future to search for a stone." Manix fisted his hands. "His sister, Evie, she's mine. With him here, I'll get her once and for all, my soul mate!"

Balor roared in his head. *Enough, ye fool! Ewan being here means the stone is close.*

She gripped his leg. "Please, he means you no harm. He's only trying to free the slave people."

He flicked his wrist, lifted, and tossed her into the tank. A splash sounded, and thrashing water met his ears when his critter changed her form. But he paid her no heed.

He needed to get to Ewan. His desire to maim and hurt the brother rose. Through the brother, he'd hurt Evie. May even gain her attention and get her back.

Balor's voice roared. *The stone, ye idiot! Ye must find the stone.*

Manix paced. *Aye, but ye said it yerself. If Ewan is here, then the stone is as well. I must get Ewan to get the stone.*

Get Ewan echoed in his mind while his pet's emotions flashed through him. Seemed she was attracted to the man. They'd even kissed. If she lured him in with her appeal and laid with him, gaining his trust, Manix could sweep in and take Ewan unaware. Torture him till he gave up the magic Iona Stone. Ewan's pain would trigger Evie to come—to him.

He rubbed his chin and turned, eyeing his little creature while she floated in the tank. Her hands pressed against the glass. Her desperate expression visible even in the distortion from the water. He chuckled at the irony—a fish for bait. She was his lure, and he planned on using her. He wouldn't be able to give her her dream. He never had the intention, not having enough power to make her human permanently. But then again, she'd likely die while he gained Ewan, then Evie. He gazed at her beauty. Losing her was worth the price.

So much to do. He must plan and prepare for Ewan's downfall and Evie's arrival when she came. Manix would gain the stone and Evie again—two for the price of one!

****

Lorelei stared at the madman as he ranted to himself. Pieces of his conversation with no one came to her, chilling her with all he spoke of.

His shoulders twisted and a shudder rocked him when his transformation began. The maniac's frame expanded while dark scales rippled over his skin. Human hands became claws, sharp and unyielding, his jaw extended, teeth lengthening into fangs. A deep growl rumbled from his chest as wings burst from his back, spreading wide with a powerful snap. In moments, his shift was complete. The beast that grew and roared before her was more like his true nature. She hated him and all he represented in his existence of life.

She swam to her cave—a rock formation he'd given her after her first successful plunder. She sat and rubbed her fin. The red gash stung a bit. She could heal herself, but some small part of her wanted the mark. Ewan said the wound would scar and she wanted a memento to remember their first kiss. Her sisters would call her silly. Her father—reckless, but she wanted something.

Reaching into her hair, praying her secret treasure was still there, her hand connected with the fabric. Sighing in relief, she pulled the handkerchief out to place her prize with her other pilfered items from the human world—her little cache of reminders of each trip to her dream world. She folded the material and set the fabric neatly to the side—her reminder of Ewan, her dream man.

Lorelei fingered the earring that had fallen from a woman on a ship Low took. She'd saved those people like all the others before Captain Low stole everything they owned. For each bad deed she involved herself in, she tried to offset it with a good one. She spied the rolling pin she'd taken from the baker in the main house. Bread, she loved baked bread.

Her lips tingled as if still touched by his kiss, a phantom warmth that traveled straight to her heart. *Ewan.* His name whispered through her mind like a wave against the shore, soft yet relentless. Tears welled in her eyes as she lifted the cloth and dabbed them away with trembling fingers. The fabric fluttered gently in the current, its embroidered initials—ERM—blurred in the water like a faded memory.

She stared at them for a long moment, her chest tightening with fear. Not just for herself. But for her people who believed in the fragile hope that peace might still come. The madman's plan was too reckless, formed in chaos. She'd felt it, sensed the imbalance in the air and the sea. The way energy shifted unnaturally around him as he slipped further into madness. If his schemes failed, if his bloodlust turned on those nearest, it wouldn't just be her world shattered. Ewan could suffer for her connection with him. The evil one—he would not forgive disobedience or failure. His wrath would fall swiftly, and it would not distinguish between the sea-born or the land-walkers.

Lorelei curled the cloth into her palm, clutching it like a talisman. Ewan didn't know how deeply entangled he'd become in this yet. He didn't understand what danger brushed so close to him now. But she did. And if fate turned cruel, she would stand between him and the storm, even if it meant baring her soul or spilling her blood.

She whispered into the water, "I won't let them take you. Not Ewan. Not anyone."

Chapter 9

His da paced as Ewan sat beside Doug in Dunstaffnage Castle's study. Why did sitting here always make him feel young and in trouble again? He glanced at Doug, who smirked at him. Aye, this was all too familiar a position they found themselves in.

His sire stopped pacing. "So, ye went back, landed in the middle of a sea battle, fought, lost, and took on damages." He huffed. "That's it? Son, ye aren't a very good captain."

Doug mumbled. "Or a pirate either. We didn't plunder either ship. In the confusion, the one with slaves sailed away, and Captain Low's ship attacked then escaped." Doug cleared his throat. "But Ewan saved the girl."

Ewan turned to his friend. "Enough, Doug!"

His da raised an eyebrow. "A girl?"

Doug grinned. "Lively redhead with the most beautiful voice." He moaned like a lovesick pup. Ewan could punch him right now.

Colin's brows furrowed. "Ye were sent back to find a stone. Remember, a *magic Iona Stone*. And ye come back from yer first mission, and all ye can show for yer efforts is a girl?" He leaned on his desk, folding his arms and feet like he always did. "Where is this paragon of beauty, son?"

Doug sat up. "Oh, she got away." Ewan's ears burned as his friend spilled every secret.

Ewan sent a message to Doug, focusing only on him like Aodhán told him. *Shut yer gob ye idjit! He doesn't need to know about Lorelei.* Doug sat back, folding his arms while a frown set on his face.

He turned to his da, who shook his head. "Ewan, ye must focus on the stone, not the women, as pretty as they may be."

"She's more than that, Da! She's there, everywhere." He ran his hands through his hair, breath catching in his chest. Wanting to scream it, he held back when the words caught like thorns in his throat. *She's the maiden, Da, from the fable—the one who gives everything, even her life, to protect the Iona Stone.*

But how could he say that out loud? Naming the maiden would be to give the label weight and make the threat real. She was Fae, aye, and powerful—but even the Fae bled, died. And if the fable was true, Lorelei wasn't just part of the story. She *was* the story. Ewan swallowed hard, trying to tamp down the dread clawing up his spine.

Every time he looked at her, he saw the shimmer of magic—yes—but also something softer. Fragile. Mortal. He couldn't protect her from the prophecy. Couldn't shield her from fate. And even more terrifying—he couldn't tell anyone. Not even his da. Because if the evil Fae found out, they might use her. Or worse…force her to go to her death, thinking it was a path to gain a stone.

He fisted his hands at his side. "Damnit Da! Ye wouldn't understand." He ran his hands through his hair. "Ye wouldn't understand."

Ewan pushed past the chair, through the door, and

walked out into the courtyard. He took off, not caring where he went.

He ran till he came to the dock. Any farther, and he'd be in Loch Etive. *The Faithful* rested easily on the waters. Ewan stood there for a moment, then a moment more. The wind blew, and the creek of the riggings came to him, the familiar sound comforting. He stepped back, needing to sit, not having to look. He'd been here many times before. The bench hit his knees, and he sat staring out over Loch Etive toward Dunstaffnage Point and the seals. His ma liked to sit here, and he'd joined her as a boy.

The seals were always there. His ma said they were souls lost trying to stay close to the one they loved, like the story his da told. His da called her a hopeless romantic. She'd chide his da but he was the one who first told her the story. Ewan smiled, thinking of the love his parents shared to this day.

A heavy footfall hit the dock. The wood creaked in a familiar deep tone when the large person came closer. His da sat next to him, folding his hands and resting his elbows on his knees. Ewan waited for the rant that would likely come—it usually did. But now his sire sat silent.

After a while, his da's voice came to him softly. "Do ye like what ye do, son? Pirating?"

Ewan turned to his da. What a question to ask now.

His da cleared his throat. "In college, yer interest was acting. I suspected ye followed yer sister out of habit. Ye two were never apart for long. But now ye finished yer schooling, and ye occupy yer time with"—he snorted—"time travel. So, I ask Ewan, ye like what ye do?"

"I like sailing on the old ship." He sighed and stared

toward the Falls of Lorne, calm now at low tide. "I like the open sea, the challenge of sailing her."

His da sighed. "Aye, sailing is a fine thing, and to conquer nature, beat her at her own game, that's something. But pirating? Stealing, do ye like that?"

Ewan sat up. "We don't steal for gain, Da. We take the slaves and free them."

His da straightened. "Aye, a noble cause. But ye are only one man. The slave trade in the eighteenth century is vast. I don't need yer ma here to tell me, and I thank God she's off seeing yer sister today and not here." A humph came from his da. "The slave history is well known. But why now?"

Ewan breathed. "I don't know. There's one captain we keep running into. Captain Low."

His da nodded and sat back, stretching his legs. "So, what of this girl?"

Ewan shuffled his feet not wanting to speak of Lorelei. "She's not connected to the stone."

A barked laugh burst from his da. "Trust me, son, she is." His sire turned to him. "Tell me of her."

He closed his eyes, picturing her the first time he saw her—last year on his first run-in with Low. "She stood tall, her bright red hair flowed around her, loose like women wear theirs today—such a brilliant color. Fire red it is, and when the sun shines on her tresses, orange then golden flames fly through like lightning."

Ewan sighed as another memory came to him. The first time he saw her face up close. "Her skin is pale, but her cheeks are like a soft pastel rose. Her face is like an angel and her eyes." When he swooped in and saved her from the exploding deck flashed in his mind. They lay on the deck, face to face. "Her eyes are the lightest shade of blue, almost white. They practically glow."

A grunt came from beside him. "Like yer brother-in-law's Aodhán's?"

Ewan gasped. "Aye, but lighter." His hand came to his lips when he thought of her kisses. Soft, sensual, and innocently seductive.

His da's chuckle had him open his eyes and turn to his sire when he spoke.

"Sounds like a beauty beyond belief, son." His da glanced at the seals. "Ye feel love for this girl?"

Ewan glanced away. "Aye. No. I don't know." He had to fess up. He'd seen a Fae in the past, making the fable about him. The possibility that Lorelei was the maiden pulled on him. He glanced at his da, whose stern glare softened. His sire had faced an evil Fae, dealt with a fable, and changed the outcome, saving his ma's life more than once. Ewan had to face reality. The Stone of Faith fable was about him making Lorelei the maiden, the victim of evil.

He needed his da's help and advice. "She has a power in her voice, but I don't know the magic's purpose."

His da turned, his expression tense. "A Fae ye have seen, like the fable."

Ewan turned, waving his hands open. "But she's a prisoner."

"Doug said ye freed her." At Ewan's affirmation, his da sat forward. "From the same captain ye keep running into?"

Nodding again, Ewan sat back, running his hands through his hair. "But she ran away. Someone has something of hers or holds something against her."

His sire scowled, tapping his leg. "Ah, now we

know the greedy one. Someone holds her, but why?" His da patted his shoulder when he stood. "Ye must search for her captor. There ye will find yer answers."

Search the seas? Ewan had enough trouble getting the ship to and from the past, let alone winning a battle. Now, he had to search the high seas of the eighteenth century.

He stood. "But Da, how will I…"

His da followed, patting his cheek and stopping his question. "Ewan, ye have just as much if not more power to do so. Yer Fae powers I don't understand. But even without them, ye can do so much."

"The greedy man destroyed the island. They cast a spell upon him, but the spell went awry. The fables tell the fate of each stone," his da said softly.

Ewan whispered as his ma's voice echoed in his mind. "The stone demands its maiden's sacrifice. The spell went awry, hit the woman, and turned her into a seal, thus launching her into purgatory. Leaving her forever separated from her true love." Ewan stepped away, refusing to believe the fable fit, but it did.

His da whispered the ending. "To this day, his ghost haunts the seas, searching for his true love."

Ewan strode back. "It can't end this way!" He paced away and then turned, yelling at his da. "So, am I to be a ghost searching for this true love? Where's the damn stone, Da?"

His sire came to him, took him in an embrace, and held him for a moment. He shifted back when he spoke. "Look to the quote, son. The love of money is the root of all evil, which while some covet after they have erred from the faith and pierced themselves through with many sorrows."

Ewan nodded. "I get yer meaning. Greed causes one's downfall. We've seen that time and time again as we hunt the stones. But how does that tell me where to find the Stone of Faith?"

His da's hand moved to his shoulder, gripping him. "Ye must look to both quotes, son. 'Faith is confidence in what we hope for and assurance about what we do not see. Everything is possible for one who believes.' "

He stared at his sire's expectant expression. His da smiled and turned him so they both gazed at the seals. "It's much like in Egypt when we went after the Stone of Hope. Some things we only saw through the Eye of Ra. Ye must have faith and believe, son. Once ye believe that which ye cannot see—ye will find the stone." Ewan stood there absorbing what his sire said.

He huffed when his naivety clicked into awareness. "Evie said the same about her search for a magic Iona Stone. One must cast out all doubt, have faith to see that which is not before yer very eyes."

Colin patted his cheek, much like pride and softness in the gesture. "Aye. Cast all doubt, carry hope, and have faith." When his da turned and headed up the dock toward the castle, he called over his shoulder, "I have faith in ye, son. Ye will find yer way."

Ewan sat on the bench as the wind rolled in from the sea, tugging at his shirt and hair like the breath of some watching force. He looked toward the seals at the point, eyes narrowed—not with doubt, but with a strange, simmering certainty.

Lorelei murmuring her poem, *united*—echoed in the back of his mind, chased by the image of her tear-filled gaze the moment she'd whispered, *It's not that simple.* Ewan shut his eyes, letting it all wash over him. Faith, hope, love. The stones were more than objects. They were truths.

And maybe, just maybe, like his da, he could find the stone and save the maiden.

Chapter 10

The Faithful approached the large port of Portsmouth, the only one on the small island of Waitukura. A favored stop of theirs over the years when they'd gone on with their adventures. Or, as his sister Evie called his time hop, *playing pirate*.

Ewan glanced up. The white shape of a man holding a knife over a red bleeding heart always made him smile when Blackbeard's flag waved in the southern wind. He rolled his hand. With the next flap, the fabric shifted to the good ole Union Jack. Ewan blew a laugh when the British flag fluttered. Can't sail into port as the notorious pirate, let alone his ghost. Or his ghost crew.

He called to his crew. "Look, lively men."

One-eyed Joe smirked. "What? Like really alive?"

Ewan smirked. "Aye, ye nim pot."

The men roared with laughter. This was something they enjoyed, interacting with live people. The contact kept their spirits happy whilst stuck in between realms. To himself, he swore one day he'd see their souls rest, somehow.

Doug approached Ewan on the bridge. "Our usual switch?" Ewan nodded as his eyes scanned the ships docked—not a sign of *The Fancy*. The boat had to dock near here. Too often, they'd run into Low in these waters.

Doug elbowed him. "Don't forget to lose the beard."

He stood taller, straightening his collar, "And ye'll be calling *me* captain."

Ewan smirked while he waved the beard away, the wiry hairs fading. They'd done this hundreds of times—switched places when sailing into port so no one would make any connection by recognizing Ewan as Blackbeard's ghost. That and their act afforded Ewan a certain freedom to roam the taverns while Doug played cards, gambling with other ships' captains. Ewan had to keep an eye on him, though. His best buddy could chat up anyone, but he was a lousy gambler and could lose hundreds if left alone without Ewan's mind powers.

Today's goal. To learn all they could about Captain Low, *The Fancy*, and his mysterious sponsor. He'd find Lorelei and hopefully the Stone of Faith through the greedy sponsor.

Doug elbowed him again when the ship rounded into a spot. "The name, ye forgot the name."

Both leaned over the side and Ewan flicked his fingers and the letters *The Faithful* faded into *Jewel of the Sea*. Doug laughed out loud as the crew tied the lines docking the large vessel.

Ewan shrugged. "She is and better."

Doug hmphed. "Ye wish."

The men lowered the plank that landed hard on the quay at the dock master's feet. Thank goodness the governor had a high turnover rate for the dock masters. Each time they made berth here, there was a new one, always influenced by the right amount of coin.

His friend rubbed his hands together. "And I'm off to the Salty Dog Tavern."

Ewan sighed. "Only after ye deal with the master there. I'm sure Abigail can wait."

Doug ambled past him as his stomach growled. "I hope the new master doesn't delay me too long. It's been weeks since I've seen my sweetheart."

Ewan snorted. "Aye, but yer stomach calls for her cooking."

Doug smacked his lips. "I do like her fish pie."

The new captain stepped on the plank heading to the dock, and the rotund dock master propped his foot on the end, preventing anyone from exiting the ship without taking a dip in the ocean. "Who makes berth before tide?"

Doug came down the plank, calling to the man. "Ho! It is finally good to make land, my mate!"

The dock master held his book open while he eyed their ship, "*Jewel of the Sea*, not a very formidable name for a ship. More like an adornment."

Doug elbowed Ewan as he spoke over Ewan's huff. "I won her gambling. Tell me, is there a fine game a captain can find here?"

His friend jingled his coin pouch, and the dock master's gaze moved to the sound of the clinking coins. "Aye, The Salty Dog has always got a game. But first your ship must be registered, and *fees paid*."

The rotund man flipped open the book. "No registry of *Jewel of the Sea*, yet you fly the Union Jack." He raised his gaze and his eyebrows.

Doug placed a coin on the open book. "Like I said, newly won. The registry's in the post." The round man sniffed once.

He placed another larger coin on the book. "I'm sure ye can make an exception." Another smaller coin joined the other two. "This once." A fourth joined them, and the pile slid to the dock master's round belly. He had to close the book to stop them from falling onto the deck, possibly losing them between the planks into the sea.

The fat man reopened the book, grabbing the coins. "All's in order, gentlemen. Enjoy your respite."

He folded his book, bowed, and strode down the deck, pocketing the coins. Ewan followed Doug off the ship to the dock, standing for a moment as he gained his *land legs* while the motion of the sea faded on land.

As both men strode toward the lively town, Ewan leaned over to Doug. "Minimal gambling this time. And focus on *The Fancy* and trying to find out who Low's sponsor is."

Doug chuckled. "After I see Abigail."

Ewan clapped his friend on the back. "I bet Abigail knows a thing or two about Low's sponsor. Ask her." Ewan turned away to the back alley. "If ye can get past that dog of hers."

His friend held his hands out. "What Salty Dog? He's a sweet boy." Doug wound his way to the front of the tavern while Ewan crept around the back, slipping through the kitchen and startling Abigail's cook, Martha, who yelped as he strode through the back door.

She batted his hand when he grabbed a roll. "Out with you, Ewan, I'll serve you proper." He shied from her when she shook her head. "Abi will be right glad to see you boys."

Ewan took a bite, mumbling from around the yeasty morsel. "Doug, ye mean she'll be right happy to see Doug."

Right on cue, the tavern erupted in cheers. "Dougie! The best captain to sail the seas!" Abi's laughter filtered in over the noise, making Ewan grin as he finished his small meal. They were a match—the tavern owner with his pirate mate and best friend. Doug deserved happiness, even if he had to find his sweetheart hundreds of years in the past. Doug used Dougie for a nickname in honor of his grandfather, who had been a captain from the future yet sailed in the past. Fond stories told on sleepovers at Ardchattan Priory by Doug's da, John, echoed in Ewan's mind. He sighed, missing those simpler times.

The cheers continued while Ewan slipped into the room. Salty Dog, the large deerhound who lay by the fireplace, stood, but he waved him down. Ewan needed to be discreet on this trip. Doug and Abigail embraced with a sweet kiss. Jacob, behind the bar, handed Doug a mug.

Doug lifted the tankard and toasted the bar. "Greetings to one and all from the seven seas!" The patrons all cheered, toasting the captain making a scene. That is, except for the three at the back table who lifted their cups, mumbling *aye*, and then set them down. Ewan scooted closer to their table as if to warm himself before the fireplace.

The heavier of the three grumbled, "Aye, what that must be like to have a captain who treats all equally."

The blond man beside him nodded. "Aye, sharing the prize, keeping to the code."

The skinniest, Ewan, mentally named Slim, chugged his ale and slammed the mug on the table. "How about a captain that wins the prize in the first place!"

Ewan slid into the vacant seat, joining the fellow Scotsmen. "Seems like ye boys have fallen on hard times. Buy ye a round?"

He lifted his hand, and the bar boy, Davey, ran to them, easily carrying four mugs, two in each hand filled to the rim yet not spilling a drop. He set them on the table, and Ewan gave him a coin. When Davey turned to leave, Ewan slipped another coin in his pocket—a little sleight of hand to help the young boy in Abi's employ.

The heavy man lifted his mug. "To whom do we toast, thanking ye for a drink."

Ewan lifted his mug using his middle name. "Ron, lads, and ye are?" Ewan beamed inside whenever he used his middle name, the same as his grandda's. Even though he had never met him, he felt he knew him well from all the tales his da told him about the great man.

They toasted and drank, the heavy one belching when he lowered his mug. "I'm Oliver." He waved his cup to the blond. "He's Al."

The skinny man beamed when Oliver introduced him. "He's Zach."

Zach nodded. "Short for Zachariah."

Oliver drank again as he eyed him. Ewan sat, drinking, allowing the men to grow used to him. Buy them a drink, gain their trust, and he might not have to use his mind powers to acquire the information he sought. A cheer came up from the bar. So, Dougie scored in his gambling game. Now, on to Ewan's assignment.

Al grunted when Oliver belched again, speaking over the grunt. "Ah, a captain with a prize. Ye come in with him?"

Ewan shook his head. "No." He sat back, setting his mug on his flat belly. "Ye men know of a ship needing some mates?" Al glanced at Oliver and then Zach, who raised an eyebrow. Ewan smiled. They only needed a little push.

Ewan sent the three a mental command. *Ye want to tell me about yer ship.*

Oliver nodded and sat up. "Aye, we do. A right easy work the job will be for a sailor who sticks with his crew."

Ewan sat forward, placing his mug on the table. "Is that so? Does she berth here?"

Al shook his head. "No, not the public port. There's a private one on the other side of the island in a secluded cove hidden by the mountain range called Roseli. Roseli Cove it is."

Ewan smirked—this was all too easy. "Private? How's that?"

Zach grinned. "We got ourselves a sponsor, we do. The sugar man, a plantation owner."

Al set his elbows on the table, waving his hands as he spoke. "Aye, rich man he is. Looking for jewels. We split the rest of the prize."

Oliver kicked Al under the table. "Enough, we don't know much about Ron here. Captain, see, he's picky about his crew."

Ewan sat back, trying to seem at ease. Picky? He sent another mind command. *Ye want to tell me why he's picky.*

The man leaned in, whispering, "There's something special about how we plunder, so ye have to be of strong mind."

Ewan almost laughed out loud. Strong of will and mind, these men were not. He easily influenced their thoughts. But he went along with them. "Really, what's special about how ye loot?"

Zach sat smiling like a silly schoolboy. "She sings. Her voice, the sound is beautiful." Oliver shoved Zach, who came out of the trance. Ewan's heart stopped when Zach said. *She sings.* He knew only one woman who sang like the gods, drawing every man toward her charms.

All three men stood, spat in their hands, clapped them together, turned around three times while rubbing their hands on their shirts, then sat obediently like little pups. They'd done the ritual in such precision that their act spoke of something they did often.

Oliver grabbed his mug, hugging the vessel to him. "Ye have to be able to resist her draw, or ye'll be sucked in, like our prize."

Ewan kept a straight face. "One woman is the same as another. I can resist any female." Ewan needed to know if this was Lorelei and Low's ship. Had he found her?

He needed to know who this mysterious sponsor was. "The plantation's name. Who is this sugar man?"

Oliver picked up his mug and drained the contents. Then held up the empty cup to Ewan, who waved Davey back over. Davey came quickly and set down four more mugs, and Ewan passed him two coins.

As Davey ambled away, Ewan sent another mind command. *The plantation owner, ye will tell me all ye know.* Zach gulped his second cup as Al drained his.

Oliver had just finished his when he slammed the mug on the table. "Right. Sugar man he's a strange one we rarely see. Black hair, black clothing."

Al nodded. "Aye, black suits him all right."

Oliver set his elbows on the table. "He showed up here last year, outta the blue."

Zach belched. "Like he dropped from the sky."

Al elbowed Zach. "He sailed in on *The Merriman*."

Oliver grunted. "He bought the Rosalie Estate at auction. Nearly two thousand acres, plus the slaves. All of it. Mrs. MacLeod owned the place before, but she died without issue."

Al waved his hand. "Aye, now this man showed up and not only has us pirating for slaves, he's after jewels. Greedy bastard he is."

Zach shivered. "He's right cruel with his slaves, not like Mrs. MacLeod, who was fair."

Oliver gripped his fist. "Can't get his hands on enough. Wants all the gems of the world."

Al grumbled. "Took the jewels. He's not letting Captain Low stick to the code."

Oliver huffed. "All fair plunder of the prize is to be divided."

Ewan nodded. "Aye, I know the code."

Ewan sent another mind message. *His name, the sugar man's name. Ye must tell me.*

Oliver shrugged. "I don't know his name." He replied so fast that Ewan glanced around, but the other two seemed too absorbed in the conversation to notice. Good, he had a strong hold on them mentally. Ewan needed to confer with Doug. He needed to know if Doug had found out the same thing, but not enough time had passed for Doug to play out his gambling ruse. Ewan's stomach growled, reminding him he'd not eaten.

He stood nodding to the men. "I thank ye for the company, but I must make my way on."

Oliver sat back. "Come, Ron, stay a bit. Ye can buy us another round."

Ewan shrugged. "I must move on, thank ye." He turned, and Al grabbed his arm. "Will we see ye on the next sail? We depart the day after tomorrow with the morning tide for another slave run."

Ewan grinned. "Aye, ye will." He'd just gained the

next step in his plan—attack Low's ship when he sailed out of the Roselie Cove. As he strode toward the kitchen, he sent his last mind command, *Ye all will forget this conversation happened.*

As he pushed through the kitchen door, Oliver yelled, "Boy, why is my mug empty?"

****

Much later into the night, Doug stumbled into the kitchen, waking Ewan from the nap he took at the cook's table. "I won. I actually won and without yer help!" Abigail followed, grabbing a bowl and scooping in fish pie.

Ewan wiped his face and sat up. "Well, what ye find out?"

Doug sat as Abigail served him, then settled on his lap, hugging him. Doug scooped up the pie, speaking between spoonsful. "Plantation owner."

He spooned another mouthful, then swallowed. "He's after jewels, but no one knows why."

Ewan nodded. "I learned the same."

Abigail spoke as Doug ate. "It's been the talk since he bought the plantation. He's increased slavery and added his pirating of jewels. His sailors aren't happy at how Captain Low's forced to turn over all the jewels. But *The Fancy* is the sugar man's ship."

Doug took a deep breath and sputtered. "Abi says the locals are worried the sugar man's upset the gods with his greed."

His gal nodded. "Morne Trios Pitons, rumbles more. The locals fear the gods' wrath. Some of his slaves speak of him using magic that keeps the gods in his favor, but no one's really certain."

Doug squeezed Abigail. "The mountain with three

peaks." Ewan raised an eyebrow, and Doug nodded in reply. *So, the plantation owner is the greedy man in the fable.*

Ewan focused on Abigail. "Does this plantation owner have a name?"

Abigail smirked. "He has everyone call him Master. No one knows his name."

She laid her head on Doug's shoulder. "The sailors speak of a siren. One they fear that sails with them." She sighed. "They boast of her voice and speak of the dangers of her allure in the same breath." Doug set his spoon down, staring at Ewan, who nodded. *Aye, it was Lorelei the men spoke of.*

He sent Doug a mind speak. *I learned much the same. So, the sugar master is the greedy man, Lorelei the Fae. But he hasn't found the stone. He hunts the gem. But does he know what he hunts? What the stone does?*

They sat in silence for a moment. Ewan kept to his thoughts as Doug cuddled his sweetheart. Ewan blew a laugh. They were lovesick for each other and a perfect match. He hoped he didn't lose his best friend to love in the past like his da lost Ainslie.

Ewan stood. "Abi, have ye rooms for a night?"

She sat up. "For you, always. I have yer room ready, and well, Doug, he's always welcome."

Doug hugged her, and Ewan almost envied them—to find true love.

He sent another message to Doug. *Ye got two days, then we attack Low's ship. I found out when and where his ship sails from. We go to hunt the stone.*

Doug eyed Abi, then raised an eyebrow at Ewan, who mind spoke again. *Aye, to find Lorelei. But is she a prisoner of Low or the sugar master?*

Chapter 11

Lorelei stood on the stern of *The Fancy* as they clipped through the chilled waters. The moon cast a white light upon the wave's tips, illuminating them. Almost like the willow lisps of the deep ocean, creatures who carried a light about themselves in the dark depths of the sea. Her people easily called the beings to them to use for light when diving into the far reaches of the deep. She smiled. The willow wisps were more like little pets, only wanting companionship in exchange for using their natural luminesce.

A hard emotion pulled at her—she sensed desperation in a lover's search for one he cared deeply for. She stared out across the sea. The tug came stronger this time. *Ewan.* Close like this, his soul called to her.

She reached for her chest, trying to dispel the ache at not being able to answer his call.

Heavy footfalls announced an unwelcomed guest. His clean scent always permeated amongst the unwashed crew—pirates and scoundrels, all of them. Why this gentleman worked for such an evil person as the madman was a mystery. Her father had the sight of a man's mind. She wished she had that now. Her powers lay only in her voice, but she didn't need her father's powers to know what this man desired. Even if any man learned how to evade her power, her lure was too much to deny.

He stood just behind her, his body's warmth breaking the wind's chill at her back. "Is there anything you require, my lady?"

There it was again. *My lady*. Like she was an aristocrat and not the creature she'd been born. She sighed. If he only knew.

She didn't turn. "I am fine, thank you."

He stepped closer, causing her to tense. "You seem chilled." He went to remove his coat.

She held her hand out, enunciating her words. "I am in *no* need of your assistance." Captain Low stood still. Was he assessing her—testing her powers? She turned her head into the wind to catch his face in her periphery. His jawline tightened.

He took a deep breath, held it, then released it. "If you would pay me heed, take advantage of my offer. I'd see you released into my care." She turned back to the open ocean and the pull on her soul. This man would not release her. No human man would. She'd only go from one prison to another.

Speaking in a firm tone, she answered him. "My answer is the same." Captain Low shifted toward her again.

She sidestepped. "Don't touch me."

His hand retreated into his coat. "I only offer sanctuary—if you were to give yourself to me. I'd give you all the world has to offer."

Lorelei stood staring at Captain Low. All human men reacted the same—attracted to the point of addiction, wanting her only to slake their lust, their need. Not one thought of her. With her powers, none were capable of reason. Not one—only Ewan.

She traveled down the rail, away from Captain Low.

"You will do your best to focus on your mission, Captain. The madman turns desperate in his search for the jewel."

The earlier tirade flew fast through her mind.

The madman, or as he commanded all call him, Master, stood yelling. She stared, still not calling any man *master*.

"Blackbeard, I want him alive. Ye will draw him in chasing *The San Miguel* again. He's due in our waters, the ship's belly full of slaves, an opportunity this pirate cannot pass up. This time ye are to capture Blackbeard and bring him to me. With him, I will find the jewel!" He chuckled. "And I will have Evie." Captain Low stood still. Lorelei floated in her tank, commanded to listen.

The captain folded his arms behind his back, seeming to look compliant, but Lorelei knew his true opinion of the madman. "It would help if I knew what the jewel looked like. You mention this gem time and again without a description."

The madman roared. "Blue, the damn thing's blue! Bright as the sun on the ocean, yet deep as a cold heart." He heaved a breath. "Points, the gem has points." He made a triangular shape with his hands, starting together at the top, widening, then cutting in at an angle, forming a tip at the bottom, the entirety the size of a man's hand. The shape reminded Lorelei of an angel fish. Home seemed like such a world away yet was so close.

Low's curt reply brought her out of her musings. "Blackbeard's crew?"

The madman's eyes settled on her. "My pet will deal with them." She stared into their blackness. Pain and torment were all she saw.

Low spoke softly. "If Blackbeard refuses or will not

come willingly."

The black gaze stayed fixed on her. "He will find his death at the bottom of the sea he seems to love so much." She shivered. His stare felt like death called for her.

Now on the ship's deck, Captain Low cleared his throat as he stood tall and straightened his coat, bringing her back to the present.

His voice clipped. "I am aware of my job." He sneered. "Are you aware of yours? Will you be able to kill as commanded? Kill the supposed ghost but real man, Blackbeard?"

Lorelei turned to face him fully, her mouth open while she set her gaze upon Captain Low, posing to bring forth her power. She'd use her powers on him long before Ewan, never on Ewan.

When his focus rose to hers, he jolted, stumbling back. "I see you are." He turned, then stopped. Over his shoulder, he whispered, "You seem to know your duty. I leave you to it."

As the captain's boots beat a retreat, Lorelei moved back to her place at the stern. Finally, alone, she took a cleansing breath. The chilled air tickled her lungs. Her body craved the chilled waters and the promised transformation to her true form. Maybe Murus was right. Maybe the Telkhines warriors, her father's fighting force, could beat the madman's powers. But Evie wasn't ready to gamble on *maybe*. Not yet. For this, it was more than duty. She had a strategy. She'd learned how to move through the plantation owner's madness, twist her words, and guard her thoughts. She had become a shadow—quiet, underestimated, invisible in all the ways that counted. And that made her dangerous. She could delay his schemes, sabotage his rituals, and unravel him from within.

She stayed because her presence kept the worst from happening. Yet, his promise that in the end she'd be human was the greatest reason of all. And still, even in the quiet corners of her soul, she remained for Ewan—because the moment this was over and the madman fell, she would find her way back to him.

Ewan's soul beckoned, making her sigh, the pull as undeniable as the tides bending to the moon. He was the one man who saw her—not the illusion, not the intoxication, but the woman beneath it all. She had spent a lifetime drowning in the hunger of others, in the way their eyes darkened, their hands reached, their wills crumbled beneath the weight of wanting her. But Ewan? He withstood it. He didn't just resist—he refused to be ruled by her power.

And that terrified and thrilled her.

Ewan was the unknown in a world she thought she had mastered. The one man who could undo her in ways no one else ever had. She didn't just want to be with him—she needed to. Because with Ewan, she wasn't a prize or a temptation. With Ewan, she was finally free.

His call came again, his mind's thoughts coming clearly to her. He wondered if she was on Low's ship, if she was still captive. If she needed saving. Her heart ached to reply, but her mind didn't have the power, unlike her father.

Did she dare defy the madman again? All she wanted was to be with Ewan. He called to her, and she couldn't stand this torture anymore. His ship secretly followed—had sensed them from the moment they set sail in pursuit. But to risk the wrath of the madman?

Lorelei centered her focus, her energy. She glanced

around. Alone. The closest human was the man steering the ship on the bridge, asleep where he stood.

Dare she risk going to him? Her heart cried yes!

She climbed over the railing and hung by the ropes. The water from the boat breaking the waves while the vessel sailed teased her senses, making her legs tingle. Her soul needed to take on her true form. She lowered herself closer, silently slipping into the cold waters with the next swell. Her body came alive. A prickling washed over her form. Her legs bucked once, then again. Lorelei's body gave a large, stretched pull, then snapped as her tail burst free. Her clothes disappeared when she drew in water, breathing deeply. Her tail flipped when she turned a full flip. She stayed suspended in the sea while the hull of *The Fancy* sailed away above her.

Ewan's soul called again, and with a smile, she turned to the south and toward her heart.

****

Ewan stood on the bow, his face into the wind as they chased *The Fancy*. She was on Low's ship again. He felt her soul reach him when she thought of him.

Doug came beside him, leaning on the railing. "All's in order. We follow based upon yer direction." He huffed. "How ye feel yer way around like this gives me chills like ye did when we were kids."

Ewan grinned. He'd honed his mind skills over time. When focused, he could pinpoint anyone within two kilometers. Hell, connecting to Evie came close to ten since they were bonded as twins. Doug sighed, tapping the railing. The beat was rapid, like Doug's heartbeat.

He took a deep breath. "Out with it. What concerns ye?"

Doug turned to him. "Ye know Low is out for ye?

This is a trap."

Ewan grinned. "Aye. I am counting on it."

His friend fisted his hands. "Ye always come out the winner." He ran his hand through his hair, looking like his da, John MacArthur. "What if this time ye don't? What if we can't get back?"

Ewan smirked. "Then ye spend yer life with Abigail in eternal bliss."

Doug grabbed his arm. "I mean it, Ewan. I have a bad feeling about this one."

Men shouting from midship had both men turning. Ewan's mind focused on the commotion—trying to discern friend or foe. He chuckled when his mind locked in on who had boarded his ship. The trespasser was both friend and foe. He strode past Doug, angry at her daring but relieved by her presence.

Doug tugged his arm once more. "Ewan…"

Ewan brushed his friend's hand aside. "All will be fine. Trust me. I've never led ye astray, and I won't now."

He marched to where two men held a struggling woman between them. The deep red hair was a dead giveaway, but Ewan played out her game, seeing what she'd do. When he moved closer, the moonlight caught the red of her tresses, making them glow blood red.

Doug's voice carried loudly. "Son of a bitch! Fate isn't with us tonight." A deckhand, Bert, an Italian, held her arm while the other deckhand, Gilbert, his friend, held her other arm. Both men had not seen her being gunners and always below when she appeared. They had no idea who or what they held, what her powers were capable of.

Gilbert spoke with a thick Italian accent. "Caugh' a

stowaway, Captain. She was clinging to the side of the ship."

Bert snickered, his accent lighter. "Naked as the day she was born." Lorelei pulled against the men. Her hair waved but still covered her intimate areas, leaving him to wonder if her waves did so naturally or if she controlled them.

Gilbert pulled her to his side. "Wanna me tak'a her below to the brig?"

Bert yanked her to him, her body jolting at the sudden pull. "No, Captain. I'll take her down. I'm the one who found her." A tug of war commenced and the men vied to possess the creature before him. Ewan smirked as they jostled her. She kept her head down, hidden from view. Was the ploy to protect these men from her spell, or did she hide from him? For some reason, he wanted to know.

He spoke in his captain's voice, stern but low. "Bert, ye will take the prisoner below."

"I wish to parley with the captain," she said, her tone sharp. Bert shoved forward, pulling her along. Gilbert followed his lead. When she pulled back, her head came up, and her hair flipped over.

Her pale face shone in the moonlight when her glowing blue eyes met his. "Parley, please." Her eyes pleaded. Her soul called to him. She'd come to see him. He held up his hand, and the men stopped. Ewan stood there, gazing at the siren as her eyes pleaded.

"Ye heard the lady. Parley is in effect." The single act took everything in him, but he turned from her radiant eyes and beauty toward the stern and his cabin.

He called over his shoulder. "Release her." He stopped without turning. "Cover her before anyone else sees."

One-eyed Joe walked past him with a blanket. Rustling sounds came from behind him.

Doug strode past him, whispering, "This is not good, Ewan. She's with Low, ye know this."

He glowered. " 'Tis perfect."

Ewan strode into the hall and stopped at the threshold of his cabin without looking behind him to see if his sea urchin followed. When her wet feet padded on the deck, he grinned. Was she here to breathe life into his soul, or did Captain Low send her? A trap to bring death to his heart.

He entered his cabin and stood for a moment, gathering himself. With all his willpower, he turned and faced the most beautiful woman he'd ever encountered. One who held his heart in her hand whether she knew it or not. Yet, if she played him false it could destroy the organ surely as Low or the man who held the plantation would send him to his grave.

Chapter 12

She stood in the doorway, concerned that she had to call for parley. Ewan didn't seem as happy to see her as she thought he would be. Maybe her abandoning him before hurt his feelings, but she had to. He had to understand. She shivered and pulled the blanket closer. Someone tapped her shoulder. She turned, and Doug handed her a bundle of clothing.

He glared at Ewan, who shot daggers back at his friend. "That is all, Doug."

Doug huffed, then turned, closed the door, and his boots sounded down the hallway.

She stood still as Ewan stared at her, then edged into the room, intent on putting on the clothing and hopefully getting warm. In her human form, the cold always permeated into her soul. Even in the warmth of the Caribbean Ocean, nights turned chilly. There was a fire going, and she advanced toward the heat.

Ewan turned, facing the back windows, his back to her. "I'll keep turned. Ye may dress, warm yerself. Then we parley." She held up the clothing. A woman's shirt, skirt, and belt she laid on his bed. Even stockings with ties accompanied the ensemble.

Setting them aside, she gasped when she pulled the shirt over her head, allowing the blanket to drop. "You keep woman's clothing?" She glanced over her shoulder and caught his gaze.

His head turned till his profile came into view, his mouth firm. "I have a sister. She likes to sail."

She turned and stared at the clothing as the madman's voice echoed. *His sister, Evie, she's mine*. She fingered the garments. He has a sister, whom the madman was after. Must the maniac harm every female he knows? Sighing, she focused on the task of getting dressed, and the parlay with Ewan. Lorelei pulled on the skirt and wrapped the belt around her waist. She sat on the bed and pulled on her stockings one at a time. She rubbed the red scar where her injury had not fully healed. The wound ached a little.

His puff came from across the room. "Ye should bandage that. It's not fully healed." She lifted her head and caught him fully facing her.

Lorelei pulled up her last stocking and replied tartly. "You were to stay turned." She tied off the ribbon and flipped the skirt, covering her human legs.

His face filled with a grin. "Ye are fully dressed now."

The cook banged through the doorway with a tray, set the offering on the desk, glanced between the two, and then closed the door when he left—the scent of steamed tea and a baked sweet filled the air. Lorelei's stomach betrayed her by growling loudly.

Ewan sat at his desk, poured a cup of tea, and picked up a different bread she'd not seen before. He sat back, placed his feet on the desk, and took a large bite of the morsel as he sipped his tea. She stayed by the fire, staring at him. She loved baked goods, any kind of bread. A sweet scent came to her. This one was different. The temptation to run to him, begging for a bite, nearly overcame her. Instead, she stood still.

He sipped his tea and exhaled. "Parley, my lady. What do ye offer?"

She inched forward, deciding to bring up a past conversation, hoping to appeal to his humor. "Meal first, then we bargain." She peeked at him, hoping the diversion would win her a piece of the sweet and some time. "Wasn't it your servant that always said life's problems seem much smaller on a full belly?"

Ewan's smile filled his face. "Aye, she did." His feet returned to the floor with a clomp; leaning forward, he placed his items on the tray. He filled a cup with steaming tea and handed the beverage to her. When he didn't offer her a sweet, she eyed the plate.

His chuckle filled the room. "I recall yer fondness for baked goods." He set the plate before her with two pieces of bread covered with a cream. "These are Abigail's creations. Cake."

She eyed the plate, more curious about the woman than the treat. "Abigail?"

He glanced at the plate and then at her. "Doug's woman, they are lovesick for each other."

Ewan pushed the plate closer. "Eat yer fill, but after we talk."

His hand brushed hers as she took the plate. "No lies, Lorelei."

Lorelei nodded and grabbed the offering. Why was she always ravenous in his presence? She answered herself. Easy, he was the only human she felt at ease with, and her body relaxed for once.

Taking a bite, sweetness filled her mouth—the taste of sugar, familiar to her from her stolen visits to the kitchen in the madman's house. The smoothness of the topping, combined with the spring of the bread, was heavenly. The sugar coating stuck to the top of her mouth, and she moaned after she sipped the tea. She savored the last piece, picking and eating the treat in pieces. First, the sugary side on top, then the bottom, to see how the bread tasted different. The sugar made her mouth water, and she smacked her lips. His snort had her glancing at him and then back at the cake, which was better than bread, all sweet and spongy.

When she finished her tea, Ewan grunted. "I like it when a woman isn't shy about her hunger." He huffed. "Now, to our talk."

He pointed his finger at her. "Ye are with Low again." She looked down and shrugged, then glanced up when his voice came harder. "I rescued ye once from his grasp, and ye ran away—to him." He pressed his fingers together as he set his elbows on the desk. "Yet ye come to me now." She picked at her skirt and shrugged again.

Ewan's voice grew hard. "Ye were out swimming in the depths of the chilled ocean, naked and alone. It's night. The tide comes from the north, bringing cooler water. Ye could have succumbed to the chill even in the warm Caribbean Sea."

She raised her head. "I wasn't cold when I was in the water."

His eyebrow lifted. "Naked?"

Lorelei waved a hand, trying to be casual; he couldn't know that she'd changed form, leaving her clothing behind. "I had to escape in a hurry. The water doesn't hurt me. I love to be in the ocean."

His glare leveled on her. "Ye were on Low's ship that we follow." She glanced down and then back at him.

Lorelei couldn't lie, never to Ewan. "Maybe…"

Stone of Faith

He stayed still when he spoke softly. "Why?" She stood and stepped to the fireplace—anything to escape his scrutiny.

Ewan stood, rounding his desk, moving closer to her. "Why put yourself in danger?"

Tears gathered in her eyes as all the reasons jumbled in her mind. Her people—the madman's powers, his cruelty—his greed for the blue stone. Could she tell him all of her problems? Would he understand how she must protect her people? She had the power, not them. A woman—needed for once. Able to do something for all of them.

She glanced over her shoulder as a tear fell down her face. Ewan edged closer.

His hand reached out, and a finger caught the tear. "Why willingly stay captive? What is it your abductor has that you must protect?"

She faced him. "It's not what he has but what he can do to me, to my people. My people need me." She turned a little. "You wouldn't understand."

Ewan brushed the back of his hand down her cheek then huffed. "Honey, there is a lot I can understand. More than you'll ever know."

He stepped closer, his eyes searching hers. "I know you have powers." He smiled and flicked his wrist. A piece of fabric from the tray flew to his hand. Her eyes went to the desk and then back to his hand. He grinned and flicked his wrist again. The cloth burst into flames, and the fabric disappeared with a wiggle of his fingers.

His gaze met hers over his hand. "I have powers as well, Lorelei. But it's yer voice that holds power." She gasped and jolted back.

Ewan took her by the shoulders. "No, Lorelei, please

don't worry." His fingers caressed her, then trailed down her arms to her hands, taking them into his.

He brought them to his lips. "Your secret is safe with me. We are alike, humans with powers living in their realm in secret." He kissed her hand. "*Ye* are safe with me." This is why he was able to resist her powers. Ewan was Fae like her. She felt so relieved and unburdened all at once. Another tear fell and another. She hiccupped a sigh, and Ewan moved them to the bed together like a little dance she'd seen people do in the village, making her grin. This was her first dance with human legs. He sat like before and took her onto his lap, holding her.

She sank into his embrace. "Your father holds your mother this way when she's sad."

He squeezed her once. "Aye, my ma says this chases her tears away." He sat rubbing her back, hugging her, and holding her till her tears faded.

His breath tickled her ear. "Have faith in me, trust me. I'll chase yer tears away." They sat for a moment more and Lorelei would be content to sit in his embrace for eternity.

Ewan whispered, "Now tell me of your troubles. Maybe I can help?"

Her reply trembled between them. "It's complicated."

As he spoke, she felt him grunt. "Something I thrive on. Come on, how bad can yer problem be?"

She fingered the hair on his arm, dark and wiry yet soft to the touch. "My people, I protect my people. They are right under his nose—he'll find them if I don't."

Ewan's voice vibrated as she leaned into him. "So, Low threatens yer people."

She shook her head. How to tell him about the

madman without saying his name, alerting her to him? He'd call her back if he knew she'd escaped Low's ship, purposefully thwarting his plans for Blackbeard and Ewan.

Lorelei focused on her people. "My captivity is essential to their survival. Their need has made me necessary for once in our world."

"Need? Need is not a necessity. Their need is greed." He sat her up, gripping both her shoulders. "Yer used for position, and yer power is used for greed, for death." She squeaked when he shook her a little.

Ewan softened his grip when he whispered. "You have your own needs, things ye dream of." He was right—she did. But to be human, she'd give all for that. Ewan seemed to understand—part of her dilemma.

She stared into his blue eyes, darker than hers, like the ocean's depths. "I must do what I can to help them, to protect them."

Ewan brushed his hand across her cheek. "One woman and ye do all this." She glanced away, not wanting to admit her true purpose. The promise the madman had to make her human. Would Ewan understand? Would he be repulsed by her true form if he found out?

He brushed his hand over her cheek and gazed into her eyes. "Lorelei, *necessary* is not something people need to survive. *Necessary* is something people can't do without." She squirmed, with the intent of moving away, but his arms encircled her, not hurting but holding her.

She spoke out, needing him to understand. "You quote necessary's meaning to me. How about necessary—an inevitable nature that no one can deny?" She could not deny her people's need—their safety.

His hand traveled to her face, his finger caressing her lips as he spoke. "Ye, Lorelai *are* a contradiction." Her lips tingled, and the sensation traveled down her body, bringing forth a shiver.

He bent, kissing her lips. "To me, ye are necessary. Lorelai, *ye* are everything."

She wanted to be his everything. She wanted to be with him.

Ewan kissed her full on the lips, then whispered into the kiss. "Don't ye see? I can't do without ye."

She whispered back, their breaths mingling. "I cannot do without you." He brushed his lips over hers softly once, then again. Giggling, she reveled in the tickle of his touch.

His beard shifted, and white teeth flashed. "I forgot the beard. It's a spell." He waved his hand, and as hair disappeared, his entire face appeared. The regal lines were sharp and attractive. Lorelei went to stand, and his hold became firmer. She shook her head and pressed against his chest to rise. He released her, his eyes following her when she pushed away.

Beside the chair, she turned her back on him and unbuckled her belt, allowing the item to fall to the ground. She glanced over her shoulder. Ewan had stood also and was in the process of unbuckling his. As she raised an eyebrow she untied her skirt, allowing the fabric to fall to the floor. She glanced down, stepping free of the garment, and when she raised her head, Ewan had stepped from his trousers.

A grin filled his face while he quickly pulled his shirt over his head. He held the garment bunched before him, covering his manly parts. Lorelei had spied on naked human men before and knew how the parts differed. Yet, seeing Ewan's chest, tapered hips, and strong legs, her imagination filled the rest.

She moved toward him, and his hand came up, stopping her. "Lorelei, is this what ye want? What is between a man and a woman?" She smiled as she grabbed the bottom of her shirt and pulled the garment over her head. Her mass of hair became caught inside, and her body but for the stockings remained bared before him. She pulled her hair free and Ewan's expression went from shock to wonder.

He dropped his shirt and came to her, gathering her in his arms. She had a glimpse of him, but the image was enough to tell her he was larger than any human she'd seen. Ewan's body came flush with hers and heated her. His demanding kiss as he lifted and spun them sent her into a dizzy spell that ended with him lying over her on the bed. With slow care, he knelt, untying and rolling down each stocking, letting them drop on the floor.

His hands roamed her body when he stood, marking each spot he touched. She became so overcome by the sensation of him touching her that all she could do was hold onto his shoulders. His lips trailed kisses to her breast, first laving one then the other. She squeaked at the first suckle, and his chuckle came when her fingers threaded through his hair as she tried to pull him closer. He kissed her lips while his hand skimmed to her center. Her legs fell open in invitation as his fingers parted her. Hot then cold flashed over her body, and a wetness covered her.

Ewan's fingers swirled, pushing against her. The hot flash came again, and his movements shifted while he pushed a finger inside. The sensation of being filled left her gasping as Ewan kissed her, taking the breath into his mouth. The spinning of the fullness had him going deeper, building a force in her. His pace quickened and his kisses grew harder. She had trouble catching her breath as heat flushed her body again. The force exploded and her body gripped his fingers. She cried out as she released that force, leaving her panting. He withdrew his finger, and he moved over her, his kisses hard against her welcome lips.

Ewan lifted his head while he pushed against her opening. "Lorelei, this will pinch a bit, but I promise sweet bliss after." He kissed her as he pressed inside. She sensed he opened her. He pushed deeper, moaning, and she felt split. He shoved, and she yelped at the sharp pain. Ewan froze, and she had a feeling of completeness. He kissed her lips softly and the ache ebbed. Ewan pushed within her again making a force build inside. The sensations from her core rose, and she imagined them joined as one. Ewan quickened while he kissed her again, and she opened her eyes, meeting his as he pressed within her.

He whispered in their kiss. "Come with me, love."

The pressure built inside her as he moved quickly. Heat consumed her, and stars danced in her vision. In a scream, the dam broke free, and shockwave after shockwave rocked her body. Her heart pulsed, and her breath caught. Ewan kept at his onslaught of her, the after waves rocking her soul. Soon, he roared, froze over her, and warmth filled her. He filled her soul.

Ewan panted while he rested his head on her shoulder. She rubbed his sweaty back as he caught his breath. Her body released him, and he sighed when he rolled to the side, taking her into his arms. They lay there a moment with her eyes closed, and Lorelei imagined she saw stars behind her eyelids.

Ewan took a deep breath, then another. "God Lorelei, ye are a gift."

She lay in the afterglow of their love. Her heartbeat slowed as his fingers drew lazy circles on her upper arm. Held in his embrace like this, she could live forever and want for nothing else.

He hummed and shifted. "The first night ye stayed with me, ye whispered a poem. What was it?"

Lorelei loved the short poem. She'd recited her prose each evening before going to sleep, thinking of Ewan. Hoping and wishing, he thought of her.

She whispered, "My body hums with energy. I sing to the gods. My love shines in my smile for you. My soul burns with the hope of our souls united."

His arms tightened around her. "United, aye."

Ewan sat up a bit. "A poem. We'll write our poem together. Each night, we add a verse." He lay there for a moment. The silence seemed like his mind wandered.

He huffed, and she felt his grin as he repeated her verse. "My body hums with energy. My faith sings to the gods." His finger dropped beneath her chin, lifting her face till their eyes met. "My love shines in my smile for you." He kissed her lips. "My soul burns with the fire of billions of stars." He sat back. "Now ye add a verse to our poem." Lorelei had worked on the verse each evening, wanting to give him a complete poem that spoke of her longing for him and the feeling of completion in his presence.

She took his hand in hers, holding them as they prayed like the humans. "I rejoice in each reunion. I anticipate the me yet to come." She did, in her form like a human, to be with Ewan always.

Lorelei took a deep breath. "I shall show you all my love. In a time when our souls shall be one."

Ewan hummed and then kissed her. "Stay, don't go back. I promise we'll figure out what we need to do for yer people. But please don't go back to Low."

She hugged him hard. "I won't." Her head rested against his chest. The beating of his heart and the warmth of his body soon had her eyes drooping.

Sometime later, a sting came to her leg, and she jolted. Ewan's hand on her, combined with the soft timber of his voice, had her easing. "Easy, *mo sìrean*, I only bind yer leg." For a moment, she feared the madman had called her, forcing her to leave again, but not this time.

She laid back. "What did you say to me in your language?"

A smile grew as a blush crept from his neck to his cheeks. "*Mo sìrean*, the word means *my siren* in Gaelic."

Lorelei tried pronouncing the words, but her version came out more like *she-ran* than how he pronounced the endearment, *sheir-an*.

Ewan chuckled. "Nice start." He patted her bound leg above the bandage. "We'll work on yer Gaelic later."

He leaned over and kissed her forehead. "For now, rest. I go to see where we are with Low and his ship." He rose, slid on his jacket, and gathered his belts, arming himself. He'd already dressed. She snuggled into the covers, his scent lingering, fresh sea with a hint of male musk. She loved being with him.

Once fully armed, he leaned over again, kissing her lips. "Stay here. We should engage around sunup. Don't let Low see ye, no matter what occurs. When it's safe, I'll come for ye." She nodded, relieved for once someone else fought the battles.

Ewan turned and left the cabin with a soft click of the door. She hoped the madman had no idea what she was up to. She wiggled her toes, no tingling. Maybe, for once, she'd stay in her human form. She prayed so.

Chapter 13

A cannon shattered the silence and jolted her awake. Her heart slammed against her ribs as she shot upright, breath hitching, the lingering echoes rattling through her bones. Bright sunlight shone into the room, and a warm breeze filtered through the open windows. Another blast from nearby boomed, followed shortly later by a splash.

Ewan's yell filled the air. "Low, I have the advantage. Leave off *The San Miguel*. She's mine for plunder!" Lorelei slid from the bed wrapping the sheet to cover her and went to the open window, intent on hearing Captain Low's response.

After a heartbeat, Low's voice came. "It's you who will leave off Blackbeard! I have my secret weapon!"

Lorelei turned, her breath caught in her throat. What would Captain Low do after discovering she wasn't on his ship? His *secret weapon* had fled in the night. She glanced around the cabin. A pile of clean clothing lay on the chair before the desk. Stockings lay neatly folded on top. When she approached, freshly polished boots sat on the floor. She smiled. Ewan thought of everything.

She quickly dressed as feet stomped on the deck above her head. When Captain Low didn't have her, would he blow Ewan's ship from the water?

As she laced up her boots, Ewan bellowed, "Gunners ready, starboard." His laughter filled the air.

Well, he had prepared to face the captain. What would happen to all on board, herself included, if Low opened fire?

She inched out the door, down the hall, and stopped short of the stairs leading up to the main deck. Bert from the night before stood beside the doorway. When she stepped up the stairs moving closer, he turned, spotting her. He put his finger to his lips, silently shushing her.

When he pulled them away, he grinned as he whispered, "Captain Low, he's not happy." He snickered. "Blackbeard made him angry."

She glanced out farther and spotted Ewan on the bow. He stood with his arms folded and his feet apart, at ease in command of all around him. His head turned and found her gaze.

He smiled when he called out. "Captain Low. I'm waiting for yer secret weapon!"

Low's response came quickly. "I'll have her soon! You will find your end at the bottom of the ocean!"

Ewan kept his eyes on her. "Really? Ye sure of that?" Warmth spread through her. Ewan would never give her up to Low or the madman. For once, a man's care and love outweighed her allure over him.

Low's call came again. "Lorelei, you bitch! Where are you?" She shrank back into the hallway at his yell—an automatic response to his summons.

Bert kept his eyes on Low's ship as he called down to her. "You stay there, sweetie. Let us deal with Low."

She inched back up to see Ewan. He stood watching Low's ship with a wide grin. He unfolded his arms and lowered them slowly. If one wasn't looking, they might have missed the signal. With a flick of his right wrist, he rolled his appendage forward as if calling someone to him.

The flap of sails unfolding filled the air. The ship lurched forward, sending Lorelei sprawling on the stairs while Ewan's crew gave a loud cheer. Variations of men yelling *Red Rover* came to her.

Bert laughed aloud. "Ewan's game! This should be fun!" He took off running. When Lorelei bent to boost herself from the stairs, strong arms lifted her, and she came face to face with Ewan.

He kissed her hard on the lips. "Ye stay here. We break the line and cut off Low to take the slave ship." A cannon blast rocked the ship, and Ewan gripped her tightly. "Stay in my cabin." He brushed his hand on her cheek. "Yer absence has saved the day. We liberate the slaves!" He let her go. His boots stomped off as he rounded the stairs to the bridge above.

Lorelei retreated to his cabin, relieved she wouldn't be required to use her powers on anyone. She sat before the desk, waiting in the same chair she'd sat before. After a few cannon volleys, the sails flapped, and calls between the sailors indicated they'd come alongside *The San Miguel* and boarded her. There wasn't any more fighting that she could tell, and soon, boredom became her companion.

She stood and began to pace. In the window, the ship's image came into her peripheral. She went closer to spy on the Spanish frigate floating beside them. Laughter filled the hallway as boots stomped toward the cabin. She turned when the door banged open, and Ewan and Doug stumbled inside. Doug carried a sizeable bound book and hefted the large volume onto the desk. She stood by the window, frozen, wondering what had happened to the Spanish ship's crew and the cargo. Did

Ewan do the same as Low—steal for someone?

Ewan came to her and took her in his arms. "All's well, Lorelei. The captain of *The San Miguel* has agreed to free the slaves."

Doug snorted. "In exchange for the large chest of jewels he carried."

The jewels. She stiffened within Ewan's arms. The large chest of jewels was what the madman was after. Was the magic stone the one he'd described there? The madman's description came to her when Ewan released her and moved to the desk, situating the papers.

The madman roared. "Blue, it's blue! Bright as the sun on the ocean, yet deep as a cold heart." He heaved a breath. "Points, it has points." He made a triangular shape with his hands, starting at the top, widening, then cutting in at an angle, forming a tip at the bottom, the size of a man's hand.

Doug's huff brought her back to the present. "Curious that *The San Miguel* captain is not only willing to free the slaves but will take on transporting them once we complete the documents for each."

Ewan barked a laugh. "The chest of jewels is worth a fortune. Now, well, he and his crew will likely never have to sail again." He stacked the papers beside the book as Doug opened the cover. "Each one could retire, maybe buy a sugar plantation in the Caribbean."

Lorelei shivered and wrapped her arms around her middle. Nausea overcame her. The madman would soon learn of her treachery. Would her time with Ewan come to an end so soon? She hoped not.

Ewan stood, crossing to her. "Ye well, *mo sìrean*?" He took her hand and led her to the bed. "Maybe ye should rest some. This task will take the afternoon into the evening for us to make each slave's freedom papers." He sat her on the bed, and she complied. Hoping her escape wouldn't come to a tragic end.

He handed her a book from the shelf. "Try reading to pass the time." She took the book and opened the front but didn't look at the words. While educated, her people could read like humans, but she didn't want to read now. She wiggled her toes, no tingling. Maybe they'd damaged Low's ship so severely that it took him a long time to return to the madman. She hoped so.

****

Lorelei came slowly awake. She lay in only her shirt on the bed. She wiggled her toes, no tingling. Where was Low? She rose to an empty cabin. More importantly, where was Ewan? She sat there a moment, trying to recall the night before. She'd fallen asleep as Ewan and Doug reviewed the slave's records, making papers for each. The rest of the evening came back to her.

Much later into the night, Ewan snuggled beside her, whispering, "We head to port, rest, *mo sìrean.*" He'd stripped her clothing to her shirt and taken her into his arms, where she felt safe and secure for the first time in so long.

Her stomach rumbled, bringing her back. She stood, and on the desk sat a tray of cakes and tea. She smiled as she ate the treat and drank the chilled tea that had been there a while. Wait. There was no movement. The ship didn't move. She went to the window, and outside was the port before her, framed by the familiar mountain range beyond. She'd recognize Portsmouth anywhere. *Home* rang in her mind. She quickly dressed, brushed her fingers through her unruly hair, and found a leather strap to tie it back.

Lorelei crept down the hallway and poked her head out the opening to the deck above. No one was about. She came topside and took a complete turn. Not a soul was on board but her. She traveled to the plank leading to the dock and trod carefully down. She stepped off and made a full turn, but there was still no one from *The Faithful*.

Many people came and went, but no one seemed to pay her any attention. She'd never been anywhere without anyone's notice, well, except at home. There, she was the ordinary younger daughter. In the human realm, as the madman's prisoner, she'd never been alone for long.

Lorelei moved with the crowd toward the village, hoping to find Ewan. When she rounded the stacks of grain at the end of the dock, someone grabbed her, covered her mouth, and pulled her behind the large sacks. A scream burst forth while she struggled, but no sound came out. A cloth wrapped around her throat, cutting off air as she gasped for breath. A second wad of material was shoved into her mouth, gagging her.

The strong arms holding her tightened. "You should have taken my offer when you had the chance." Low's familiar voice sent her over the edge. He loosened the cloth around her throat as she gasped for breath around the fabric.

His breath blew on her ear. "No singing, no tricks, and you will live to see another day." He pulled her closer and his body came flush against her back.

His hardness rubbed against her rear. "You went to Blackbeard, didn't you?" He held her away, turning her around to face him. "I'll forgive your transgressions if you tell me one thing." She eyed him as her saliva dripped from the cloth down her chin.

She knew what he'd ask for before the words left his lips, and he would not like her answer. "The jewels. What has Blackbeard done with the jewels?"

She shook her head. He nodded to the man behind her, and the cloth around her throat tightened, cutting off her airway. She gagged and fought for air. Her powers rose inside her, but she had no outlet with no air. Blackness flashed, and her head floated. Then nothing.

****

Ewan returned to the ship with Doug.

Once they stepped onto the deck, Doug grabbed his arm. "Ewan, Aodhán calls."

Ewan turned. In his mind, he heard the call. *Ewan, ye must come to the future now. Ye've been there too long.* Ewan took off for his cabin, bursting through the doorway to find the space empty.

Doug followed. "Now, Ewan! Aodhán says now!"

Ewan yelled, "She's gone!"

His friend gripped him. "Now, Ewan!"

Ewan quickly gathered energy as worry built inside. He channeled the emotion and power into the portal, focusing on the Chapel in the Woods at Dunstaffnage Castle. He sent him and Doug through and called his ship, not caring where the vessel landed. His boat flew overhead and overshot the castle dock, landing farther into Loch Etive, rocking from the impact. Both he and Doug tumbled on the floor.

Ewan came up, roaring into the rafters. "God Damnit!"

Doug sat up. "I don't think God has anything to do with this one, Ewan."

Aodhán materialized at the altar. "Must ye tempt

fate? With each trip, ye stay longer and longer. My ma, Brigid, summoned me to get ye."

Ewan turned, facing his brother-in-law. "Aren't ye supposed to be acting like a human?"

His glowing eyes glittered with his smirk. "A Fae living among the humans, Ewan." He stepped off the pulpit, coming closer. "Much like ye." Ewan gave him his back, waving his hands and gathering energy to transition to the past.

Aodhán came to him fast, grabbing his hands. "Ye can't. Ye must wait here for two, no three days."

Ewan jerked his hands from his brother-in-law. "She's gone! In danger, I must save her."

Aodhán's expression softened. "I see why my ma scolded me about tracking yer time. Ye lose control, much like yer da." Ewan roared out his fear about Lorelei. He paced as anger built inside him.

Doug moved next to Aodhán. "Maybe she escaped to hide?"

Ewan rounded on them both. "Lorelei committed to stay with me. He has her. The greedy one. I feel it!" He ran his hands through his hair and waved his beard away. "Ye don't understand. She defied him." He fell to his knees, staring at his hands.

Hands that held so much power yet were unable to save his love. "He'll hurt her. I fear for her." He raised his head. "I know he will."

Aodhán tilted his head. "Lorelei? The siren of the sea?" He scratched his chin. "Legend says her song draws men toward her, to their death."

Doug blew a laugh. "Sounds like the tale of the mermaid. *This* Lorelei really sings men to the sea."

Aodhán's smile grew. "I haven't heard her fable

since childhood. Even then, the tale was nothing more than a bedtime story."

Ewan's da's voice echoed, and he repeated the words spoken by his grandma. *The Fae fables are our bedtime stories. Some tales haunt, and some make ye laugh. Ye'll never understand them until ye are full grown, and then, my son, they will become yer sole existence.*

A chill swept down his spine. "I will find her. Lorelei is my love. She *is* my sole existence."

Chapter 14

Lorelei's vision swam. The cold of the stone floor seeped into her making her shiver while her body ached.

A slap echoed, and the madman's voice roared. "Ye damn near killed her!"

The pain in her throat was unbearable. Swallowing proved impossible—a dry mouth made the effort futile. Fire scorched every inch of her throat. As she lay curled on the floor, pain radiated through every limb. Never before had such agony taken hold. Sickness was rare among her kind—understandable, given how little contact they'd had with other species until recently.

Low's raspy reply made her cringe. "She was with him! Snuck away from me!" He growled the last. "Defied your orders, Master."

The force of energy encircled her, gripping her body and lifting her off the ground. She tried swallowing again and met dryness and she shut her eyes, wanting to be anywhere but there. The force shook her, and she opened her eyes, meeting the cold black ones of the madman. His mind crawled through hers, and she was too weak to stop him.

Ewan's face swam before hers. His loving returned to her, making her smile as the dryness cracked her lips. Her thoughts about the madman wanting the jewels flashed. The stone her people protected came to her mind. Blue and pointed.

The force squeezed hard, and she cried out, but no sound came. She struggled as the pain continued to grip her. Unable to breathe, blackness threatened again. The force threw her. She landed in the blessed salt water and sank into the heavy embrace.

Lorelei's body tingled and jolted. Too tired to react and so weary, she allowed herself to float to the bottom while her body returned to her natural form. The fabric of her clothing floated away, disappearing as she drew in deep pulls of water. She sighed when the nourishment her body needed to retain consciousness flowed through her.

The madman approached the glass, tapping the wall, and the vibrations repeatedly shook Lorelei with each knock.

His mind spoke. *Ye were with Blackbeard. Fucked him too.* His chuckle was low. *Ye even liked it.* He hissed, *My pet, ruined, first by Blackbeard, then by Low.* With a wave of a hand, her throat heated. Her hand went to her neck, and the area burned hot.

The madman scowled and lowered his hand as the pain and heat receded. *I've healed ye fish, restored yer voice.* He pressed his face against the tank. *With yer magic, ye will kill Ewan MacDougall. With yer power, ye will get me the Stone of Faith.* Lorelei shook her head, a denial of the stone she'd seen in her mind.

He tsked. *I know ye've seen my gem. The Stone of Faith. Ewan has what's mine and will give the stone and his sister to me.*

The madman turned and strode to Low, grabbing him and strangling him. "Ye will not fail me again. Ye will kill Blackbeard and get me the jewel!" With a twist of his shoulders, the maniac shifted into the black demon that lived inside. His body stretched while jagged horns burst from his skull, and his skin darkened to an inky void. Clawed hands tightened around Low, who stared in shocked fascination as leathery wings unfurled with a sharp snap. The monster roared and shook Low. In a blink, the madman stood before them in his human form. His release of Low had the man stumbling to his knees.

The evil one straightened his cuffs. "I hope my message is clear, Captain?" Low's eyes traveled to Lorelei in her tank, then back to the bad man. He nodded and backed away. After a few steps, he turned and ran from the room. Lorelei sat at the bottom, stunned. The madman even turned on his own people. The lunatic turned and sat on his throne before the fireplace.

He picked up a goblet, drank deeply, and then chuckled. "Everything is turning out so well."

****

The following day Ewan paced the study's length as Aodhán perused the *Fae Fable Book*. Evie leaned on their da's desk, and Doug lounged in a chair. How his friend could remain at ease at this time was beyond Ewan's comprehension.

Aodhán flipped the page again. "There must be more to this fable. I feel ye miss something."

Evie folded her arms and crossed her feet much like their da. "I'm happy for the trip here. A day where Mrs. A spoils Annie is a welcome break for me."

Her husband glanced at her, a smile on his face. "Ye love our wee bug, terrible toddler stage and all."

Evie grinned. "And her budding Fae powers. She stole another cookie the other day. Had the treat floating across the room."

Aodhán barked a laugh. "I did the same."

Ewan stopped his pacing. "Focus, please. I am stuck here for another day before I can go back. There must be something more on Lorelei in the fable."

Aodhán tilted the book as he reread the page. "Too bad yer parents are in Edinburgh today. Ye sure yer da caught all the quotes, Ewan?"

Evie groaned. "I'm glad they are gone. We can read the *Fae Fable Book* without their interference."

Ewan strode to Aodhán, studying the book from over his shoulder. "My da said they are in a story marked separate from the rest of the text." Ewan ran his finger down the left side. "The first was about the greedy merchant." His finger stopped when he found the quote, separated from the text. "The love of money is the root of all evil: which while some coveted after, they have erred from faith and pierced themselves through with many sorrows."

Ewan flipped the page to the end of the fable. "My ma said the second is the last line of the story. 'Faith is confidence in what we hope for and assurance about what we do not see. Everything is possible for one who believes.' "

Aodhán tilted the book into the sunlight, then grunted and tilted the book farther. "Ye don't see the words, do ye?"

His brother-in-law glanced back at him. "It's here in a different ink. One we use in the Fae realm." Aodhán pointed to a space beneath the last line. "Be on your guard against all kinds of greed. Life does not consist in an abundance of possessions."

Aodhán took a breath. "There's a second one. 'Those who want to get rich fall into temptation and a trap and into many foolish and harmful desires that plunge people into ruin and destruction.' "

He tilted the book again. "Ye complained before of no direction. This is it. When the greedy man falls into temptation, his gluttony will be a trap that will plunge people into ruin and destruction."

Ewan puffed. "That's not a direction, not even a place and time. Only a situation I do not know when and where something might happen."

His brother-in-law set the book down. "Yes and no. This tells ye the final straw—the last thing that will break the greedy one. That combined with what comes next, well, this tells ye the end."

Aodhán bent as he read from the mysterious ink. "When all is said and done, the life of faith is nothing if not an unending struggle of the spirit with every available weapon against the flesh."

Ewan growled when he stormed away. "That tells me nothing." He leaned on the chair before his da's desk, almost wishing for his presence and wise advice, even if his being here meant risking his wrath.

Aodhán strode with the book to the case in the wall, set the volume there, and waved his hand over the *Fae Fable Book*, making the Fae glass cover the valuable book again. "Ewan, ye must read between the lines. The greedy one will use all he can against you mentally and physically."

Evie went to her husband, taking his hand in hers. "He will use those ye love against ye as well, Ewan. The evil Fae always do."

Lorelei. The greedy man and Low have used her to the end of the realms and back again. He huffed. *Even her people, whoever they were, used her as well.*

Aodhán hummed. "Ye think of her, Lorelei."

Evie grinned, her teasing tone coming through. "Yer siren from the sea."

Doug sat up in his chair. "She is a Fae. Her voice is like an angel's. Her stare is one that ye cannot turn from—haunts ye. She makes me want to leave Abi." He shook himself. "Dash, I'd never leave Abigail."

Evie stood taller. "Abigail?" She shoved out of Aodhán's embrace, punching Doug on the arm. "Abi, is it, Doug? Someone ye got the hots for?"

Ewan's eyes met Aodhán's over their exchange while Ewan sent a mind speak only to him. *Lorelei is Fae. Do ye know of her people? She mentioned having to save them.*

Aodhán shook his head as Evie went back to his embrace. *A siren from the sea. What do ye know of her powers?*

He closed his eyes, picturing her on the bow of *The Fancy*, her voice carrying over the waves, calling all to her. Her beauty was a draw, her voice—hypnotic. Aodhán nudged him.

Ewan opened his eyes and stared at Aodhán. *She sings, and the melody draws people in, like yer bedtime story of the mermaid.* He blinked, and the image of her sitting in his cabin, speaking about her people, flashed. *She swims naked.* Aodhán chuckled.

Ewan stared him down. *The water, she loves the water.*

He blinked again as another memory flashed, her tear-stained cheeks. *Her people, she protects them. Said they were right under his nose.* He grunted, recalling her take on *necessary*. *She claims she's necessary. Her captivity is necessary for their survival.*

Aodhán nodded. *Under, really? I must consult with my ma and grandda. If her people are who I think they are, they've been lost for a long time.*

A sense of urgency overcame Ewan. Lorelei was in danger; he sensed her call for him. He couldn't take the torture anymore. He must go to her now!

Ewan marched past Doug, slapping him on the head. "We head out today. I must get back to Lorelei. She's in danger. I feel the evil."

Aodhán shifted out of Evie's embrace. " 'Tis a full day early. Ye must wait. Ye will not have much time this trip if ye go too early." Doug ambled up from his chair, yawning as he shuffled toward Ewan.

Ewan stopped at the door. "I fear if I do not go now, I'll lose Lorelei." He shivered. "But more importantly, I fear Lorelei will lose her life."

****

Lorelei stood on the stern of *The Fancy* while the ship clipped through the sun-warmed waters. The sunshine cast bright lights on the waves, much as the moon had the night she last stood alone. In the daylight, they sparked bright silver. She was thankful for the baggy hat Low made her wear. The shade was welcome to her light skin.

Much like before, a firm emotion tugged at the soul. Desperation radiated—an aching search by a lover for someone cherished. Eyes fixed on the sea, where clouds gathered fast, and a powerful storm brewed. The pull grew stronger this time. Ewan. So close now, his soul called out once more.

Boot steps sounded from behind. A heavy footfall announced an unwelcome guest again. His clean scent soured her stomach. He was no longer a gentleman in her eyes now that he'd shown his true colors—greed.

He stood just behind her like he had many times before. His body's warmth heating her back despite the extra clothing she wore. "Is there anything you require, my lady?"

There it was again, *My lady*. Like she was a woman of society and not the creature he knew she was—one he desired to control. Why he kept at her like this when she continually denied him…she sighed knowing the answer, her allure.

She didn't turn. "I am fine, thank you." Captain Low stepped closer, bringing a tightness to her shoulders. Lorelei turned her head, catching his face in her periphery. As before, his jawline tightened.

He took a deep breath, held the air, then released a puff. "You should have taken advantage of my offer. If you were in my care, I wouldn't have hurt you."

She turned back to the open ocean and the pull on her soul, knowing no human would release her ever—one prison to another. "My answer is the same." Captain Low shifted even closer. Like before, she sensed his hand close and felt the warmth in the quickly cooling air.

She stepped away farther. "Don't touch me."

His hand stayed out. "I offer sanctuary. If you were to give yourself to me instead of Blackbeard, I'd give you all the world has to offer. With your powers, we'd live like kings, ruling over all."

Lorelei stood staring at Captain Low. All human men reacted the same—attracted to the point of addiction. Greed was all they saw when they learned how her powers worked and how they could use her for gain. Not one thought of her. Not one—but Ewan.

She moved down the rail, away from Captain Low,

repeating the same warning. "You will do your best to focus on your mission, Captain." The tone shifted, haunting, as she drew on her powers, hoping to persuade this pathetic human. "The madman turns desperate in his search for the jewel." The latest order from the lunatic flew fast through her mind, given just before their departure hours ago.

The master stood yelling. "Blackbeard, Ewan! I want him dead or alive. I care not! This time ye are to capture Ewan and bring him to me. With him, I will find the jewel!" He chuckled. "I will have Evie." His sister, what was she to him?

Captain Low folded his arms behind his back, seeming to look compliant. "Your stone, the blue one you still seek?"

The madman chuckled. "Aye, my blue diamond. The Stone of Faith."

The blue stone her people protected flashed in her mind again. She'd not thought to make the connection until she lay nearly unconscious. That's when realization hit her: the diamond-shaped stone that protected her people, shielding them from all and keeping them invisible was what the madman was after. She was now more of a necessity than Ewan or she had realized. Without the blue stone, her people became visible to all, to the madman.

Captain Low cleared his throat, bringing her back to the present as thunder rumbled in the distance and the wind picked up.

His voice clipped. "I am aware of my duty." He sneered. "Are you aware of yours? Will you be able to kill as commanded? Kill a man you have lain with, Blackbeard?"

Lorelei, like each time before, turned to face him fully, her mouth open while she set her eye intent upon Captain Low, posed to bring forth her power. She hated him and, for once, relished using her powers over men.

When her eyes met him, he stepped back. "I see you are." His gaze rose over her shoulder. "Your time has come. Your precious savior has arrived for his death at your hands."

Chapter 15

Ewan's ship quickly came up on *The Fancy*'s stern, intent on coming alongside. His goal—get to Lorelei at all costs. Wind thrashed at his face, and the rigging creaked under the strain, but *The Faithful* would hold steady. She always had.

Davy's high-pitched voice shouted from the crow's nest. "Ship to starboard, Cap'n." Like he didn't know, they practically rode up her ass, but the crew and the ship had just time-hopped, so Davy did his job.

Doug stood at midship, feet braced apart whiles he yelled, "Storm's rolling in. We need to stay close to the inlet."

Ewan wrapped a rope around his hand as he bellowed, "Crew, strap yeselfs in. We're about to have a blow!" He kept the line loose so when the time came he could swing over and grab Lorelei. He'd swing back and tie them both down for the storm.

One-eyed Joe laughed into the wind. "Ye mean ye and Doug, Cap'n. We's already dead!" Ewan's eye caught Doug, who had tied himself to the main mast. He nodded, and Doug nodded back. They knew their duty and were ready.

As Ewan glanced at the mainland, spotting a cove, he grinned. He'd found the hidden inlet that led to the sugar plantation's private dock. And here he found Low sailing from it into the open waters. His plan was perfect. Take his ship, save Lorelei. Portsmouth was a short sail around the island. How he had ever missed this inlet was a mystery. From the open sea, one only had to sail in from the west and steal a glimpse past the jagged mountain range. For the briefest moment, the hidden cove revealed itself—a perfect, peaceful sanctuary cradled between towering cliffs, its well-fortified dock standing firm against the tides. Then, just as quickly, the mountains swallowed the sanctuary again, concealing its existence from all but those who knew where to look. And from the looks of the berth, Low kept the place well-stocked, ready for whatever—or whomever—might come calling.

Bert shouted over the splash of the waves when the surf turned angry. "He's got his guns out, Captain!" The ship rose and fell hard with a bang as saltwater washed over the deck.

Ewan shouted over the crash. "Guns out starboard. One-eyed Joe, take us alongside."

The Faithful climbed and descended with a crash again while they gained on the smaller ship. Ewan grinned, knowing the modern steering on his boat would outmaneuver anything from the eighteenth century. He had this in the bag.

As they came closer, each ship rose and fell like a merry-go-round while the swells grew. A cannon shot boomed from *The Fancy*. As *The Faithful* rose high on a wave, the shot fell short, the ship uneven from the waves, leaving the cannonball crashing into the surf. Scanning the sky, Ewan smirked. The weather worked to their advantage. Now, he just needed to hold out till he could get to Lorelei and make a fast getaway. The closer they came, he searched the deck for her but didn't spot the flames of her hair. Another boom came from *The Fancy*. This time, glancing off his bow, taking some railing down into the waters.

Doug yelled from midship. "Guns, Captain?"

The ship rose and fell as the sea sprayed them all. Ewan shook the water from his eyes. "No! I won't risk hitting Lorelei. Try to get us closer, Joe! I must see where she is to know where to aim!" One-eyed Joe laughed again when he turned the ship, the bow coming alongside *The Fancy*. Ewan spotted Low on the bridge.

When their eyes connected, Low sneered as he shouted, "I see you haven't had enough, Blackbeard!" He turned, yelling, "Fire all guns!"

Cannon booms erupted from *The Fancy*. *The Faithful* rocked under the barrage of fire. The bow splintered, taking out a corner of the bridge. Another cannon ripped into the ship's side, likely taking out a gunner's area. No cries came from *The Faithful*, only laughter. The men, spirits serving Ewan, weren't affected by the attacks. Ewan took this time to scan the deck, his arm wrapped around a line, ready for him to swoop in and swipe Lorelei from the ship the moment he spotted her. No woman stood on the decking. He scanned again, and there was still no dress or red hair.

Low called out as his gunner reloaded, and *The Faithful* came even alongside. "Searching for something Blackbeard? Lost a lass, maybe?"

Ewan grinned. "Not lost, come to claim."

Low's sneer filled his face. "Then you shall have what you wish for." He turned, patting the shoulder of the shorter man beside him, who kept his head bent with a hat covering his face. Ewan's breath left him in a whoosh when he lifted his face. Lorelei's eyes connected with his as tears streamed down her face.

He whispered. "*Mo sìrean?*"

Low's voice carried while the ships rose and fell with the growing surf. "She has come for you! The sea you love so much will be your doom!"

Low hit her, and she stumbled but righted herself. Lorelei opened her mouth, and a sound Ewan had never heard came out. Her voice came out screeching and haunting all at once. Her shrill made his eyes water and his insides churn. He sensed her denial in the song, the spell she cast unwillingly. His heart bled for her.

Ewan's crew stood still, transfixed by her song but unaffected by her spell. The men on board *The Fancy* all bent, covering their ears.

Low bowed, covering his ears as he yelled, "Fire them all!" Cannons boomed, hitting *The Faithful*. Wood splintered, and Ewan's ship rocked beneath him. He stood upright, his eyes never leaving Lorelei's as her voice sent out her magic, meant to tempt a man to his death.

Doug yelled, "Fire!" and *The Faithful*'s cannons let loose on *The Fancy*, filling the space between the ships with flying wood.

Ewan gripped his line and launched toward her, determined to sweep in and scoop her from the deck. Mid-swing, something hit him, causing him to lose his grip, forcing a tumble into the ocean. The impact of the water made his breath leave. The chill of the water stunned and the surf gripped—tossing his body with the sea's fury. He couldn't find the light, losing track of where up and blessed air was. With the line wrapped around his body, it dragged him lower. The water pushed in as his lungs begged for air. He closed his eyes and black spots danced before him. This was it. His doom was to be the sea.

****

Lorelei watched in horror as Ewan's body hit the water. Her heart threatened to stop when he sank below the surface.

Low ran up beside her, jolting her from her trace with his yelling. "Well, the sea really is his doom."

Lorelei dove off the ship's side, uncaring of the consequences. One thought burned—save Ewan. The water struck like the madman's blow, leaving her stunned. Tingling in the legs stirred awareness. The change would come soon, and the new shape would easily cut through the depths.

Fire seared through muscle as lungs pulled in water like air, power flooding every limb. The form tightened, then snapped into place—her true form, fluid and strong. No hesitation followed. Downward, she surged, hunting the rigging that bound Ewan to the wood, dragging him toward death.

The mast dragged Ewan deeper and deeper—so fast catching up proved nearly impossible. Once close, Lorelei came even with his face, hands bracketing his cheeks. The beard had thinned, his magic—nearly gone. A life force faded before her eyes.

Every ounce of power surged forward. Mouth opened, clamped over his—not a kiss, but a seal, a conduit for breath and magic. Her song flowed through locked lips, driving air and energy into still lungs. Down they sank, but the spell had to hold and keep pouring life into a body slipping too far, too fast.

As Lorelei breathed more magic air, the bubble

encircled his head just like the elders had described—a helmet of air for a human. This deep power was the only thing that could save him.

Ewan breathed once, jolted, then breathed again. She gave him more—magic air created for him. A jolt ran through his body. Eyes snapped open—shock flared, then softened at the sight before him. Recognition settled. Hands fought the ropes, limbs finding strength. With effort and urgency, the bindings loosened, then fell away.

The mast and rigging sank as they stayed suspended in the water, lips locked and Lorelei breathed into him.

Only once had she heard a tale of the air bubble for humans—an old fable from times when humans visited the Telkhines Fae in the sea. She waved her hand around Ewan's head, forming magic as she filled the bubble with air. Pulling her lips away with a kiss, and they floated holding hands.

Ewan's mind spoke in her head. *How?*

She giggled. "It's an old spell. One I've never tried until now. Try speaking." Her speech sounded clear even in the water.

Ewan took a deep breath and another, then spoke aloud. "Will the spell sustain me? Can I cast one myself?"

Lorelei nodded. "As long as you like. To cast the bubble spell, you only have to focus on air from your lungs, create magic inside, and then blow the magic breath around where you want the bubble to be."

He glanced up, following her gaze while the hulls of the ships parted, going their separate ways. He sighed, and she sensed his regret at leaving them. His duty—fighting against his desire to remain with her. In her true form, her full powers returned.

Lorelei took his hand in hers. "Please come. I wish to show you something." She swam down fast.

Ewan pulled back. "Where do we go?"

She turned and came face to face with him. Slipping inside his bubble, she pressed a kiss to his lips. Arms closed around her, and the kiss deepened, fierce with relief. His gaze swept over her when their mouths parted—taking in every inch. The full tail, glimmering where human legs once were, undulated in the water as she floated free of his embrace.

Would revulsion follow recognition? The truth of her form now bared. Silence lingered. She drifted back, heart clenched against the answer in his eyes.

He grabbed her, pulling her to him, his hand caressing her face. "*Mo sìrean?*" Then he chuckled. "This is who ye truly are? A siren from the sea?"

She nodded, pulling him deeper into the sea. "Come, come see my home."

Her tail flipped, taking them deeper into the ocean, to her home under the Morne Trios Pitons, and to the Fae kingdom of the Telkhines.

Chapter 16

The wind built as *The Faithful* sailed fast, leaving *The Fancy* damaged and listing in the rough surf. The sea churned, and Doug knew they needed to wait out the storm. If not, he'd lose the ship and all with her. He worried about Ewan, but when he caught sight of Lorelei diving after him, an ease washed over him. She cared for him—Doug sensed it in his bones.

He called out to One-Eyed Joe. "To Portsmouth Joe. We need to find a cove to ride out the storm." He glanced up as the sky grew darker. "Might have to beach her to survive."

Bert strode past him, patting his shoulder while Doug untied himself from the main mast. "And ye wouldn't mind spending the time with your sweetheart either!" He rubbed his belly. "Her cakes are mighty good."

Doug called after Bert. "Yer dead, ye can't eat!"

Bert yelled back, "One can dream!"

Gilbert came up from the hold. "We're taking in water, but the men tarred the hole, which'll keep for a bit." Doug's trained eye roamed the deck. The battle had blown away the railing from most of the starboard side.

When Gilbert came up, he spied a hole in the ship's side large enough for a man to fit through but rode above the waterline. "Board up what ye can. The work doesn't have to be extravagant, just functional. Once we get home, we'll see to the proper repairs."

Davy swung down from the rigging. "Home, ye can't go without the cap'n."

Doug stared out over the land as the cove with Portsmouth came into view. He sighed and turned, glancing over the open ocean and the dark black clouds moving slowly toward Waitukura Island. He couldn't leave without Ewan. His magic made time travel possible. But this storm looked like more than a little blow. If Aodhán came for him, he would still refuse to leave his best friend in the past, even if Ewan insisted. Their place was in the future.

The air shifted, and nature's energy filled the area. Doug knew a strong storm when he saw one. They'd sailed around a hurricane once, and this one was not only too close but barreled toward them.

He turned to One-Eyed Joe. "Get us into the port fast, Joe."

Abi would weather the storm fine. She had many. But Ewan… He'd not seen either Ewan or Lorelei surface. He prayed Ewan's magic would sustain him. If not, Doug feared he'd lost his best friend in the depths of the sea.

****

Lorelei pulled him deeper and deeper as they followed the island's base. Coming upon a cave opening, she turned to enter.

Ewan pulled back, his mind refusing to enter out of pure survival instinct. "A cave, I won't be trapped down here to drown. This isn't yer powers, is it?"

Lorelei swam to him, circling her arms around his neck and moving into his air bubble. "My powers passed from my ancestor. I don't kill. I refuse to." She kissed his lips. "I do not have frustration or revenge for humans in my heart as she did, only a love for them. I show you my home." Lorelei released him leaving the air bubble that encircled his head. When she bent her head, whispering echoed in what sounded like a prayer. When her eyes lifted, she smiled wide.

Lorelei swam, pulling him along and they traveled through the opening into a tunnel. Twisting and turning, Ewan lost count of rights and lefts as he tried to keep track should he need to exit. His heart pleaded to *trust her* while his mind screamed *swim for air*.

The tunnel opened into a vast underwater cavern with a glowing central earth-like cylinder in the middle. Ewan pulled up, marveling at the sight before him. Situated around the red-orange pulsing duct of what must be the center of Waitukura's volcano sat a city constructed of carved rock and various sea resources. Cave dwellings sat amidst coral buildings and seaweed-woven structures, all using the natural resources available at the ocean's depths. Merfolk like Lorelei swam about in what was a bustling underwater metropolis.

Lorelei pulled him alongside her, their bodies touching. "My home. The kingdom of the Telkhines." Ewan stared, stunned. An entire kingdom of Fae in the ocean. Did Dagda even know they existed?

Two long-haired creatures like Lorelei, yet male and enormous, swam toward them, each carrying a long-jagged spear. Ewan tried to shift Lorelei behind him, but she shoved herself before him, moving more agile in the water.

As they neared, the larger one with darker hair

addressed them first as he floated before them with his arms folded. "Lorelei, what is wrong with you? It is forbidden to bring humans here."

Lorelei straightened her back. "Murus, I bring one who is a friend to me and the people."

The merman's face grew red. "You bring evil here. He's no different than the madman plantation owner above. All humans are the same selfish beings."

Ewan had heard enough. He sent his mind speak to the fool. *I am nothing like the madman, and I am not necessarily human, either.* So, they knew of the plantation owner and feared him as they should. The warrior shied back, unfolding his arms as he shoved the sharp edge of the spear into Ewan's face. When the sharp end passed Lorelei's cheek, the blade would have nicked her had she not moved out of its path.

Ewan grabbed the pole just below the blade. "Careful *friend*, ye nearly cut Lorelei's face in yer battle heat."

Lorelei reached up and eased the spear down, forcing Ewan to release his grip when she spoke. "As I said, he is a friend. I bring a human to show him my home."

Murus did a complete flip, brandishing the spear in a defensive position. "You court this human?" He lowered the weapon, coming closer to Lorelei and whispering, "Have you taken him as your one?"

The guard behind Murus drew in water in a gasp, as did Lorelei. "As I said before, and I repeat now, Murus." She grabbed Ewan's hand and quickly swam past both guards. "What I do with my life and who I choose to live it with is my business, not yours." Ewan eyed them while they swam away.

Murus turned to follow, and the guard behind him grabbed his arm. "Leave her. I shall follow them as a guard. Report to the King. Lorelei has arrived."

Murus called after them. "Your folly will be your end, Lorelei. Only death comes from the humans!"

She led him into the thriving area while the other guard followed just behind. Glancing back, she hissed, "I need no guard, Vinnis."

He replied with a chuckle. "Your father would disagree." As they traveled through the busy area, many groupings of merfolk floated back while others fled the area. Ewan shook his head—nothing like being the new guy in town. Smiling at himself, Ewan thought of an old Western movie where the bad guy walked through the middle of town and everyone ran, closing doors and windows. This wasn't much different.

Lorelei turned right and swam away from what must have been the main area, heading toward what looked to be rows of smaller buildings, all similar. Ewan mused this must be the area for individual homes.

As they whirled along, Lorelei spoke over her shoulder. "How is my sister, Vinnis?"

He grunted before replying. "Her same high-spirited self, just like her sister."

She slowed. "And yer daughter, she fares well?"

Vinnis pushed closer, coming alongside Lorelei. "She was ill." Lorelei stopped drawing in water and gasped.

The guard's hand rested on her shoulder. "Adredyn is fine, a minor flux." Lorelei sighed and nodded.

Vinnis tilted his head. "Why don't you visit your sister? Dathamyn would love to see you."

Lorelei shrugged, looking down as she gripped

Ewan's hand harder. "I don't know. I mean, I'm unsure how long we will be here."

The warrior's eyes traveled Ewan's form. "You have mastered the bubble spell. I've only heard of the hex from the elders."

Lorelei straightened and made a bow while still holding Ewan's hand. "I make known to you Vinnis, mate of my sister, Ewan of…"

Ewan smiled at her formal introduction. "The MacDougalls." His gaze moved to Vinnis. "Your brother by marriage, Vinnis." Ewan bowed, duplicating their greeting. "I am glad to meet ye."

The merman squinted. "What is marriage? He speaks strangely, but his manners don't match what we know of humans."

Ewan smirked. *Does a human speak in yer mind as I do?*

Vinnis shook his head. "I wouldn't know. You are the first human I've met. It's been eras since our kind has associated with the species." His eyes slid to Lorelei. "Until now."

Murus approached them at a fast rate. When he came upon the three, he flipped a summersault and bowed before Lorelei. "Your King welcomes you home, Lorelei. He extends a welcome to your…Fae guest." When he rose, his eyes glittered. "You are to take your rest and report to him in the morning."

Vinnis bowed to Murus. "I make known to you Ewan of the MacDougalls."

Murus bit out his reply, "I care not to make him known to me, Fae or human." He flipped his tail into Ewan's face as he swam away. Ewan had to turn from the force of the water moving against him, his air bubble shifting.

Lorelei groaned. "Well, he hasn't changed much."

Vinnis laughed. "Yes, he has. He's gotten worse since you left." He grumbled. "I take by his leaving that I am to guard you till the morning."

Lorelei opened her mouth, but Vinnis raised his hand. "Our home is not far. I'll ask Dathamyn to bring provisions, and we promise to leave you"—he glanced at Ewan and then back at Lorelei—"in peace." Vinnis swam away, calling over his shoulder, "Stay inside tonight. You have the entire kingdom in hiding." He swam farther, then stopped turning with a flip. "Lorelei, try to stay out of trouble. If you are able." He flicked his tail, and with the wave, his body floated away, leaving them alone in the middle of what must be a street. Rows of houses rested on either side of the cliff. Ewan's eyes drifted to a home across from him, and a leaf fluttered in the window as a form shied away. Some welcome. Vinnis had said humans had not been here in a long time. He tried to imagine what it must be like, a strange new being amid their peaceful home. He wondered why they didn't attack him outright.

Lorelei turned, pulling him with her. She swam so well through the water that Ewan didn't have to kick. He grinned as her arrival in her kingdom revealed much about her and her people. His conversation with Aodhán flashed. He'd mentioned they may be a long-lost kingdom, but he wasn't certain. That explained why only elders knew of humans. He wished Aodhán was here now to answer some questions.

Lorelei waved at the houses. "These are our dwellings." She glanced over her shoulder while she swam. "The area before was the main center. You'd call that area a market, and we have a castle for the king with a court." She giggled. "Taverns for drinking like the humans as well." Ewan pulled back, stopping her. She came to him with an open expression on her face.

He squeezed her hand once. "Lorelei, shouldn't ye see yer father, yer family? Ye've just arrived."

She pushed within the bubble, kissing him full as arms wrapped around him. Her tongue danced with his, and his hands wrapped in her hair and the strands floated in the water. This woman could kiss all his cares away, and Ewan would ask her to kiss him again.

When she finished the kiss, he almost forgot his question. "Nice try at distraction, but yer family?"

She shoved out of his embrace. "See my home and take our rest. The time to retire for the day is upon my people. Tomorrow, we meet them."

She pulled him with her while he spoke. "Ye mean dodge them tonight and face them in the morning." She flipped her tail, knocking him, but held his hand as he jostled in the water. She glanced back with a grin that left him chuckling. Soon, they stopped before a smaller hut made of what must be white coral. Light from inside glowed in the window openings and seaweed waved like curtains.

The door or rather a curtain of darker sea grass, waved aside, and a larger, older merwoman engulfed Lorelei in an embrace, forcing her to drop his hand. "It's good to have you home, sister." She moved back while her eyes traveled Lorelei's form. "You look well." Her gaze slid to him, and a smirk filled her face. "A human! Vinnis said you had one." She swam around him, poking him here and there with her finger. "He's a warrior if I ever saw one, and Vinnis said he's mannered."

Lorelei bowed. "Sister, Dathamyn, I make known to you Ewan of the MacDougalls."

When Ewan bowed, her sister waved her hand in dismissal as she studied Ewan. "Such a nice form." Her eyes dropped to his legs, laughing. "Till you get to the fin, he's got none!"

Lorelei pushed her sister away. "Yes, well, thank you for the food. You must get home now!"

Dathamyn swam away with her eye over her shoulder, staring at Ewan. "Just wait till I tell Elyn and the others. A real human!"

Lorelei called after her giggling sister. "You don't have to tell all my sisters!"

When she turned back, Ewan raised an eyebrow. "How many sisters do ye have?"

She swam past him into her home. "Eleven. Come inside."

Ewan blinked. The thought of eleven siblings blew his mind. As he traveled through the curtain into her home, his focus shifted, and he stopped to examine all around him. To the right was a counter and a bar of sorts. Fish and seaweed sat in a neat pile. To his left, another curtained doorway fluttered with Lorelei's movement, revealing a large shell with more seaweed that must be a bed. Lorelei swam about, picking up various objects and gathering them. His eye caught a fork, then a piece of fabric he couldn't make out. Her next grab was a brush. When she turned to the corner, he kicked his legs till he floated toward her, bumping her in his attempt to get close. She dropped the items and floated before him with her hands behind her back. Ewan glanced behind her, and his guess was correct. In a pile was a cache of items from the humans above.

Stone of Faith

He chuckled. "Treasures from the humans?"

Her smile wobbled. "Research." She swam past him, babbling as she did. "There's food for us made of fish and grass, modest compared to your baked bread. We don't cook here." She glanced over her shoulder while she gathered the food items. "No fire." Her laugh came out in a forced chuckle. She was nervous, but why?

Ewan kicked toward her, grabbing the bar to pull himself near without bumping her this time. "Lorelei, your home is lovely as you are." He caressed her face. "*Mo sìrean.* Show me what yer people eat." Ewan glanced down. "Whitefish and raw." He chuckled. "I like sushi." He pulled his knife and took a fish from her.

She grabbed his hand. "You must thank the gods first." She was right, and her earnest expression enchanted him.

Ewan sheathed his knife. "Ye must show me how yer way." He tilted his head, smiling at her with what he hoped was encouragement. Lorelei nodded, raised her hands, palms up, and hummed.

Ewan shied back, and she stopped lowering her arms. "Do not fret. I sing without magic, thanking the gods for our bounty." She lifted her arms again and hummed softly, reminding him of a lullaby.

When she finished, she lowered her arms and handed him a fish. "What is sushi?"

Chapter 17

Lorelei bit into the fish piece wrapped in a seaweed leaf Ewan had made for them, calling the dish sushi. Seemed sushi was basically a word for raw fish. Earlier, he'd taken the fish and *filleted* them, as he called it. He only cut them by separating the bone from the meat, tossing the innards aside that she wrapped up saving for her sister. With the meal ready, he awkwardly pushed to her collection of human things and picked up two silver items he'd called *forks*. He handed one to her with the fish on a leaf, and they rested against the bar. He used the *fork,* spearing the fish and shoving the bite in his mouth. Under Ewan's smile, she repeated the process only to discover the pieces were too big for her smaller mouth. Lorelei had to bite them, but being able to use an item from the humans excited her. She had to admit that the cleaner preparation made eating easier. Plus, she hated bones and scales anyway.

She turned the remaining piece and examined the fish, trying to picture what Ewan had told her about the humans. "You tell me there are many types of humans you call nationalities."

He nodded as he swallowed. "Aye, like the ocean has different fish, there are different humans. Sushi is from Japan. The Asians come from the other side of the earth. They thrive eating fish. It is a main part of their diet." He popped the last bite into his mouth while speaking around his chewing. "Although they serve the fish with rice, which makes the meal more filling."

Lorelei stopped at another new word. "Rice? What is rice?"

Ewan squinted. "A grain they grow in water, then dry only to boil again, making the kernel soft."

She sat up at the word *grain*. "Grain, that's what they grind to make bread." She sighed, thinking of fresh bread.

Ewan's chuckle had her turning. "I love bread but can't bring a loaf here." She waved, making the water move between them. "The soft food melts away." She stopped trying to envision what Asians looked like and couldn't. She opened her mouth and then closed her jaw with a click.

Ewan raised an eyebrow. "I sense ye want to ask something." He pushed to a ledge lower in the wall, attempting to sit, but only floated. "Ask me anything ye wish."

She placed her meal on the bar and swam before him, back and forth, trying to organize her thoughts. So many questions about humans, and they all jumbled at once. She stopped and then swam again. Stilling, she opened her mouth and lost track of her question, wanting to know everything at once.

Setting his food aside, Ewan pushed off from the ledge, gathering her in his arms. "I sense yer confusion. We have different nations, different languages, and different people. It's like the Fae."

She tilted her head. "The Fae have different people? We only know of us, but my father speaks of others, long gone."

Ewan frowned. "There is the good Fae, the Tuatha Dé Danann ruled by Dagda. There is the Fomoire Fae, the evil Fae who has a new ruler. There are other kinds I've not met, but I am certain they exist. I serve Dagda, the good Fae." He chuckled. "Hell, there's even dragon shapeshifters."

The dragon, the madman, had a black evilness inside him. She shivered as she gathered the courage to ask, "A dragon, what do they look like?"

He must have sensed her quiver. His gaze moved quickly to her and he held her tighter. "They are men who have an animal inside. When they want, they change into a large flying reptile." He closed his eyes as he spoke, seeming to see something in his mind. "Kind of like yer seahorses but larger with wings and more dangerous."

The black monster the madman changed into flashed in her mind, his roar echoing, making her shiver again. "Are they evil?"

Ewan brushed her face with his hand. "Some are, some are not. Good or evil depends on what the person they embody is like." He stared at her for a moment.

She twisted away, and his hand brushed her face till she turned back, and their eyes met. "Ye haven't seen one, have ye Lorelei?" She stayed still, fearing what he might do if he knew of the madman.

Ewan's eyes roamed her face, then rested on her. "The plantation owner, the one who lives above. Ye are his captive. The slaves speak of him having powers. What does he hold that has ye a prisoner?" Lorelei tried to pull from his embrace, and he gripped her tighter. She wiggled and slipped from him, leaving his arms in an empty circle as she swam away.

From across the room, she spoke softly. "Nothing, he has nothing."

Ewan crossed his arms and freely floated before her. "He has something that has ye using magic ye have vowed not to use." He kicked closer this time, not bumping her but encircling her again. "What Lorelei, what does the evil man hold over ye?"

Eyes closed, a silent plea banished thoughts of the madman, yet they came. The monster roared, a great body arched, light glinting off massive scales. Her eyes opened, meeting Ewan's—steady, full of care. Lips found his without hesitation, seeking comfort in each kiss, a balm against the vision clinging to memory and heart. The only desire was to feel human again, to remain with Ewan. His response came in a moan, low and unguarded. Hands clutched his form close, seeking solace in warmth, in affection.

Ewan lifted his head. "Ye distract me as before." He smiled. "I will have an answer before the end of the night. But for now, I'll enjoy yer diversion." She swam quickly into her sleeping area, pulling Ewan's hand.

He laughed aloud. "Want something, dearie?"

Lorelei stopped at the shell, her sleeping area, wanting to come to Ewan as a woman and a human. She released his hand and formed a ball with hers, gathering energy for the bubble spell. This had to work. When her body encountered air, she changed—a spell from the madman, the tease that kept her returning to him. She prayed that away from the plantation, she could conjure the magic now. For Ewan, she'd do anything.

Focusing on the ball of energy creating air from water, her magic commanded the sphere to grow. A small bubble grew between her hands. She spread them wider, and as the bubble grew, she turned to the shell, encasing her bed inside the bubble. Once she'd covered the shell bed, she pushed inside and waited. Soon, her legs tingled, then burned, and her body stretched and snapped into the form of a human. Lorelei stood naked before him, her wet hair clinging to her body.

Ewan shifted within the bubble. Once he reached the air, he stepped on the seaweed floor and approached her. "Ye bring forth air and make a change to human form. What kind of a power is that?"

She shrugged his question off as he took her into his arms. "Turning human. Is that something ye can maintain? The shape that is?"

Lorelei looked away, unable to meet his eyes. "I…I wish to come to you as a woman." Her eyes moved back to his, tears gathering in them. "I wish to be human." As a tear fell, she whispered, "I'd give anything to stay this way."

He gripped her shoulders. "What do ye mean, ye can't?" He couldn't know. No one could know. She threw her arms around him and kissed him while she pressed herself along his body. His hands sculpted down her back to her rear, molding to her curves as he pulled her against him. His hardness attested to his desire for her. She kissed him and undid the buttons on his trousers. As she slid them down, his audible groan filled the area.

He pulled her up and pressed flush against her body. "Lorelei, ye distract me, but I will have my answer." He kissed her hard. "Later." He shifted back and stripped his shirt off, then quickly returned to kissing her.

She returned his kiss, pivoted them, then pulled away and slipped back into the shell where she slept. The bedding squished with a step onto the seaweed, still wet from the water. In the dry air of the bubble spell, wet seaweed didn't seem like a soft resting place. She waved her hand, and a pillow-like shape replaced the seaweed. When she turned back, he stood naked like her. Her human warrior, all muscle and hard. Her man with a soft heart.

Lorelei stepped, laying on the softness, hoping she would appeal to Ewan.

He stood gazing at her, "Lorelei, my siren of the sea. Ye take my breath away." He moved onto the bedding, coming over her body. Her heart hammered at his declaration as she sighed into his kiss. His hands skimmed over her hips and then rounded her rear, squeezing the back while he nudged her closer to him. He brushed her curls, forcing a gasp from her as heat spread from her core.

He chuckled into the kiss. "Come, *mo sìrean*, show me yer love." Her love, she loved him from the moment she first set eyes on him. To show him her heart brought tears to her eyes.

Ewan pulled back, the concern evident on his face while he wiped her tears. "Tears?"

She shook her head, "Not sad, happy tears. I show you my love."

His fingers brushed down her cheek to her neck and her breast. He bent and licked the tip, then suckled the point, sending shock waves through her. Ewan moved to the other breast, giving it much attention. She ran her fingers through his hair, marveling at its beauty. He kissed farther down, tickling her belly and making her flinch.

Ewan glanced up with a smile on his face as he progressed lower. "My sweet woman, lay back and let me love ye." When he moved even lower, her hands came free, and he nudged her a bit, placing himself between her human legs facing her juncture. He blew on her curls, lightly tickling them. She shifted her hips and her arms came over her head. Ewan stared as his tongue flicked out, licking her there.

She jolted, and his hands held her hips in place. "Trust me, *mo sìrean.* Ye will like this." He repeated his tongue movement, and desire shot over her. He closed his eyes and covered her with his mouth. The warm wetness flushed her with heat. His tongue swirled around a nub, teasing her senses. He sucked on her, and her hands gripped his head. He held her in place while he rotated the swirling and sucking, making her breath pick up. Something built in her, a force she'd not felt before. Her fingers gripped his hair, and he built a pace. Swirling and sucking over and over, faster and faster. She panted as the force rose inside her, making her nearly out of breath. Ewan delved into her softness, exploring with slow, deliberate strokes, and her world burst when she screamed from the intensity. His mouth moved away, and another filled her when the pressure built and his pace picked up. She panted little gasps as that force built again, harder now pushing against her—she knew not what. She had to find her release. Her fists grasped the bed, pulling on the fabric.

The fullness slipped out, and he came over her. "God, woman!" He glided his man-part into her, and stars burst behind her eyelids. She screamed his name. He sat seated in her for a moment.

He kissed her softly. "*Mo sìrean*, I love ye."

She flipped him to his back, wanting to take control. "And I, you, my one."

Lorelei rose, pushing him into her till she sat on him. He stretched her to the edge of bliss, leaving her aching for the last piece of him. Ewan's hands trailed to her hips and lifted, then lowered her on him as a moan escaped his mouth. He repeated the motion, going faster this time. So, he liked this. She placed her hand on his chest and followed his lead, rising and lowering, enjoying his groan with each stroke. He gripped her harder and pushed her to a faster pace. The feeling of him loving her had that force building again. They surged together, bodies finding a rhythm that deepened with every thrust. Soon, that energy built, and her core exploded as she froze from the intensity.

Ewan sat up and guided her as he turned her beneath him, never breaking their connection. His hand brushed her cheek and kissed her softly as he moved slowly, and her body clenched around him, the exquisite friction making her tremble. Lorelei gasped with each movement, and the sensitivity was intense. He kissed her again and pushed harder. Her body gripped him and the force built again. Her hands moved, gripping his rear, pulling, asking him to fulfill her needs.

Ewan chuckled and shifted with the next stroke. His pace became frantic, his movements harder. He grunted with effort, and her hips met each push. The force inside her built, and she pulled him harder, wanting him closer to her heart. Ewan thrust deeply once, then again as he lifted his head and bellowed her name into the night. He froze, shaking a little. He pulsed inside her for a brief movement, and wetness filled her. He collapsed on her, gathering her in his arms. Ewan lay on her with their bodies still connected while he seemed to catch his breath.

As Lorelei lay still, her body hummed like she had a power beyond her understanding. The sensation left her with scarce a breath and feeling so—alive. This joining rocked her to her core. She held Ewan close, savoring the feeling of being in his arms—her human body pressed against his. At that moment, nothing felt more right. She would give anything to live like this forever.

Lorelei whispered as she lay her head on his chest, his heartbeat slowing against her ear. "I find my glory in rebirth's glow. I anticipate creating my new tomorrow. Forging a new life with my true love. When I shall embody the earth."

Ewan hummed, the sound echoing in his chest. "I like that one." He tilted her chin till their eyes met. "My true love. Aye, *mo sìrean*, I love ye."

She smiled. "My one."

Chapter 18

The next morning, Lorelei led Ewan through the central area of the town. Merfolk floated about, some stopping as Ewan and she sped past. Others only glanced at them. It seemed word had traveled around that the human stranger was no danger. Ewan smirked at his rhyme.

Lorelei stopped at a shop, and the female keeper came to greet them. "Lorelei, glad I am to have you home." She turned quickly, disappearing behind the leaf of a door, and returned on a wave with both hands full. "Seaweed rolls, freshly made."

Lorelei took them from her, smiling. "Your sister, Elyn, came by already." Her focus moved to Ewan when she placed her hands on her waist. "He's a fine specimen of a human." She giggled, eyeing his form. "All muscle and handsome." She laughed aloud. "Till his tail." Ewan wiggled his legs as he glanced down. Were they so odd?

"Thank you, Estelle. I'll send coin later."

As they swam away, Estelle called out. "No need. Feeding the human will be a great story to tell."

Near the pulsing tube that traveled through the center of Lorelei's village up into the island and a park-like area, a bench made of seagrass and weed made a nice place to sit as Lorelei sat and bit into her meal. She eyed Ewan, who floated before her, unsure what to do.

She patted the seat next to hers. "Come break your fast."

Ewan kicked closer to her, trying to sit, but he floated just above the seat. Lorelei grinned and she pulled on his hand until he rested beside her. The two sat in comfortable silence, munching on the leafy meal. Ewan huffed. They called this a roll since they rolled the leaves together. He felt like he ate a salad, not bread, understanding why Lorelei craved the delicacy. The crunch echoed in his head a little. He glanced around as her people wandered past. A merwoman with a baby in her arms, then a group of women moved by. When Ewan made eye contact, they giggled and swam farther away. A pair of men floated by, eyeing them. Ewan glanced at Lorelei, who sat eating, unaffected by the attention. He finished his meal and brushed his hands, unsure if there was something to clean up or if he did the motions out of habit.

He turned to her. "So, this is yer kingdom, yer people."

She smiled, blushing. "Yes, the Telkhines. We are merpeople under the rule of Poseidon from the Water Realm. King Triton rules this kingdom. Lore has us Sea-daemons and powerful but malignant sorcerers of the Aegean Islands who Zeus buried beneath the sea." She shrugged. "Bedtime stories told to our youth setting Zeus as a god that will punish us for wrongdoings. Really, we are only people from the sea."

Ewan's eyes traveled to the giant cylinder before them while the tube pulsed with red energy, heat flowing from the mass. "This feeds the volcano on the island?"

Lorelei pushed off the bench, floating before him as her eyes roamed the tube, "Yes, the locals believe the earth disruptions are their god telling them they do wrong. They speak of the creatures from the deep and fear them. They think we power the Morne Trois Pitons. The power of the mother earth creates this heated lava, not us."

She swam higher, waving Ewan to follow. "We worship the great stone." She stopped about five feet from the ground and floated before a stone attached to the side of the red tube. A blue diamond that glowed and pulsed with the red lava in the tube.

As he stared at the glowing gem, his ma's voice echoed. "At least we know what this stone looks like. I've held the gem once, a blue diamond." Ewan's breath left him in a whoosh. This was what he searched for: the Stone of Faith.

He turned to Lorelei, who floated and gazed at the stone. "It came to us from the gods. The stone's power is too much for one to hold—even for our King. We worship the gift from the gods, protecting the gem. In exchange, the stone hides us from evil, from the humans." She turned, looking at him. "It keeps us invisible to the human eye."

Ewan shook his head. "Wait, I see ye." He waved his hand to the settlement below. "Them."

She nodded. "I asked permission when we entered, and the gods granted you approval." At the arch in the cave, she had stopped and prayed before entering.

Ewan stared at the gem while it glittered on the tube's red light, making the moment eerie. The pulsing lava inside the cylinder matched the flash of the gem as if the stone powered the gods' wrath through the volcano. Lorelei and her people had no idea what they had or what an evil Fae might do to them should they find the magic stone here. Her desire to help her people against the plantation owner, the world—hell, the realms was a more significant duty than they could imagine. His eyes went to hers as she floated, gazing with reverence at the gem. She had no idea the danger she placed them all in or the risk to herself.

"Lorelei…" his voice cracked, and he had to clear his throat to gather his thoughts. How to tell her? *Should* he even tell her? Under the sea, the stone might hide them, but the entire kingdom was still vulnerable. A warrior swam to them quickly.

Vinnis approached. "Your King awaits Lorelei." His eyes moved to Ewan, then to the blue diamond. "He refuses to wait any longer." Lorelei nodded, her head lowering.

She took a deep breath and lifted her eyes, meeting his with a new resolve in her expression. "Come, Ewan."

Vinnis led them through the city area and past the cave entrance he'd come through the day before. A turn to the left had them in another mountain range with a large castle structure carved into the rock. Ewan's gaze went over the large gold structure as they swam closer. Turrets, much like castles in the human realm, shot up from the main building they headed toward. The closer they came, the golden structure glittered like a glowing rock. Merfolk gathered around the base, all making an opening when Vinnis escorted them through the crowd.

Whispers reached Ewan when they swam by. "It's the human." Another came to him. "She's returned bringing evil with her." Ewan took Lorelei's hand and squeezed her once for encouragement as another whisper hit him. "She'll get not only herself killed but us all."

As they swam behind Vinnis, Lorelei glanced at

Ewan and gave him a wobbly smile. Ewan would not allow her or her people to face this alone. His mission was to retrieve the Stone of Faith, but he also felt a duty to the people who had protected the gem for some time. Hell, he had to protect Lorelei. She had no idea what they faced with the power of an Iona Stone.

They cleared a grand arched entrance and floated into what seemed to be a traditional throne room. Merfolk lined the sides of the room, much like retainers in the King of Scotland's throne room he read about in history class. They floated farther into the room, and a large merman with long silver hair held a staff with a trident. Ewan's mouth fell open. Was this truly Triton, King of the Seas?

Vinnis floated aside, positioning himself opposite Murus, the one from the day before who had refused his introduction. Murus' glare met Ewans as the guard floated beside his King.

Lorelei pulled him forward and she bowed before the King. "Triton, my King." Ewan copied the gesture, hoping his etiquette matched their customs—not wanting to insult them before he had a chance to explain what he needed.

Triton floated to them and cupped Lorelei's cheek when she rose. Ewan floated with her as she gripped his hand.

Triton's voice came soft and deep, the tenderness resonating. "Daughter, you have returned."

Ewan barked before he could stop himself. "Daughter? Triton is yer da?"

Her father's focus traveled to Ewan with a smirk on his face. "I see you brought us a guest." Murus growled from his place.

Her father's eyes moved to their clasped hands. "And you seem to have selected your one."

Triton turned, shaking his head while he spoke loud enough for everyone in the room. "I welcome Ewan of the MacDougalls to our realm. He is an honored guest." Then last, her father spoke when he turned, glaring at Murus.

Her father waved as he floated to his throne. "Come sit. We have much to discuss." Another merman set chairs of seagrass and weed for him and Lorelei. She gripped his hand as they sat.

Triton eyed them, then lifted his eyes to Ewan's when his mind speak came clearly. *Ewan from the humans. Should I worry about you, Fae boy?* Ewan's eyes bulged and his gaze turned to Lorelei's, wondering if she had heard.

Triton's chuckle echoed in his head. *You have yet to master mind speak well. Only you and I converse.*

A merwoman appeared with drinks, first offering one to Triton, who took his. She served Lorelei next and Ewan last. He took the cup and waited till Triton took the first sip.

When he did, Ewan sipped his, keeping eye contact with Lorelei's father. *I am not here to harm.*

Triton smirked. *I know.* He set his cup aside, speaking aloud. "Ewan, what Fae kingdom do you serve?"

Ewan placed his cup on the chair arm and tried to stand in the water, pulling his hand from Lorelei's while he bowed. "I am from the realm of man. I serve the Tuatha Dé Danann, the good Fae." Ewan added as he rose, and his regard met Triton's. *And never call me boy.* He sat, taking Lorelei's hand and bringing her to his lips, kissing the back, never taking his eyes from her father.

Triton's grin went wide. "I bid you welcome. Dagda still rules the good Fae?"

Ewan nodded, still holding his love's hand. "Aye, he does. I'm here on a mission on his behalf." The mountain rumbled, and echoing knocks of rock filled the area.

Triton growled. "Your mission is the least of our worries. The madman, the plantation owner, has angered the gods." He settled his glare on Lorelei. "Daughter, you will tell us all you know of the madman who forces all to call him Master." He sat forward. "The Morne Trois Pitons grow angry. The wind gods bring a great storm to the island." The last, he growled, "Enough of your games, daughter. The time has come." Ewan's eyes went to Lorelei, who sat with a wide-eyed, blank stare.

Ewan's focus swung to her father. *Ye don't understand what ye hold. She's in danger. You all are.*

Triton's glare turned menacing. *No, it is you who don't understand.* He turned to his daughter. "Tell us of the monster above."

She pulled her hand from Ewan's as she rose and swam back and forth before her father, who spoke softer. "The truth, always the truth, daughter."

Ewan sensed her agitation, and he pushed before her, taking her hands in his. "Lorelei, whatever the challenge is, we face the issue together. Find courage in my faith and love for ye." She blinked and floated for a moment, staring at him. He squeezed her hands once and let them go to await her report. She twisted her hands.

Ewan whispered, "My da always said it's easiest to start from the beginning. Tell me of when the plantation owner arrived."

Lorelei turned to him and nodded, keeping her eyes on him as she spoke. "He came to us shortly after the blue stone arrived. We,"—she waved to the people around her while she spun, stopping to face Ewan—"Protect the stone as the gem protects us." Her focus shifted to her father. "Our King quickly realized as the madman pillaged treasure, he hunted our stone for its magic. Triton knew we had to keep the magic stone safe." Her gaze lowered. "When I secretly visited the humans, the plantation owner caught me. I tried to escape using my gifts."

Her father huffed. "Visiting them against the law. Gifts? A curse is more like it. Passed down from your ancestor who caused our falling out with humans in the first place. A mistake that had a human take my love's life."

Ewan's gaze met Triton's while he continued, "The mermaid folktale of her singing men to their death is my sister scorned by a human lover. She killed so many in her hunt for the one man who broke her heart that we had to stop her. A human mistook my wife for my sister, killing her. We cut off all contact with humans." He sighed. "Lorelei inherited her gifts, if you call them that."

Lorelei floated as a tear fell, and she wiped the dampness away, squaring her shoulders. "I agreed to an exchange. I work for him, and all the while, spy for my people to try to find a weakness. Someway for us to beat him."

Murus growled from his post. "At the cost of your life nearly. An evil Fae never keeps his promises. Your obsession with the humans will get us all killed."

Triton's voice boomed. "Silence! Murus, you will stand guard and keep your opinions to yourself." Ewan gasped. The plantation owner was an evil Fae. Had he been sent to hunt an Iona Stone? His focus flew to Lorelei, who gasped and covered her mouth as tears filled her eyes. When Lorelei lowered her hand and tears fell freely, her situation hit Ewan.

He floated toward her. "That's it. The power the plantation owner holds over ye. That's why ye keep going back." He waved his hand to the side. "This is as ye said for yer people but more." He cupped her face. "Ye go back to learn more to gain knowledge and how to beat him."

Lorelei choked a sob. "At first, I snuck away to be near the humans. I love them so. He caught me, and I turned my captivity into an opportunity. But then you came along." She hiccupped. "I fell for you when I first laid eyes on you. My human warrior, I prayed to come save the day."

She gazed at him, tears in her eyes. How they formed separately in the water was a mystery to Ewan. He wiped them with his hand, and the warmth spread to his heart. A quote from the Fae fable echoed in Ewan's mind. *The love of money is the root of all evil, which while some coveted after, they have erred from the faith and pierced themselves through with many sorrows.* The quote was the evil Fae and Lorelei. She put herself at risk for her people and to be close to Ewan. She loved him.

He bent and kissed her, whispering into her lips, "I love ye." The words trembled with urgency, heavy with the weight of everything he hadn't yet said. This had to stop. The danger looming over her people was grave—he knew it like he knew the rhythm of his heartbeat—but the threat to Lorelei, his love, was far greater. The evil coiled around his chest like a vise, suffocating in intensity. She didn't even see it. She moved among them with quiet courage, focusing on saving others, blind to the shadow stalking her.

Ewan's sense of duty flared hot in his chest—not just a warrior, but a man who loved fiercely. These people were hers, and by extension, they had become his. He would not see them fall. But more than that, he would not lose her. He would face fire, blade, storm, and evil if it meant shielding her from harm. War, betrayal, or fate itself—the evil Fae would have to go through him first.

He released Lorelei and turned to Triton. "My mission for Dagda, the good Fae, lies in line with yers." He pushed, swimming closer. "The stone ye worship, the gem is no mere stone but the Stone of Faith, an Iona Stone from the Tuatha Dé Danann. The evil Fae above hunts this stone to use to control the realms. Ye cannot allow an Iona Stone to fall in the hands of evil."

Triton sat back on his throne. "A Stone of Iona? I have only heard their tale. I've never seen one with my own eyes." He huffed. "And we've worshiped one for eons. Hell, since near Lorelei's birth, shortly before my beloved died when we fled Atlantis and went into hiding." He sat up. "You are right. We cannot allow an Iona Stone to fall in the hands of evil."

Ewan folded his arms and floated as if he stood tall. "My mission comes from the good Fae. I am to confront and fight the evil Fae." He omitted that the task came from a fable, not wanting to mention the maiden part. There was no need to worry Triton or alert Lorelei. She might have a greater purpose. If she knew of a way she could help, that's what she'd do. Try to help and get caught in the middle, harming herself in the process. He glanced at Lorelei. He could easily keep Lorelei safe if she stayed with her father's people. She needed a duty, and he needed her and the stone away from the evil Fae. He had the perfect plan. He'd fight, and she'd be safe. Triton offered his hand to Ewan, who grasped his.

The King leaned forward, whispering. "You truly come to fight the evil above? The good Fae remembers us?"

Ewan nodded while he replied. "Aye, before I left, the good Fae discussed a long-lost kingdom. The *sirens of the sea* they called ye."

Triton grinned and spoke in his booming voice for all to hear. "Elders, I call you forward." The crowd of merpeople shifted as one, and then another older person floated to the front. There were a couple of men, then three women, each with graying hair and a knowledgeable look about them that spoke of ages of existence. Ewan turned a full circle. Twelve in all stood in a circle around him, Triton, and Lorelei. Triton floated for a moment.

Whispers echoed in Ewan's head, some of which he couldn't quite grasp and others of which he caught portions. *He's sent from Dagda.* Another came, *Our destinies are combined.*

Ewan turned another circle till he faced Triton, who squared his shoulders. "It is decided. I vow before the kingdom this battle will be a trial for the seat of King. If Ewan is successful, he will be the future King of the Telkhines."

Ewan jolted, speaking for all to hear. "I do not covet yer kingdom to rule, only to save ye. Leadership should come from yer own."

Triton sighed and sent him a mind message. *You're my daughter's love.* He pulled Ewan's hand till they floated side by side. "All hail Ewan of the MacDougalls as we send him into battle. May the gods be with him." Ewan nodded when the crowd cheered. He floated to Lorelei, who rested near their chairs. He took her hand in his and she sniffled.

Ewan brought her hand to his lips. "Not to worry, *mo sìrean.*"

She shook her head while he lowered her hand. "He is evil. Something lives inside him."

Lorelei shivered and she opened her mouth to speak again, and Ewan placed his finger over her lips. "Worry not. I am prepared to battle an evil Fae. Brigid, my Fae prepared me." He kissed her. "But please, I beg of ye, Lorelei, stay here to guard the Stone of Faith. I need you here. No matter what happens, stay with yer father." He took her by the shoulders. "Promise me."

She nodded and a tear slipped. As long as Ewan kept her safe, it did not matter what happened to him. The Iona Stone he'd retrieve after the battle, but Lorelei would not be the maiden's sacrifice. Even if he had to give his life for hers, he wouldn't let that happen. His da changed the outcome once. Even at a great price, Ewan vowed to change the result again.

Chapter 19

Manix stood at the window beside the fireplace, having retreated from the flooded caves below. The wind howled against the panes with a force that rattled the glass in its frame—a strength Manix had never seen before. The storm had risen like a beast from the sea, surging inland with a fury that turned trees into whips and the sky into a thrashing, boiling cauldron. Rain slammed against the house in sheets, not falling so much as flying sideways, driven by gales that shrieked like mourning spirits.

Lightning cracked across the heavens, illuminating the dim room in sharp flashes that made the shadows leap and twist. Thunder followed like cannon fire, the sound so close it reverberated through the wooden floorboards and shook the stones of the hearth. Smoke from the fire curled reluctantly upward, tugged by the drafts sneaking through unseen cracks in the old walls.

Manix's eyes stayed fixed on the chaos outside. The trees beyond the hill bowed low under the storm's weight, some uprooted entirely, their gnarled roots exposed to the wild air. Water pooled in the fields below, dark and roiling, rushing in torrents where gentle creeks had once meandered. His breath fogged the glass as he leaned closer, searching the shadows outside for movement. This wasn't just weather. The moment rang of a reckoning.

Balor growled in his mind. *Ye've done it now. The storm will blow us to bits.*

Manix growled. "It's called a hurricane, and in the future, people survive them all the time." He grumbled. "I should have taped the glass. Should have installed storm glass from the future like my critter's tank." He grumbled as he tried calling her again. *My pet, siren of the seas. Come to me now!* Silence. His every summons met with stillness.

The wind howled and took on a whistling sound while the air blew around the building. Manix hoped since his house sat higher on the hillside, they'd be out of the storm's full force, but maybe he'd need to take cover, just in case. The caves had flooded since they sat at sea level, and he had no cellar. Another gust of wind had something hitting the building with a bang that had Manix jolting.

Balor roared. *Boy, ye better know what ye are doing.*

Manix growled. "I always know what I am doing, old man!"

Balor laughed. *No, ye don't. Ye should have found the Iona Stone before this came.* The volcano rumbled in the distance as Balor growled. *The gods are not happy, boy. Ye need to find the stone. I sense magic nearby.*

Manix barked at nothing. "I'm not going out in this. Flying is impossible, and I'll not survive without shelter in a storm like this."

Balor whined. *Flying is impossible.* Then chuckled. *Ye have no idea the power ye possess.* He inhaled a gasp. *Prepare, boy, ye have a visitor.*

Manix turned from the window. "In this storm? My servants fled when the winds picked up, and I doubt any human can travel the hill in this." A door banged open, and the wind blew from the foyer, blowing out the candles and sending the room into shadows.

Balor chuckled. *The prodigal son has come to meet his match.* He growled, *Be ready, boy, yer time has arrived.*

Manix turned a full circle, finding no one. When the wind blew again, he spun his focus to the foyer. A figure stood, feet braced apart as his coat whipped in the wind.

Lightning lit the room, and his uninvited guest stood at the entry to the great room. A frown marred his face, but Manix recognized his nemesis—the familiar shape of Ewan MacDougall, the brother of his fated lover. Balor was right. His time was upon him. Manix turned, hiding his face, hoping Ewan hadn't recognized him in the dark room.

Ewan folded his arms, yelling above the wind. "They call ye master. The sugar plantation owner come to labor the good people of Waitukura to death." He blew a laugh. "Ye are from the evil Fae, the Fomoire. Tell me, evil Fae, what name do ye go by?"

Manix sneered, so Ewan did not know who he dealt with. A fact that Manix hoped to use in his favor.

Balor chuckled in his mind. *Stupid MacDougall. He's just as daft as his father.*

Ewan strode to the large tank Manix used for his pet, thumping the thick glass three times. The dull thud sounded in a lull of the wind. "Tell me, evil Fae, where is yer powerful Captain Low?" As Manix crept closer to the fireplace, Ewan tapped the glass harder this time. "Yer precious secret weapon?" Manix growled when he tried to read Ewan's mind, yet all he came up against was a block—a wall of blackness.

Ewan chuckled, "Aww, come on, evil Fae. Ye can do better than that, can't ye? Reading my mind. How juvenile. I know I can't read yers. Tried before I entered."

Manix yelled, unable to control his temper. "My pet is hiding, but she will see ye to yer doom."

Ewan turned, smirking. "Ye sound so certain, but I am not so sure." Ewan flicked his wrist, and the tank broke open. The water rushed around Ewan, leaving him dry. Manix stood still, allowing the water to cover his feet. Damn, Ewan.

Ewan held his hands to his sides. "Yer *pet* ye have no more. She will no longer be yer prisoner." So, Ewan had her, that's why she didn't respond to his summons.

As Manix returned to the shadows, Ewan turned fully and faced him. "Come, evil Fae. This is not like Balor's underlings. Others tell me they do not hide like cowards."

Manix threw a force at Ewan, who quickly blocked the energy with one hand. "Yer power is strong but not controlled. Are ye new to this Fae?" Manix threw another spell and another, each blocked by Ewan while he remained unaffected.

Ewan's white grin glowed as the wind howled from the foyer, blowing more leaves and rain into the vast room. "I recognize yer power, an evil Fae ye think ye are, but there's a goodness underlying yer magic—a sign of betrayal to yer kind." Ewan stepped forward and the lightning lit the room. "Come, Manix, come out of the shadows and fight like a man."

Balor roared in his head. *Are ye going to let him call ye that? A coward is what ye are!*

Manix roared as he charged Ewan, casting energy

with a crackle that split the air like a lightning strike. The force hurtled across the room in a searing arc of light and heat—but Ewan was faster. He threw up a shield that clashed with Manix's spell in midair. The collision burst like a star between them, sending shockwaves rippling through the chamber. Light fractured across the walls in shimmering veins, and the air thrummed with a high, unnatural hum that prickled the skin and tasted of ozone and ancient magic.

Energy rebounded off the shield in a shockwave that struck the window. The glass didn't just shatter—it exploded outward in a thousand glittering shards, each catching the light like a falling star. The blast sent a cascade of sound rippling through the room, a haunting, crystalline chorus that echoed like magic unraveling at the seams. In the next instant, the storm outside surged like a living creature, furious and wild. The wind tore through the room, rattling the rafters and sending glass and loose wood flying. Rain came in sheets, driven sideways, soaking everything in its path.

The storm drenched Manix, leaving his hair plastered to his face and making his clothes cling to his body. The fire sputtered in protest as droplets hissed against the flame, smoke billowing from the fireplace.

But Manix didn't care. Let the storm rage. Let the wind scream, and the sky fall.

He had only just begun.

****

Doug and the crew easily beached *The Faithful* near the port. The storm blew harder, picking up speed and power in the last hour. One-eyed Joe patted him on the back as they stood on the beach. Joe did not need to shield his face from the stinging rain flying sideways like

Doug had to.

Doug wiped his face while he yelled over the wind gust. "Joe, I must seek shelter. I'm off to the Salty Dog." Doug gazed at *The Faithful* for what he feared might be the last time he'd see her whole. His eyes traveled beyond the inlet to the open ocean and the torrent in the surf. The feeling of returning to the future overcame him. The time to go back was now, but time travel was impossible without Ewan. Doug didn't have Fae powers.

One-Eyed Joe patted his back. "Not to worry, Dougie. We'll keep watch as we always have. The storm won't bother us." He chuckled, "Ye go on to yer sweetheart and hunker down." He climbed the rigging to the deck, calling over his shoulder. "See ye when the blow is over!"

Doug waved as the other crew members peered over the railing. His eyes traveled to areas blown away in the last battle. Just when they seemed to fix the old girl, Ewan entered another fight that tore her apart. Another gust hit him harder, this time knocking him sideways. He needed to find shelter and fast. He took off at a run to the port. The distance had to be only a short jog, but his trek took longer in this deluge.

As he ran, he prayed for his friend, Ewan. They'd seen a lot together, spent their lives side by side as best friends, as cohorts in every prank they played. They took part in each other's adventures, mishaps, and everything in between. He hoped Ewan was safe. Doug cleared the docks and quickly went to the Salty Dog Tavern as the feeling of doom and an earnest need to return to the future overcame him. Ignoring the sensation, he burst through the doors and ran into the back kitchen area. The cellar door was open halfway, and Abi stood half in and out.

Her shocked expression at his sudden appearance had him chuckling. "Ye didn't think I'd come by to wait out the storm, did ye?"

She barked at him. "Well, damn glad I am to see you, Doug. Here I thought Davy Jones dragged you to the sea forever." She waved to him. "Get your good-looking ass in here. We have enough provisions to ride out a good gale." He followed her down the ladder, and when he landed at the bottom, she threw herself into his arms, holding him tight. Her sniffles echoed in the room while her cook, Martha, and Davy, the bar boy holding Salty Dog's collar, looked on with a smile.

His arms quickly encircled her. "I have ye, Abi, I have ye."

She pulled back and wiped her tears away. "I don't know what I'd do without you."

Doug grinned. "And I ye, my sweet." They shuffled to the corner as Abi helped him dry off with a rough cloth. He stared at Abi, heart thudding like the thunder outside, not wanting to imagine her caught in the storm. The thought of her, vulnerable and alone, twisted something deep inside him. It wasn't just worry—it was something more primal, more personal. The more he stood there, the more his resolve to leave unraveled. The urgency that had driven his need to go to the future dulled beneath the weight of something he couldn't quite name. A sense of doom had haunted him each time they time-hopped, had clung to him like a second skin, but now…now it loosened its grip.

All he could feel was her. Her presence grounded him and made the impossible seem suddenly possible. While the wind howled outside, the need to return to the future faded, replaced by a quiet, terrifying truth—he didn't want to leave her behind. Not now—not ever.

When she let out a huff and another sniffle, he took her in his arms, kissing her. As he settled her in the crook of his arm, they sat in the corner among some blankets. Staying here in the past did not seem like such a bad idea after all. His mind and heart warmed to the idea, and a grand plan for restoring the island that history told a storm destroyed formed in his mind. He'd rebuild the port, making it bigger to accommodate more trade ships.

If Ewan succeeded in his mission to rid them of the greedy one, as Doug figured he would, the sugar plantation would go up for auction. With the land and buildings damaged, the property would come at a fraction of the land's total value. He mentally prepared for the next part of seafaring history—the end of pirating and the entry of merchant shipping as a profitable business.

The wind howled above them like a furious beast, ripping through the cliffs with a voice that shattered silence. Then it came—the thunderous crack of splintering beams followed by a heart-wrenching groan. Doug's breath caught. A booming roar split the night sky, and in its wake came the sound no seaman ever wished to hear: the agonizing collapse of wood and stone.

He turned just in time to catch through a crack a cascade of debris—shattered timbers, slate shingles, and once-familiar shutters—tumble into the storm-slicked bay. Abi's pub—gone. The warmth, the laughter, the memories built into every corner of that weathered heaven—all of it swallowed in a single, merciless breath of nature's wrath.

Doug staggered forward a step, chest tight, rain mixing with the salt on his cheeks. Davey sniffled, and Martha held him. Salty Dig whined while they all sat out the storm. In Doug's mind, he visualized a new beginning with the woman he loved.

She hiccupped a sob. "Well, that's the end of that."

Doug cuddled her as he kissed her head. "Naw, Abi, this is the beginning." He placed his finger under her chin and tilted her face till their eyes met. "Marry me, please?"

She hit him. "Marry you? How can you ask at a time like this?"

He grinned. "It's the perfect time. A new beginning with ye by my side."

As he kissed her, she smiled. "I want a proper wedding, Douglas."

He squeezed her tight. "Anything for my Abi, anything."

****

Ewan shifted his feet as the maddening gale blew into the room. A lump came under his toe, and he glanced down to find a dirtied piece of fabric. He bent and picked the scrap up. The corner flipped in the wind. When the ERM came into view, he recognized the handkerchief he'd given to Lorelei when she was on his ship.

Stone grated against stone, making Ewan look up. The bookshelf beside the fireplace stood open as he caught the flash of Manix moving down some hidden stairs. So, the weakling ran. Good. The chase was now on. He pocketed the fabric as he crept toward the secret door, keeping his hand ready to block a spell or any advance Manix might make. In the darkened stairs,

Manix's boots mixed with the sound of lapping waves filled the area.

When Ewan rounded a corner, a spell came full force. He sensed the hex's energy coming, and he dodged the flash. The spell's force broke rock in the wall, the pieces tumbling down the stairs to crash into the water below. Water, this must be a sea cave, flooded from the storm. What was Manix's goal, to head into the water, or was he fleeing in panic? There was only one way to find out. Ewan progressed farther down the stairs toward waving torchlight, intent on reaching Manix and ending this farce of a fight. As he rounded the next corner, the water lapping grew louder. Manix roared and threw a spell. Ewan threw up a block, the spell dying.

Manix turned, yelling, "I know, old man, I know."

Ewan glanced around the large cavern he'd entered. Multiple scones lit the cavern, which was half full of seawater. *Old man? Who?*

Manix bared his teeth as he focused on Ewan. "Ye, it's ye who ruined all my grand plans. I would have had my reward, the Stone of Faith and all the riches." He tossed a spell that went wide, hitting the cave wall. Ewan grinned. In Manix's haste, his aim got worse. All Ewan had to do was distract Manix, find an opening, and strike.

Ewan stood ready while he called out to Manix. "Have it all? Ye mean like when ye coveted my sister?"

Manix yelled, "She's mine!"

Ewan chuckled. "Really? I attended her wedding in the Fae realm. She and her true love, Aodhán. Theirs was a glorious event binding two true loves."

Manix roared. "No!"

Ewan grinned wide. "Aye, their little daughter is so cute. The perfect family that isn't yers." Sensing another spell, he ducked and yelled the last. When the force came, Ewan was ready to use a deflect spell, hitting Manix as he roared.

Ewan yelled when Manix bent over in pain. "Careful Manix! Be on your guard against all kinds of greed. Life does not consist of an abundance of possessions. Those who want to get rich fall into temptation and a trap and into many foolish and harmful desires that plunge people into ruin and destruction." He threw the fabled quote at Manix, hoping they neared the end. He felt the resolution near in the air. Another spell came from Manix, aimed too high. When the force hit the rock wall, making debris fall on him, Ewan bent, covering his head.

When Ewan glanced up, Manix quickly recovered and stood in the waist-deep water. "I have mastered the water, Ewan, have ye?" Wings flew out from Manix's back, but not incandescent and clear like Brigid's butterfly wings. In the cave's dim light, they looked batlike, black with a leather texture, just as Evie had described after her encounter with Manix. The span alone was over thirty feet, spreading the width of the cavern.

His body swelled, muscles stretching while his limbs thickened and realigned, his fingers curling into razor-sharp claws. A tail shot from his spine, lashing through the surf. His skin darkened, hardening into gleaming black scales as his face elongated into a fearsome snout. Manix twisted his shoulders, and with a flash, the transformation was complete—a full-sized dragon stood where he had been, his obsidian scales shimmering in the torchlight. When Manix exposed himself as the plantation owner, Ewan figured the dragon would show himself. At least Ewan was prepared.

Ewan backed up the stairs while Manix's red eyes leveled at him. The dragon took a deep breath and, in a swirl, dove into the ocean. Not one to let his target out of his sight, Ewan leaped off the stairs and onto the dragon's back, gripping the horns tightly as he did so. Just before he dove into the surf, Ewan took a huge air gulp, filling his lungs. The cold water hit him hard, nearly knocking him out of his seat. But he held onto the dragon and the air, needing the resource for the next spell.

Lorelei's voice echoed in his head. *To cast the bubble spell, you only have to focus on air from your lungs, create magic inside, and then blow air around where you want the bubble to be.* Manix twisted when he dove, breaking Ewan's concentration as he held on to the horns. When Manix stopped underwater, Ewan gathered energy, focusing on the air in his lungs. They heated, and he blew, pushing the mass in a circle around his head. The bubble formed, and he gulped in the air as he held on.

Water splashed, making a loud whoosh, and Ewan ducked when Manix's horned tail slashed nearby. He missed Ewan and hit himself on the head, knocking them both sideways. As they floated there momentarily, Ewan breathed a deep breath and then another. Manix likely waited, hoping Ewan couldn't hold his breath this long, but the dragon couldn't see him on his back. Ewan pulled his hand back and threw a spell at Manix's head. The force hit full-on, causing the dragon to arch and push toward the surface.

As Manix's dragon roared into the wind, they broke free from the water. They flew higher and the island spread out beneath them. The wind died as the clouds lightened and the rain let up. Ewan gazed over the top of the hurricane, its eye over the island and the back side's tempest yet to come.

****

Lorelei floated to one end of the throne room, turned, and swam to her father and the elders who all seemed to wait patiently. How could they be this calm? Lorelei was beside herself with news of Ewan's confrontation with the madman. She inhaled, deeply trying to push the next thought from her mind—his potential demise.

"Please, Father. I have a bad feeling."

Her sire, looking the part of king holding his trident, shook his head. "No. Ewan said you must remain here."

She gripped her father's hand, holding his spear, symbolizing his leadership for all the Telkhines. "Please, I fear for him. The emotions swell inside me. Like something's gone wrong."

Triton's free hand pulled hers to his chest. "Daughter, I am certain Ewan of the MacDougalls faces the enemy with courage. He will succeed." Lorelei's heart lurched. Something was wrong. She felt the shift deep down in her heart.

She pulled away from her father, heading toward the exit. "I feel the evil. He's failed."

Her father swam to her, grabbing her arm. "You promised him you'd stay here. You must let the man fulfill his destiny, no matter the outcome."

She pulled back tears in her eyes. "I cannot, Father. Not when I know I have the power to help him. Possibly save him." She swam out of the throne room and through the castle as her father called after her. "Lorelei, you must let Ewan do this alone. We don't surface during the storms. Going up is too dangerous. You know this."

She stopped turning a flip to face her father. "Not if my lack of action costs him his life. Not the life of my love, my one. Ewan said the stone from the gods is magic. The Stone of Faith. I go give him my faith and love." She flipped again, speeding away. *The stone, the stone, the stone.* Chanted over and over again in her mind. Ewan needed the magic stone. She felt in her heart.

****

The volcano rumbled louder than Ewan had ever heard. Manix circled while he flew to the top as if to peer into the massive ridge. Heat flew out of the gaping hole in waves while the rain and steam covered the area. Manix's wings beat a steady rhythm while they hovered above the red, orange opening. Deep from within the earth, a vibration began, and the rumble grew. Ewan sensed the earth's energy shift as the roar grew louder. In a vast eruption, red and orange lava shot from the top, flying into the sky. Manix had to shift aside quickly to avoid being hit, nearly knocking Ewan from his seat. They floated suspended, and Manix's wings beat an even drum while lava poured from the mountain, leading a trail from the top down the side. The melted earth quickly flowed as steam rose when the rain hit. The bottom of the flow caught vegetation on fire, burning everything in the lava's path.

Manix's dragon roared and flew, turning a full circle of the devastated area. When the lava river reached the beach, the torrent seemed to split the island in half, one side the village and the other the plantation, taking out primarily unused jungle land, avoiding areas where people lived.

The mountain rumbled again, and lava shot from the

top, sending a ribbon toward them. Manix shied, avoiding the burning liquid as the chunks fell near the beach. The dragon's head swiveled a little, and Ewan caught the dragon's eye. A grin and a low growl came from the creature, the only warning Ewan had before Manix's dragon dove for the earth. At the beach, he landed with a jolt that sent Ewan tumbling head over heels into the surf. The impact knocked the wind from him making him flounder in the waves. Ewan came up gasping for air, and a force hit him. He dove into the shallow waters, gathering energy. When he burst from the surface, another spell hit him harder before he could block the force. As he raised his hand, another hit him again, making him fall into the waves. He crawled from the water exhausted and lay on the beach.

Manix's dragon soared overhead. Weak from the tumble and the power of Manix's spells, Ewan prayed for a miracle. He feared that's what it would take for him to beat Manix's dragon as he lay frail from the spells—a perfect target for the flying dragon above. Faith, he needed faith.

Chapter 20

The sea fought against her as she swam to the surface. Cresting the rough waves, Lorelei had a hard time searching the beachline. She sensed him nearby. He had to be here. A roar echoed into the sky, shooting through Lorelei's heart. Only one creature sounded like that. She searched the skies, only finding angry storm clouds and the rain hit her like the sharp pricks of a knife. She dove under the water, trying to focus on her inner senses. Ewan's feelings flashed through her—hurt and tired his endurance spent. Ewan was at his end. She gripped the Stone of Faith close to her heart and swam toward the emotions. Ewan needed faith. Ewan needed her.

****

Manix flew over Ewan as he lay on the beach. The wind picked up and the rain grew heavy again. He smiled; the second half of the storm approached, coming in at a whole gale. That second wave in the storm usually hit harder than the first. He glanced down at Ewan as the surf engulfed him, tumbling him on what little the storm left of the beach. He roared again, relishing Evie's brother's imminent demise. Hurt Ewan, and he'd hurt Evie. The same way she hurt him.

A gust of wind rocked him in the sky, but he steered into the gust. Balor said he could fly in this, and it turned out he could. He circled again, setting up for another attack, hoping to end Ewan in a blast of a spell or two. The rain blew sideways now, harder than before. He paused midair, trying to see Ewan in the rain. When he caught a glimpse of the figure on the beach, the blob wasn't one but two huddled together. Manix circled lower as he focused on the forms, and damn it, a form with bright red hair hugged Ewan while he sat up. Lorelei in her human form!

Manix roared, and the two figures turned their faces up to him. Each with the same expression of shock. Lightning flashed, and in the light, a blue gem in Ewan's hands winked from the momentary light. Ewan had the Iona Stone! He held the Stone of Faith. Manix roared again as he circled closer. It couldn't be, but there it was, a blue gem. When Ewan stood, Manix quickly gathered power. Manix must strike fast, or Ewan could blow him out of the sky. From his encounters with Evie, both brother and sister knew how to use the magic Iona Stones.

****

The storm grew heavier, and Manix flew above with the advantage of the overhead position. Lorelei shouldn't have come.

Ewan gripped the stone to his chest as he yelled over the storm. "Lorelei ye must leave now. Ye risk yerself by being here!"

She hugged him and a wave hit them, nearly toppling both into the sea. "No! You needed me. I felt it."

Ewan pushed her into the surf. "Go now! I must fight!" He sensed energy gather. Manix must be getting ready to cast a spell. He held the stone to his chest, allowing the gem's energy to meld with his own. Ewan needed to have his block ready, but combining the energy between him and the stone took longer. The spell would be more powerful, but would he have the full power in time? Manix roared as lightning struck close by. A ball of energy formed in his claws. It was now or never.

Lorelei screamed while she ran to Ewan. Manix threw his spell too soon; Ewan didn't have his block ready. Lorelei launched herself into him as Manix's spell hit. They tumbled into the surf. When his free arm grabbed Lorelei, Ewan nearly dropped the Stone of Faith. Her body jolted as her form heated. As Ewan righted them, she glowed bright white. Ewan dropped her into the ocean, hoping seawater would rejuvenate her and bring her to her true form.

Ready or not, Ewan had to act fast. He had mere seconds before Manix could gather energy for another spell leaving him with only one chance.

Ewan thrust the Stone of Faith forward, his entire body trembling with the surge of emotion coursing through him—grief, rage, desperation, and something deeper still, something ancient. The magic responded in kind, not in a trickle or stream, but in a torrent. Power exploded from the stone in a brilliant blue light too immense to contain. The spell tore through the space between them like a spear of burning judgment, carving a searing path through the air that scorched the wind.

The sky split with a crack that shook the mountains. A blinding flare lit the horizon, casting jagged shadows and turning night briefly into a white-hot imitation of day. The spell struck with such force the air itself convulsed as it tore open in ragged lines, recoiling from what he had unleashed.

A deep, rolling boom followed—not a sound, but a force that moved through the chest, the bones, and the soul. A ring of raw, trembling silence expanded outward after the blast.

Ewan staggered back, breath stolen from his lungs, and pulled his arm to his chest, cradling the Stone of Faith as though it might crumble in his grasp. Steam hissed from the scorched grass around him. The air reeked of magic—sharp, metallic, volatile.

He raised his eyes to the sky, searching through the dissipating haze of power, the crackling remnants echoing. Where was Manix? Was it enough? Or had he only angered the monster further?

As the rain abated, a roar resounded, the clouds parted, and Manix flew suspended overhead.

His mind speak came to Ewan. *Fool. Yer spell hit lightning. But missing me is not the best part of this.* Manix's dragon nodded his head to something behind Ewan. Ewan turned, and in the shallow surf lay a white seal.

Manix exhaled. *Well, I kept my promise, fish. I made ye into something.*

Ewan moved toward the seal. "What?"

Manix's chuckle echoed in Ewan's mind. *Of all the things she could have asked for, all she ever wanted was to be human. I made her one for a while, but the spell would never last. She kept returning for a promise I never had the power to grant.* He huffed. *Naive thing she is.*

Ewan stepped closer to the seal. "Is this true? Is this what kept ye coming back to him? Doing his dastardly deeds?" The seal blinked, bowing her head. Ewan sensed

Lorelei as he neared the animal. Her feelings came clearly to him—her fear, hurt, and embarrassment. The seal lifted her head and rose a bit, looking prouder.

Manix circled. *Oh well. That's too bad. As a mermaid, she was much prettier.*

Keeping his back to Manix, Ewan clutched the Stone of Faith to his chest, drawing power into it with every breath. The stone pulsed warm against his skin, responding to his will and desperation. He felt the shift behind him—the subtle change in the air as Manix prepared his strike.

Ewan spun, eyes blazing, and released everything. The stone's energy surged forward, braided with his own, forming a spell so fierce it shimmered in the space between them like a living force.

Manix's spell met it midair. The clash ignited in a burst of raw magic that cracked the sky and sent a shockwave rippling through the ground. The cliffs groaned. The tide recoiled. And Ewan was thrown backward, crashing into the cold surf with a grunt, arms wrapped tightly around the Stone of Faith.

He lay there, soaked and gasping, the world still shaking from the impact. But he still held the magic Iona Stone.

When he righted, Manix flew above him. *Well, I can tell when it's time to cut loose and bail.* With a wave of a wing, a portal opened mid-sky that Manix flew through. As the opening closed, a lightning bolt struck through the closing hole. Ewan sat in the surf, blinking at the sky and the clouds parted farther and the sun shone on the decimated island.

Lorelei! Ewan turned to the seal who sat in the surf, and Aodhán's voice echoed in his mind. *Yes and no. It's the final straw. The last thing that will break the greedy one is what this is. That, combined with what comes next, well, this tells ye the end.*

The end. Is this the end? Lorelei as something she's not? He ran toward her, fighting the waves to get nearer to the one he loved. He didn't care that she was a seal. He'd find a way. He loved her. When he came closer, the waves washed over her, then again. One moment, she was the seal; the next, she was the mermaid.

He fell on his knees, the surf covering them, and took her in his arms. "Lorelei!"

She shook her head as tears streamed down her face. "I brought the stone to you so you'd fulfill your destiny." Ewan shoved out of her embrace, holding her hand and dragging them onto the land.

She pulled out of his grasp, but he kept walking through the surf. "Lorelei, I told ye to stay behind for yer own safety." He cleared the waves and turned, expecting her to be behind him. The sight before him froze him in place. Back in the surf sat the white seal blinking at him. Ewan glanced at the magic Fae stone in his hand. This couldn't be. He stomped through the surf toward her, fighting the waves again as tears threatened. No, it couldn't be. When he came upon his love, her body quivered. Her form melded over itself and morphed into the mermaid. Ewan stood with a lump in his throat.

Lorelei offered him a smile that wobbled as another tear slid down her cheek. "You succeeded. What's happened to me is of no matter." Away from the Stone of Faith, Lorelei was a seal, close to the magic gem, she became her true form, a mermaid.

Aodhán's voice echoed again. *When all is said and done, the life of faith is nothing if not an unending struggle of the spirit with every available weapon against the flesh.* Manix had used the flesh against him, against them in the cruelest way. Destiny or not, Ewan knew at that moment what he'd do. In his mind, there were no questions. Fae duty or not, Lorelei was all that mattered. His love that he'd never leave—not whole.

Ewan pulled his handkerchief from his pocket as he tried to swallow past the lump in his throat. He held the same square of fabric he'd found near her tank, her prison. The one he'd gifted to her to wipe her tears. Ewan wrapped the Stone of Faith inside, leaving the embroidered ERM on top. The initials wavered through his tears. He took her in his arms and kissed her hard and long—a last kiss from one love to another.

He handed her the wrapped stone and whispered. "I give ye my heart, my love and my soul. But most of all, I gift ye yer life as ye should live it."

Chapter 21

Ewan came through the portal. A simple step was all it took this time. Each time he and Doug had gone back and forth in their escapades, they'd barreled through the opening powered by the force of pushing and pulling his galleon back and forth. No ship this time, no extra force, just a simple step from the past to the future. His head spun a little as the familiar ringing in his ears faded.

Ewan turned, expecting to see Doug and Abigail where they stood on the beach beside *The Faithful*. In the future, all Ewan saw was the pulpit. He stood in the Chapel in Woods at Dunstaffnage Castle alone while his goodbye to his best friend echoed in his ears.

Doug held Abi's hand as she petted Salty Dog, whose head nearly reached her waist. "It's what I feel, Ewan. I must stay here. Plus, I don't think I'd make it back. That feeling is strong." Abi cuddled into Doug's side. Ewan huffed. It wasn't the Fae powers of time travel Doug felt. His best friend had lost his heart to a woman in the past. Ewan's gaze scanned the island, torn apart from the storm. The trail of cooling lava steamed as the mountain rested, no longer spewing hot molten rock. It seemed the gods had their say. When he turned back, Doug and Abi embraced, kissing. Ewan cleared his throat, and the two jumped apart.

Doug moved forward, gripping him with a tight hug

that brought tears to his eyes. "That's for my parents." They stood there for a moment, hugging. Doug stepped back and punched Ewan hard on the arm, making him flinch. "That's for my sister, Kat. Ye look out for her as yer own." Ewan fought the lump that formed in his throat. Doug put his hand out, and Ewan took it.

They gripped hands as Doug spoke. "Thank ye, friend—for everything." Ewan turned, unable to look at his best friend without tears in his eyes. The thought of leaving him forever overwhelmed him. He gathered energy and opened a portal easily from his desire to return home.

When he stepped through, Doug called back. "Look me up will ye? I'll leave a mark!" Ewan nodded, keeping his face away as the tears streamed down his cheeks. He waved his hand, closing the portal.

He sighed. That was mere minutes ago, and it already felt like years. He brushed a tear away as he pushed open, then shuffled through the chapel door toward the castle. The day was mild, and the breeze wafted through the leaves in the trees—the sound soft like someone tried to soothe Ewan's troubled emotions. He ambled through the foyer and passed his ma, Bree.

His ma stopped and glanced between him and the castle doors. "Ewan, I didn't know you were back. There wasn't a boom or a whistle of wind." She went toward him with concern etched on her face. "Ewan, you are all wet." Coming closer, she sniffed and coughed. "Honey, you smell like dead fish. I'll get you a towel, dear."

Ewan could only muster a nod and proceeded with his head down, the weight of what was to come pressing heavily on his shoulders. His steps toward the study felt longer than they were, each echoed with the promise of confrontation. Trepidation twisted in his gut—he knew his da would be furious. Walking away from the Iona Stone, from the legacy entwined with their bloodline, would be seen like a betrayal. Cowardice, even. But Ewan didn't see it that way. Every step forward was a choice. Leaving the stone behind had been his, not made in haste or fear, but in clarity.

He paused outside the study door, heart thudding against his ribs, and lifted his head. He would face his father not as a boy looking for approval but as a man owning his truth—his decisions, his mistakes, and his chosen path. It was time to stand up for himself.

The study door he found cracked. Ewan pushed on the wood. A slight creak sounded when the entry moved, exposing his da who sat at his desk looking over some papers in the same position Ewan had seen since childhood. Laird Colin MacDougall had aged gracefully. His salt and pepper hair glittered in the sunlight from the window, and his skin had taken on a weathered look, but his body remained fit.

His sire didn't lift his head but called out. "*Mo chridhe*, yer back so soon?" *Mo chridhe*, my heart, that's what he called Ewan's ma, Bree—my heart. Ewan's throat closed as he thought of his heart, his love.

Ewan stood there momentarily, and the man sniffed, then lifted his head. "What is that I smell?" His da's eyebrows rose. When their eyes connected he frowned. "So, it's ye who smells like dead fish."

Ewan nodded. "Aye, it's me."

His sire set his papers aside. "I didn't see yer ship come flying through the sky, landing in the loch distributing all around." He waved his hands to mimic the ship flying and crashing in the loch. Ewan used to find the sarcastic pantomime of his antics humorous, but not today.

Ewan stood there ready for his reckoning. "No, da. The ship didn't come back."

His da waved to the chair before him. "Well, sit, son. Tell me what has happened."

Ewan proceeded to the chair as his ma rushed in. "Not on the chair." Ewan jumped up and she placed a towel on the seat. "They are antiques, Ewan." Everything in the castle was an antique. He huffed; everything in their home was something his ma had collected from the past.

He stood, allowing his ma to help settle him as familiar clinking sounds filled the room. His ma's care, his da's typical tot. The routine of it all he found comforting and depressing at the same time. The thought of not having them, his parents, in daily life made his eyes water again. He sat a moment and took a deep breath, then another. When his gaze came up, his da rounded the desk and held out a whisky for him. Ewan took the sniffer and stared into the golden-brown liquid, not finding the answers to get through this discussion. The thought of whisky soured his tongue.

As his da sipped his drink, he leaned on the desk, folding his arms and legs in his usual pose. His ma went behind the desk, poured her a glass, then shifted and leaned on the couch. They all had positioned themselves in the same places where this began—yet seemed so far away now.

His da took a deep breath. "The beginning, Ewan. Always start at the beginning."

Ewan inhaled, took that sip he thought he didn't need, and then exhaled as he spoke. "It's not so easy,

Da."

His ma's voice came softly. "Where's Doug, Ewan?" Ewan glanced at his ma.

Her expectant expression made what he had to say so much harder, but he had to tell them everything. "Doug stayed. He fell in love. Abigail. They plan to rebuild the island, Waitukura."

Bree gasped. "You mean like Ainslie?" That day, he'd found out Ainslie wasn't returning to their time, echoed now.

Ewan stared at his mother as she lay in her bed. She'd been gone for some time, taken by a bad man. He recalled calling her a bruised peach, and Evie had scolded him, calling her a princess.

He spoke over the lump in his throat. "Da said Auntie Ainslie had to stay. She had to stay with her true love."

His ma had smiled. "Yes, that is true, but she gave me something to give each of you."

She bent and kissed Evie and him on the head. "For each of you from Ainslie. She said to watch for her in your dreams." Ewan had cherished that kiss for a long time—the thought of never seeing someone he loved ever again burned his chest now as it had then.

Ewan's chin wobbled. "Will we ever see her again?"

His da's voice held a confident ring to it, lifting Ewan's spirits. "Aye, someday."

The four had sat together for a short time, chatting and hugging.

Who would he sit with now that he'd left his best friend he'd had his whole life? Who would he talk to share his innermost fears and desires? His confidant was now gone. Ewan felt the emptiness of Doug's absence deeper. Never was so—permanent, yet, Doug looked so happy to start anew.

Ewan nodded, unable to look at his ma. "I left him *The Faithful*. Said he would start a new life as a sea merchant."

She sniffled and sighed. "Marie and John will take this hard. And Kat…"

Ewan sat staring into his glass. "I promised to look after Kit Kat for Doug, and I plan to keep it."

His sire grumbled. "The crewmen. They were a spell, ghosts of yer ancestors. What of them?"

Ewan smiled, proud of what he'd done. "I set them free." Tears blurred his vision as he raised his gaze to his da's, "Like Evie does with lost spirits. I set them free so their souls would find rest."

Colin huffed. "Well, that's a relief." He sipped his whisky and smacked his lips. "The greedy one, the plantation owner?"

Ewan sat up quickly, blinking his tears away. This next bit would come as much of a surprise to them as it had him. "Manix is in hiding."

His da stood. "No! This can't be!"

Ewan nodded. "Aye, we battled. First him—then as his dragon."

He had battled a dragon shapeshifter, not just any Fae, one of Balor's sons. The battle rang in his memory. The spells flung without care reminded Ewan of when he and Evie trained with Brigid as children. Manix is in the early stages of using his Fae power, struggling with control. Though his abilities were raw and untamed, there was a fierce, potent energy within him, hinting at immense potential once he mastered it. The portal opening in midair was a power Ewan had practiced until all his energy drained. The power to possess portal skills like Balor. A vow he'd made as a child—to master a force to use to battle Balor and save his ma that, in the end, Balor's son used to evade him in a loss.

Ewan grunted. "In the end, he ran like a coward." Manix's magic signature lingered in Ewan's mind. "His magic is like Evie said. Good lies under all that hate."

His da crossed to the fireplace, leaning on the mantel. "The stone? Ye did find the stone?"

Ewan stared into his glass. The last few drops of whisky glittered there as his memory flashed.

Lorelei showed him the stone, sharing her people's prized possession that they worshipped in exchange for protection. Her face was so innocent, her expression so hopeful.

He remembered staring at the gem as the stone glittered in the tube's red light, making the moment eerie. The pulsing lava inside the cylinder matched the flash of the gem as if the stone powered the gods' wrath through the volcano. It was an omen of the evil to come.

His voice came out cracked. "Aye, the merfolk had the stone all this time. The gem sat under the island."

His ma stood as she gasped. "That's right, I remember. The stone fell into the ocean!" She turned to his da. "They must have found it in the sea. Merfolk, another Fae?"

Ewan could barely nod. "Aye."

His da leveled his gaze on Ewan. "The stone, Ewan. Where's the stone now?" Ewan drank the last of his whisky. He sighed, but his breath got caught in his chest, and the memory of discovering Lorelei's fate echoed.

He cleared the waves and turned, expecting her to be behind him. The sight before him froze him in place.

Back in the surf sat the white seal blinking at him. Ewan glanced at the magic Fae stone in his hand. This couldn't be. He stomped through the surf toward her, fighting the waves as tears threatened. It couldn't be. As he came upon her, her body quivered. Her form melded over itself and morphed into the mermaid. Ewan stood with a lump in his throat.

Lorelei offered him a smile that wobbled. Another tear slid down her cheek. "You succeeded. What's happened to me is of no matter." Away from the Stone of Faith, Lorelei was a seal, close to the magic gem. She became her true form, a mermaid.

He rose, blocking the memory as he stormed to the whisky, poured another measure and chugged the potent liquor.

His da growled from the fireplace. "The stone, Ewan!"

Ewan rounded on his sire, roaring. "I couldn't. I couldn't do it! Taking the stone from her meant she'd be something she's not! Manix tricked her, tricked us."

His da bellowed. "Ye left a Stone of Iona behind? What the hell for?"

Ewan's memory flashed against his will, her tears tearing him apart inside.

He handed her the wrapped stone as he whispered. "I give ye my heart, my love, my soul. But most of all, I gift ye yer life as ye should live it."

She'd refused, using his own profession of love against him. She whispered. "To me, you are necessary. Ewan, you must complete your destiny." She kissed him on the lips, then whispered into the kiss. "Don't ye see? You must take the stone."

After kissing her one last time, he turned, giving her

his back, and strode from the surf, leaving the stone and his love forever.

Ewan yelled back, "For her! Just like the fable, she took a spell meant for me. Without the stone, she'd be a seal. With the stone, she'd be whole!" Ewan threw his glass at the door. With a crashing ring, the glass shattered into pieces. "Damn it, Da. I thought ye, of all people, would understand! Sacrifice for yer love. That's what ye did for Ma!"

His da threw his glass in the fireplace; the crashing sounded like light bells. "Aye, but I came back with the stone, Ewan!" Both stood staring each other down, panting—the older faced off with the younger, much as they'd done before.

His ma spoke softly. "I came back with the stone, Colin. You sacrificed yourself for me."

Ewan fisted his hands. "Aye! That's what I did for Lorelei! Sacrifice myself for her."

His da's face grew red as he waved his hands while he spoke. "Don't ye get it, Ewan. Ye left the stone behind. The gem must come here, join the other stones. Apart, they are strong, but together they are all-powerful." He moved his hands apart and together as if he'd bring the stone there now.

Ewan yelled back. "The stone is safe. The Telkhines have guarded the magic gem and will guard it well. Close to Lorelei so she can live as herself!"

His da roared. "We must guard them all—together, or they will fall into the hands of evil!"

Ewan ran his hands through his hair, fists trembling. "Ye don't get it!" He turned and bolted, making the heavy door crash against the frame. His boots pounded across the stone of the castle yard and down to the loch.

The chilled air bit at his face, but he didn't slow down, not stopping until his boots hit the dock. The sea opened before him, and the scent of salt and kelp filled his lungs. As his chest heaved, eyes scanned the quiet stretch of water. Loch Etive should've calmed him—it always had. The sea, the steady rhythm of the waves, the timeless hush of everything. But not now. Not this time.

Ewan stumbled backward, barely registering the creak of the wood beneath his boots. The familiar bench caught the backs of his knees, and he dropped onto it hard, elbows to his thighs as he hung his head. It wasn't his da he ran from. Not really. When Ewan saw how to save Lorelei, he thought he could outwit fate, thinking he could protect her and keep the world from falling apart. He'd believed he could carry both burdens.

The wind picked up, tugging at his hair, and a seagull cried overhead. But the usual comfort—the creak of his ship, the slap of the sails, the hum of a vessel ready to answer his call—was gone. Silence met him. Emptiness.

He'd given it all up for her—his ship, oath, and status in the realms. And damn it, he'd do it all over again. Even knowing what he knew now. Because it wasn't giving Lorelei the stone he regretted, he'd underestimated the cost.

Chapter 22

Ewan sat at the dock trying to find solace. The wind blew, disturbing the silence as he gazed at Loch Etive, blind to its beauty. The seals sat on the point as they usually did, just lazing in the afternoon sun.

The dock creaked lightly, so slight he almost missed the sound. A movement came from the corner of his eye, and he turned, spotting his ma standing there. She gave her typical wobbly smile. The one she used when she tried to hide her emotions. Ewan took a deep breath and released it as she stepped closer, sitting on the bench beside him.

They stayed in companionable silence as the clouds moved over the sky, turning the loch water light then into a darker blue. The seals bathed in the sunlight. One sat up, almost staring at them.

His ma's voice came out softly. "I used to sit here for hours on end. The wind would blow. It was chilly at that time of year, but I couldn't feel it. That was when your father was in purgatory."

She sighed. "I was pregnant with you and your sister. The seals sat perched on the point as they have for centuries. I came here daily, sometimes daydreaming about my days with Colin."

He sensed her grin and heard her smile in the tone her voice took on. "I would daydream of us together, but it was the present instead of in the past, as if he were here with me that day. He didn't know when he took the Stone of Fear, sending me to the future with the Stone of Love that I was pregnant with you kids."

She glanced at him and then back at the seals. "I'd dream of him holding my stomach and how he would kiss the mound, telling me our babes would be beautiful."

They sat silently for a moment, the seals still waiting for his ma to finish her story. "I'd sit here and ask myself which seal he was. Which one was my love stuck in purgatory forever?" She blew a laugh. "Auntie Ainslie would join me. We'd joke about what Colin as a seal would look like."

Ewan smirked. "Da as a seal? I couldn't imagine it."

His ma laughed when she spoke, duplicating a Scottish accent when she got to Ainslie's quote. "Oh, his sister was good at describing him. She'd say, 'So, which one do ye think he is? The fat one lazing in the sun, or the one that jumped on the rocks and is trying to run.'" Ewan stared at the seals when his ma spoke easily, picking out which seal might fit Auntie Ainslie's description.

His ma caught her breath. "Then we'd filch some of Mrs. A's cookies. Like you and Doug did as children." Ewan warmed at the memory of him and Doug as kids sneaking into the kitchen unnoticed by Mrs. A. When he thought back on it, she was there the whole time and likely knew what they were up to.

He turned to his ma. "Doug, his choice. It seemed so easy for him to make."

She smiled and nodded. "Yes, it was the same for Ainslie. Even though I was injured then, her path was clear for all to see if one just looked." She grunted. "Ainslie was so stubborn. She was the last to admit it. That she fell in love with Rannick, and he, with her. They belonged together."

Ewan nodded. "Aye, I saw the same in Doug and Abi. Imagining them apart, I can't."

She patted his knee. "Well, those were their decisions, so they were right for them."

Right for them echoed. Were the choices Ewan made right for him? They didn't feel right for him but made sense for others. Still, none of anything he'd done felt—right.

Ewan glimpsed at the seals and then his ma. "But what if I haven't made the right decision? What if I made a mistake?"

Bree took a deep breath and released a puff. "Then you find a way to fix it." She leaned over and hugged him, holding him like she had when he was younger. "Ewan, we all make mistakes. It's how you learn." She sat back, holding his shoulders. "Give it time. All will work out in the end." The last she said while she patted his cheek. Ewan nodded as they took each other's hands and sat for a while, staring at the loch and the seals.

His ma huffed, and he turned to her as she tilted her head. "There's a new seal. That all-white one in the front." When his ma pointed, his gaze followed, and the seal shifted as if to sit up and stare at them. The wind blew, and a chill came over Ewan.

His ma patted his leg, bringing his attention back to her. "I'd best get back. Your da called Marie and John when I came out. They'll likely be here soon. Ardchattan Priory isn't far." She rose, bent, and kissed his cheek. "Ewan, it will be fine. Have faith."

His ma stepped away, and her footsteps faded as birds chirping overtook the sounds. The wind blew again. Have faith. Ewan blew out hard. Faith in what?

Doug had done what he thought best. Hell, he probably had the island cleaned up, rounded up some sailors, and had a crew already repairing *The Faithful*. All the while, Abi proudly fed them from her newly built pub. Ewan glanced out over the loch again. Aye, Doug had chosen well.

He'd done what he thought best. Leave the stone for Lorelei even if that wasn't what the Fae decreed or his da wanted. The stone would be safe. Triton had kept the stone safe this long. Close to Lorelei, the stone was where it needed to be—providing a life for his love.

Ewan glanced at the sky, wondering if his grandda looked down, would he approve? If this was so right, why did it still feel so wrong? And why did he not have faith in his choice?

Footfalls beat the dock hard and fast. Ewan stood and turned.

Kat, Doug's sister, came to a stop as her chest heaved deep breaths. "It's true? Doug's gone?" Ewan stood immobile. He knew he'd have to face Doug's sister, but so soon. Her parents had to have rushed from Ardchattan Abbey right over. Kat must have been home visiting from college in Edinburgh. Tears streamed down her face, making a lump form in Ewan's throat. He cleared it as he gathered the courage to say everything—all he needed to for Doug.

"Aye, Kit Kat."

She crossed her arms as she stifled a sob. "Doug didn't say goodbye."

Ewan stepped toward her, taking her in his arms.

"Aye, he did." He rocked back and forth as Kat sobbed into his chest. She was so young and naive yet had the most brilliant minds, being an expert on physics and trumping all her professors in college with her theories on time travel and other dimensions. She should be able to understand Doug's plight when he made his choice, but her emotions likely overrode her logical mind. Emotions were such a hard thing to contend with.

She hiccupped as she rocked back. "Tell me." She wiped her eyes and moved out of his arms to the bench he'd just left. She patted the seat beside her. "I want to know what he said." Ewan smiled. The logical Kat had returned and waited for news.

As he sat, it seemed Ewan's turn to get emotional. His eyes watered as he thought of Doug's parting, of his promise. He had to pull himself together for Kat but more so for Doug. Kat sat with her eyes bright and her mouth set firm. He patted her leg as his ma had done for him. The act did seem oddly comforting.

He breathed deeply. "Doug fell in love." Ewan glanced at the seals as he spoke. "Abigail's her name. She runs the Salty Dog Tavern." He glanced back, smiling. "Named after her enormous hound."

Kat grinned. "Let me guess, the dog's named Salty Dog?"

Ewan chuckled. "Aye. He planned to rebuild the island. Waitukura. The isle still exists today."

Kat sighed. "That sounds grand."

Ewan nodded. "He said to give ye this." He hugged her hard, and memories of his ma hugging him when she told him Auntie Ainslie chose to stay in the past flashed in his mind. Of how she brought him Ainslie's last goodbye, he now delivered to Kat for Doug. Kat huffed and hiccupped. So, Ewan held her longer, like his ma did for him. It had made him feel better. When Kat shifted, he released her and sat back.

He punched her arm but not as hard as Doug hit him. "That's also for ye from Doug."

Kat blew a laugh that came out like a half sob. "Aye, well, that I believe."

They sat side by side for a moment. The wind rustled the trees as birds cheerfully chirped. The crisp ocean scent blew off the loch like it usually did. Life seemed to have moved on.

Kat sat up when she spoke. "I finished college."

Ewan glanced at her. "Congrats."

She shrugged. "Ma and Da. They're taking Doug's news hard." She exhaled. "I don't have plans or a job. Maybe I'll hang around here for a bit." His promise to Doug rang in his mind. Kat needed someone, and Ewan would be there for her like Doug had been there for him.

Ewan took her hand in his. "I left *The Faithful* with Doug. I've got no plans either. Maybe we'll hang out, like brother and sister."

Kat gripped his hand. "I'd like that."

Ewan nudged her shoulder. "Ye know, Doug told me to look him up. He said he'd leave a mark. Maybe there's a trail?"

Kat grinned. "We can get our mas' to help look him up. They'd like that."

Ewan gripped her hand back. "Aye."

Kat nudged his shoulder. "Mrs. A baked cookies."

She pulled him to stand, and he followed. "Chocolate chip?"

Doug's sister smiled. "Aye." She dropped his hand and started down the dock. Someone called his name from the distance, and Ewan stopped. He turned to the seals on the pier, and the white one his ma pointed out was still sitting at the front. As he stood there momentarily, he felt, for the first time, faith that he'd done one thing right. He'd kept his promise to Doug.

Kat called, "Come on, slug-a-bug, or I'll eat them all."

Ewan blinked, and the seal slipped into the water. He turned, following Kat, hoping his faith was enough.

****

The following morning, Ewan entered the kitchen to Mrs. A, making breakfast. His ma sat at the breakfast table sipping her coffee and reading her cell phone. His da sat next to her with coffee and a bowl of oatmeal. Everyone seemed so normal, as if the world hadn't upended yesterday.

Ewan woke up this morning feeling like a failure. He missed his friend, worried about his love, and felt awful over explaining to Kat that she would never see her brother again. He stood there glaring at them all. How could they act like everything was okay when reality was so far from it?

His ma scrolled her phone. "The historical society has already begun a search for Douglas MacArthur. Odell says there are some promising leads." Ewan froze. Already? He'd just left him yesterday. He sighed—time travel. They were in the twentieth century now. Doug was dead—history.

His ma glanced up and rose, crossing to him. "Ewan, breakfast?"

Mrs. A turned from the stove. "I can whip ye up something." Ewan glanced around, expecting Doug to stroll in at any moment. But he didn't.

"No, Mrs. A."

His da sipped his coffee. "Ewan, ye will need to meet with the Fae. I suspect they know what has happened." He pointed his finger at him. "Ye'll have to answer to them for the stone." Ewan sat at the bar, resting his head in his hands. Answer to the Fae for what? His failure?

Ewan faced his end, and the finalization of it all hit him at once. He was a failure—a complete disappointment at all he'd done. The Fae fable was true. He'd end up as a ghost searching the seas for his love who had the stone. This was not how he wanted any of this to end. Everyone involved with the stones found true love and happily ever after. His happily ever after was a happily never at all.

He turned, yelling at his da. "Answer to the Fae, for what? My failure! Of course, they know. Aren't they all-knowing?" He paced. "I'm surprised Aodhán isn't here now." He pulled on this hair. "Shit, I'm surprised even Dagda, the King of the good Fae, hasn't shown up."

His sire stood. "Language, Ewan. It's not failure but choice. They need to know where the stone is."

Ewan slid off the stool, needing to get away. "Aye, Da. I get it. I failed to save the day. I didn't send Manix to hell. I didn't recover the stone. A failure!" Pounding his chest, he yelled, "But I save her! I saved my love." His ma crossed to him, and he backed away. "Fine, I'll meet with the Fae, face what consequences my failure will bring me." He turned to the door, then stopped speaking over his shoulder. "Tell Dagda I'll be on my boat."

His ma breathed. "Ewan, honey, you left your ship with Doug."

He knocked his head on the doorframe. "Fine, I'll be at my dock by the sea."

Ewan strode out of the castle, each step echoing in his mind like a war drum down the empty corridor behind him. All he found in those walls now was emptiness—no honor, no redemption, only the shadow of what he might've been. The morning sea wind chilled as he crossed the courtyard, the scent of salt growing stronger with every step.

Aodhán had survived the Fae prison. If his brother-in-law could endure that cursed place, then so could he. And if not? Then let this be the end. A fitting punishment for the failure he'd become. His fingers curled into fists at his sides while he marched on, not from fear, but resolve. He would face what Dagda had in store for him—not as a warrior, but as a man stripped bare of everything but his will.

When he came upon the dock, someone sat there making him come up short. When he came closer, the white iridescent suit glittered in the sunlight, which hugged the fit form of the large man sitting there. His long white silky hair fell down his back, telling Ewan who sat in his spot. Well, the Fae *were* all-knowing. When he neared, the man didn't turn to greet him. Ewan slid onto the bench beside him as an easiness overcame Ewan. A sudden awareness that all would be right.

Dagda, King of the good Fae, picked up a familiar glass and decanter and poured a measure into the glass to quarter-fill the sniffer—Ewan's typical portion.

He handed the glass to Ewan, and when he took it, Dagda filled his to the rim. "I stopped by yer da's office. Swiped us a tot for our chat." The King of the good Fae took a generous swing, swished the liquor around his mouth, swallowed with a gulp, then sighed audibly. "Sometimes I wonder if I come here just for yer da's whisky."

Ewan took a sip before he spoke, not wanting to have this conversation. "I told da I left the stone with the Telkhines. Ye should know being all-knowing. I don't have anything else to say."

Dagda held his glass between his legs. "Aye, 'tis true. But I'm not here about the stone or yer da. I'm here about ye."

Ewan waved his glass, spilling a little. "Me, what now? A punishment from the Fae like Aodhán? Fine, it's more than I deserve failing the Fae as I did. I'll take it. Anything to rid me of this heartache."

Dagda grabbed his hand holding the glass, stopping it. "Don't spill the whisky, Ewan. This is the good stuff." He released him, chuckling. "Love bug bite ye, eh?"

Ewan groaned. "It's not a mere bite."

They sat there for a moment. Each took a sip of whisky. Then Dagda took another. The birds chirped, and the wind blew the salty scent of the sea. A sign to Ewan that time still passed.

Dagda filled his glass, took a sip, and blew his breath out. "The one. The Telkhines never told ye what it meant, did they?" Lorelei's first mention of the term flashed in his memory. So caught up in the new realm, the merpeople, and trying to keep up with customs, Ewan had not noted the term till now—the one. Or Murus' reaction to it. The word must have meant something. Then, another memory hit. Triton mentioned *the one* as well.

Ewan turned to Dagda. "Her da asked that. Am I her one? I am her love."

The Fae King chuckled. "She never explained it, did she? Even after ye made love, eh?" Ewan's face heated. So, the Fae knew everything.

He shook his head. "Explained what?"

Dagda sipped his whisky. "Not all Fae view courtship the same. They each have their own way of courting, love, and marriage." He waved his free hand. "Ye see, the merfolk, they don't have weddings. For them, what we think of as marriage to them is an agreement only. In their realm, the woman chooses her mate, calling him her *one*." He held up his index finger like a number one. As he spoke, he waved the appendage in the circle. "They declare her choice to the tribe, and then ye are mated forever." When he finished speaking, he pointed at Ewan. Ewan eyed the finger when Dagda slowly lowered his hand. The implication of what he said settled in his mind.

Ewan gasped. "Her one? She chose? Ye mean I'm married to Lorelei?"

He gulped his whisky when Dagda nodded. "In her kingdom, aye. 'Tis why Triton offered ye the King's seat. Ye married his daughter." He blew a laugh. "He sees ye as the son he never had, having only daughters. Twelve of them." Daga sat up taller. "But that doesn't matter now." Dagda poured the remainder of the decanter into his glass, frowning at the half-full vessel.

Ewan turned to him. "Why not?"

He sipped and choked. "Damn it all if they didn't take yer advice. Elected a King from the people they did."

Ewan smirked as Lorelei's statement to Murus about the King's seat echoed. "Who, Murus?"

Dagda laughed. "No, too hot-headed. Vinnis."

Vinnis, Lorelei's sister's husband's calm, cool demeanor, came back to Ewan. "He will make a fine leader."

They sat for a moment more as a sailboat glided by them. The sails flapped in the wind, reminding Ewan of sailing on his ship. He loved sailing. He should get another boat. Maybe a clipper this time. Something smaller but an antique. He could share something with the people of the future, his knowledge of the past, like his ma.

Dagda set his glass aside, folding his hands before him. "She came to me."

Ewan blinked, almost forgetting that Dagda sat next to him. "Who?"

The Fae King whispered. "Lorelei." As he spoke her name, his hands rotated one over the other till a ball of blue light formed, which then faded as Dagda cupped something in them. Lorelei came to the King of the good Fae.

Ewan swallowed, almost fearful to ask but needing to know. "What did she want?"

Dagda took his hand and placed a heavy stone in his palm. The points at the ends pinched his skin. His eyes watered. Ewan knew which stone he held before he opened his hand. He bent his head. She didn't. All he sacrificed was for her to have the gem so she could live a happy life with her people. Tears gathered in his eyes. He rotated and opened his hand as he set his glass on the bench. He cupped the blue stone that blurred as tears fell down his face. If he had the stone, Lorelei would forever be a seal.

Dagda sat back, picking up Ewan's glass with the remaining whisky. "She wanted yer mission to be complete, saying *no one person is more important than the safety of all the realms*." He sighed. "She wanted ye to know ye had succeeded."

Ewan stood yelling. "At what price? Now I've not only lost her to the merfolk, but she's gone as a seal! Away from the people who care for her, who love her!" He gripped the stone between both hands hard, allowing the points to hurt. "God, could I be any more of a failure? She's out there alone!"

Dagda sipped Ewan's whisky, eyeing him over the rim. "She chose to leave. Going to the one place to be near the one she loves." As he lowered his glass, he toasted the seals at Dunstaffnage Point. Ewan's eyes followed his movement. No, it couldn't be. He took a few steps forward.

As Ewan searched the seals, the Fae King's voice came from behind. "All she ever wanted was to be human. To be with humans and after meeting ye, to be with ye. Manix knew this and used the fact against her. She knew he used her but thought he held the power to make turning her into a human happen. That one day, her sacrifice would make her dream come true."

Dagda moved beside Ewan and stared at the seals. "Ye know spells are merely spoken words with energy supporting them. Much like yer ability to change a person's mind, ye can change a person's form."

Ewan turned to Dagda. "Changing a person's shape, their being is impossible. No human possesses that much power."

Dagda chuckled. "Says the man who is half Fae." He patted his shoulder. "Just as ye call ye ship to ye, with enough power, say from true love, ye can also call a soul. But the question remains…is yer love strong enough?"

He tapped his arm. "Maybe yer siren from the sea desires to be human, eh? Maybe with yer powers combined, both yer love can make the impossible—possible."

Ewan gazed over the seals, searching. His ma had mentioned one pure white one that had appeared recently. He had stared at them the other day. He gripped the Stone of Faith and sensed the stone's power surge through him. Was it possible?

A seal burst from the water, lumbering onto the rocks, and shook itself off. Slowly, the mammal turned, gazing in their direction—a pure white seal.

Aodhán's voice echoed from the day they'd discussed the Fae fable. *Faith is confidence in what we hope for and assurance about what we do not see. Everything is possible for one who believes.* As Evie said, maybe he needed to believe to have faith.

Dagda nudged his shoulder. "Go to her, have faith and love, Ewan. Go call yer siren back."

Call her back. Doug's parent's poem, was it a spell? He sensed the stone in his hands warm, then felt a power surge up his arm. *Call her back.*

Ewan walked a few steps toward the loch, nearly toppling into the water at the end of the dock. He blinked and turned, running to the back end of the pier and the path to the point favoring a run over a dip in the loch.

As he ran by Dagda, the Fae King finished his whisky and called after him. "Oh, Ewan. Put my stone away when ye are finished with it."

Chapter 23

Ewan ran from the dock around the bend and onto the point. As he came closer to the seals, he faltered but righted himself. When his eyes fell on the cluster, the white seal moved from the group and sat facing him. Ewan stood immobile, staring at the creature. It all seemed too much to expect that Lorelei sat before him in a seal form locked in some spell. In their training for the guardianship of the stone, his da mentioned that an evil Fae's spell cannot be undone, yet with true love, his da and ma had overcome one. Manix cast this spell, and his power signature echoed in Ewan's mind. There was good underlying the hate. Maybe changing the spell wasn't so far-fetched after all?

He gazed at the seal, who stared back and then blinked. The seal lowered her head, and Ewan took a moment to examine the creature. Mostly white, unlike the others, with a small area of gray at the bottom near the animal's tail. When she flipped her fin, a scar near the bottom caught Ewan's attention. The cut on Lorelei's ankle flashed in Ewan's mind. His eyes moved to the seal's face, and the seal turned her head, almost as if she blushed.

The stone warmed in his hand, and Ewan brought the gem to the chest, gripping the jewel with both hands. Human will and emotion power the Iona Stones—true love, being the most powerful of them all. He closed his eyes, praying their love would be enough. He gathered all his energy, making his breath even as he did so to maintain the high level of power he needed. Changing a form was no simple task, and Ewan hoped there was enough magic in their love. The energy climbed as another swirled within him. A pure blue energy that made him gasp. Was it?

He reached out with his mind and heart, casting her name. *Lorelei.* At first, the answer was silence, an aching emptiness where her essence should have been.

And yet—the blue energy stirred. What began as a flicker surged, rushing into him with a force that stole his breath. Not answering with words but with *feeling*—grief, love, fury, hope—raw, sacred, and vast. The spell collided with his magic, not gently, but with the violence of longing unmet, of connection too strong to fade. The merging of their energies overwhelmed him as if Lorelei's soul reached through time and space to embrace his, to remind him that something of hers remained. Ewan cried out, not from pain but from the sheer *magnitude* of the magic's power.

He dropped to his knees, the world tilting around him. His arms clutched the stone as though letting go would shatter him. The gem pulsed beneath his fingers, alive with light and memory, holding pieces of her—of *them*.

He bent low over the stone, forehead touching its surface, grounding himself before it consumed him whole. But he felt her, his one.

A whisper came to him. "Ewan."

He took a deep breath and chanted with a strong voice, sending all the power through his words and out to the seal. "The sea fairy swam fast away, safely over the wave and sea. Gave her heart to her human love, will she ne'er come back to me. Will ye come back to me? Will ye come back to me? Better loved ye canna be, will ye come back to me?" Ewan peeked as the seal sat still. He took another breath and concentrated on his love for Lorelei. "Ye trusted yer heart to yer lover, I trusted ye, dear sweet Fae. I ken yer hidin' in the glen, your crying echoed my way." He changed the next part from Doug's da's version. He needed Lorelei to know his intent—the full measure of his love. Taking another deep breath, he held one hand out toward the seal.

He kept his eyes closed and focused inward on the spell's power. "I begged her to be my bride, an' even tho' purer we may be. Silver canna buy my heart, that beats hard for her beauty." He glanced up, and the seal shifted, bowing her head as he bent his head, taking a deep breath, adding more power to the spell. "Sweet the love stone's note held long, lilting wildly up the glen. But aye to me I regret she has gone, will she not come back again?"

The stone cooled in his hand, but he gripped it till the points hurt, fearing the spell would fade before it could work to bring his love to him as her dream form.

Lorelei's voice came to him in a whisper. "Come back to my one?" Ewan nodded as he opened his eyes, lifting his gaze. The seal pulled itself up, standing on the tail fin. The side fins morphed into arms that were fair, thin arms like a woman's. Those arms reached up to her head and pulled the skin away, revealing bright red-orange hair. When the seal skin fell from her head, Lorelai's face greeted Ewan. Ewan gasped and stood, not believing his own eyes. The seal stripped away its skin, revealing a human woman. His love's form. Lorelei as a human. She stepped from the seal skin and stood there naked, her hair artfully covering her woman's parts. He still wondered how she did that, but the thought faded when she moved toward him. His heart fluttered to his chest, and he took a deep breath.

****

Lorelei stood before her love. He'd pulled her from the spell, away from the seal's grip on her, allowing her to strip the spell away and come to her true love as she had in her dreams. She'd sat on the point watching him, begging the gods for a chance to speak to him to tell him of her undying love. Now, she had her dream come true two-fold. She was human and with Ewan. She wanted to share her heart with him and knew only one way.

She started the beginning just as she had on his ship while tears formed in her eyes. Her voice cracked at first, and Ewan's grin went wide when she spoke the first verse.

Lorelei stepped toward him as the words took on strength, and tears formed in her eyes. "My body hums with energy. My faith sings to the gods. My love shines in my smile for you. My soul burns with the fire of billions of stars."

When she finished the verse, Ewan took a deep breath, speaking the next as he moved toward her. "I rejoice in each reunion. I anticipate the me yet to come. I shall show you all my love. In a time when our souls shall be one."

With each step, they came closer until they stood not but a breath apart. She glanced over Ewan's face. Her heart warmed as she saw him close. He shifted closer, and his free hand came to her cheek, cupping it.

Tears formed in his eyes while he kissed her and breathed the last of their poem into another kiss. "I find glory in rebirth's glow. I anticipate creating my own tomorrow when I shall embody the Earth. Forging a new life with my true love."

True love, destined to be together—his siren of the sea and her pirate savior. She finished the last verse, hoping her love brightly shone for him to see. "My body hums with energy. My faith sings to the gods." She lifted her hand to the sky and brought her palm to Ewan's cheek as she spoke the rest, finishing with a kiss. "My love shines in my smile for you. My soul burns with the fire of our love."

Ewan moved back. "Ye are here."

She beamed. "I am here, Ewan of the MacDougalls."

He brought her hand to his lips, kissing the back. "Yer one? Ye never told me what that meant. I am truly yer husband?"

Lorelei tilted her head at the new word. "Husband, what is husband?"

Ewan grinned while he held her. "If we are *one*, as mates, husband is what I am, and wife is what ye are."

She giggled. "Husband and wife. Bound. Yes, you are my one, my soul mate." She liked the sound of it. Ewan was hers.

"Well, *mo sìrean*. Lorelei, wife to Ewan. I welcome you to my home." He stepped back, waving to the large castle behind him. "Welcome to Dunstaffnage Castle." She grinned as they walked hand in hand. Ewan tossed the blue gem she'd given to Dagda, King of the good Fae, up and caught it. "Although, ye'll need to get dressed before ye meet my parents. Humans don't run around naked, *mo sìrean*."

Epilogue

Ewan led her through *the house*, as he called this place. The building was more extensive than her father's castle. Outside his bedroom, where they'd stayed a cozy night, photos of MacDougalls lined what Ewan had called *the hall*.

She stopped to eye one resembling Ewan, but he pulled her along. "Come, ye must meet my parents. We missed them last night." She tugged on the *pants* he'd given her to wear, swearing she was the same size as his sister, Evie, but the shirt and bottoms fell off her body.

After many twists and turns through halls, passing room after room. Then, down a set of stairs crossing a room larger than her father's throne room, they stopped before a door. Ewan took a deep breath and squeezed her hand. He lifted her palm, kissing the back, then burst through the doorway and stopped as three people, two women and a man resembling Ewan, stared back with equal expressions of shock on their faces.

The heavy-set woman holding a pan by the stove reminded Lorelei of the cook at the plantation owner's kitchen. When the woman smiled, it dawned on her who she was. Mrs. A.

Mrs. A slammed the pan down and came round the bar with her arms outstretched. "Aw, would ye look at her? What a gorgeous thing she be. Look at all that red hair, like flames it is!" She engulfed Lorelei in a warm, tight embrace. The scent of sweet baked bread tickled her nose. When the woman shifted back, Lorelei's stomach growled loudly, making her face heat.

Mrs. A pulled her to the table and sat her in a chair. "Why she's starved." When she sat, the nice woman pinched her arm. "And skin and bone." She turned, glaring at Ewan. "Have ye not offered to feed yer guest, Ewan? Where are yer manners?"

Ewan stood at the doorway with a grin on his face. "Mrs. A, may I introduce Lorelei Telkhines." He moved to sit beside her, across from the man who wore a frown and beside the pretty lady, each of the occupants taking a side of the square table.

As he sat, he patted Mrs. A's arm. "And she'd love a Rowie if ye have one."

Mrs. A bustled back into the kitchen. "Why, of course, I do, fresh this morn." She hummed and stopped. "Ewan, ye'll be wanting yer usual?"

Ewan nodded as he took Lorelei's hand in his. "Aye, I have a hunger about me this morning." He lifted her hand, kissing the back, making her face heat before the others at the table. He'd spoken of hunger last night but not the kind eased by food. She giggled, thinking of their night's activities. The man cleared his throat, and Ewan shifted his focus to him, smiling wider.

With Ewan's silence, the man's eyes bulged. "Ewan, don't be rude. Introduce us to yer guest."

Ewan's fingers played with hers as he spoke. "I just have. This is Lorelei." He waved his other hand to the man while he spoke. "Lorelei, I make known to ye my da, Laird Colin MacDougall." Ewan waved his hand to the woman, who gave a wobbly smile with tears in her eyes. "This is my ma, Bree, short for Brielle."

Ewan's da, as he called him, grunted. "This is the woman ye spoke of? The one distracting ye from yer mission?"

His mother, Bree, slapped the man's arm. "Colin, don't be rude." She rose, moving to Lorelei. "Dagda visited this morning. We know all about where you come from, Lorelei." She took her free hand and pulled her into her embrace. "Welcome, siren of the sea." She pulled back, tears in her eyes. "I am so happy you both found true love and changed the ending of the fable. The need for a maiden's sacrifice is now over." She sighed as she released her. "And a happily ever after for us all."

Bree moved and sat again as Mrs. A returned to the table, a glass and plate in hand, setting them before Lorelei. "Here ye are, dearie. Fresh juice and a Rowie." The nice woman set before her a bright red liquid in a glass and on a plate a flatbread with a glittering covering.

Ewan leaned over, whispering, "Ye'll love this. Sugar covering baked bread."

Lorelei picked up the bread and stopped setting the treat down. "I must sing and thank the gods." She took a deep breath and let out a sound for the gods. But what came out was nothing like her usual song. Her voice howled and squeaked off tune. Ewan's father covered his ears, and his mother, Bree, bent her head.

Ewan let out a yelp as Mrs. A called out over the noise. "My goodness, I've never heard a song like that!"

Lorelei turned to Ewan. "My song is gone."

Ewan took her hand in his, holding her to his heart. "A good sacrifice for the gift of being with the humans."

Mrs. A filled a plate and returned, setting the meal before Ewan. Many items piled high, each looking interesting as the smell of freshly cooked food filled the air.

As Ewan picked up a fork and scooped food into his mouth, Lorelei took her first bite of the Rowie. Sweetness with flaky bread filled her mouth. The sweet taste of sugar brought a smile to her face. She picked up the glass and tried the juice, and its sweet flavor burst into her mouth. She swallowed with a moan.

Ewan turned, winking at her as his father spoke. "So, ye return from the past with a woman and the stone. Job, well done, son, but did ye think about what ye and Lorelei will do here in the future?" He waved his finger at her and back at Ewan. "Have ye thought of how to explain her appearance and how to get her identification in this time?"

They sat up last night discussing this very thing. Ewan set his fork down and took her hand. "Aye, Da, we have. I wish to purchase an antique boat."

Colin huffed. "And what do ye plan to do with it? Shift between times again?"

Ewan shook his head. "Naw, Da. My time travel days are over. I no longer feel the draw to go." Lorelei giggled as Ewan glanced at her, wiggling his eyebrows. "I'm to follow the fable, Da. Become Blackbeard sailing Loch Etive searching for my lost treasure. Along the way, I find and rescue a mermaid."

Bree sighed as Colin's gruff voice rose over the soft sound. "What do ye mean by this, Ewan?"

Ewan sat taller in his chair. "I aim to merge my talents of acting and sailing. I'll give tours each summer on the loch in my pirate ship. As we search for treasure, we find a mermaid."

His mother gasped. "You don't mean to tell me she can…I mean, shift still."

She turned to Colin. "Dagda said she was human."

Colin's eyebrows lowered in a frown. "No, Bree, Dagda said she was no longer a seal."

Lorelei's face heated as memories of last night in what Ewan called a bathtub surfaced and all they'd done together after their little discovery.

Ewan squeezed her hand once when he spoke. "It turns out that the change from a mermaid to a human is a power of the merfolk. Something they'd kept hidden since they'd forbidden contact with humans. She can still shift."

Colin sat back with his eyebrows near his hairline. "A mermaid?" They moved down with his frown. "Ewan, ye can't go showing the humans her Fae form. They will all panic, call the police, have her arrested or, worse, incarcerated!" He waved his hand with the last statement.

Bree sat forward, taking Colin's waving hand in her own. "We can say it's an elaborate costume. They have them these days. Mermaids swimming in pools have been a featured entertainment for years." She turned to Lorelei, smiling. "I think it's a grand plan, and Dominic, my brother, can fix her identity like he did for Aodhán."

Ewan's father yanked his hand from Bree's. "Well, since ye all have it figured out, I won't worry." He picked up his cup and sipped his drink, smirking over the rim.

Bree beamed at her. "Lorelei, well, have so much fun planning the wedding."

Lorelei finished her last bite of the sugary goodness, glancing at Bree. "What is a wedding?"

****

Doug stood at the altar of the framed-out chapel—no roof or walls, just a wooden frame which suited him just fine. He waited for Abi to make her appearance for their wedding. It turned out Monroe, the head servant to the plantation, was also a practicing pastor and proudly stood beside Doug as they awaited his love's grand entrance. She'd planned this day for months as they'd helped villagers and townsfolk rebuild the port and village. Doug lent much advice and counsel to the structures to ensure a modern, prosperous merchant port. When the plantation came up for auction, he got the land for the steal of a price he'd hoped for, even better since Manix left without anyone to pass his wealth to. Doug freed the slaves, who all came with the property, and offered them land in exchange for labor to rebuild the island, forming what he hoped would be a long-lasting partnership.

A fully repaired *The Faithful* sat in the harbor, managed by a crew member from Captain Low's ship named Bert. He had two new mates, Oliver and Zach, that came with him. They promised fair work for fair wages, claiming they'd finished with pirating and Captain Low's unfair share. Doug liked them and hired them on the spot.

His thoughts turned to Ewan. He hoped and prayed all was well in the future. In his full human form, Triton had paid a visit to Doug, nearly making Doug mess his britches when he told him of the Fae merfolk beneath the island and how they wanted to reestablish their relationship with the humans again. How Doug would manage that, well, that was something for another day. Lorelei was now in the future, human and with Ewan as fate meant them to be. But what Triton had to share from the future was what Dagda said was to come for the Iona Stones. He hoped Ewan and all in the future would be ready.

People moved into the chapel, and everyone turned, facing the back. When Doug lifted his head, Abigail stood in a light blue dress, clutching fresh pink hibiscus. The sun shifted and shone behind her head, forming a halo, and Doug's heart warmed. He stared at his love and future and knew everything would be right in the world.

****

Ewan held Lorelei's hand as they walked toward the Chapel in the Woods in the afternoon sun.

She leaned into him. "So, this is where all the stones are? In the worship house?" Ewan chuckled at her wording.

She still used phrasing from her people, which warmed Ewan's heart as she held on to her heritage. "Aye, they are protected by many Fae spells."

The birds chattered, and the wind rustled the leaves, telling Ewan time passed. He grinned, enjoying a stroll with his love. His mind wandered to Doug as it often did since learning what the historical society had found. Douglas McArthur became not only a sea merchant but also a successful businessman. He bought the sugar plantation at auction for a fraction of the land's worth, freed the slaves, and offered them land ownership for work rebuilding the village. Doug had made a huge profit from his shipping business and the plantation. As captain, he called himself Dougie after his grandda.

Lorelei hummed off-tune, making Ewan smile. Doug had married Abi on the plantation, calling the place Parras, which meant paradise in Gaelic. They had four children: two boys, John and Ewan, and two girls, Gail, likely after Abigail, and Katherine, likely after his sister, Kat. Kat had taken the news well. Marie and Bree had searched for their offspring, who were due to visit John and Maire's home, Ardchattan Priory, the next month. Ewan blinked back tears thinking of Doug but took heart in the fact he'd lived a happy, full life well into his nineties before a natural death. He'd left a mark and even named a ship *Jewel of the Sea*.

Someone tapped his arm. He blinked, turning to his side where Lorelei stood smiling. "You have stood at the worship house door for a moment."

Ewan glanced back, and the large wooden chapel door stood closed before him. "Aye, well, let's get on with it." He opened the door and pushed his way inside.

Lorelei lingered in the doorway. "It's dark."

Ewan flicked the switch, turning on the lights.

Lorelei jumped and squeaked with a hand to her chest. "I still cannot get used to that electricity." Ewan came to her and took her hands in his as he led her to the chapel center. He took the stone from his pocket and held the gem between them.

She touched the stone. "Must we give the stone back? I've worshiped the gem for so long."

Ewan bent and kissed her. "Aye, it belongs here with the others. Apart, they are strong, but together they are all-powerful." He stepped back, and when Lorelei moved her hand away, he took her hand and held her palm to the stone. "Together, my love, we always do things together."

She nodded as she held her side of the stone and Ewan's his. Ewan folded energy over itself inside him and the stone warmed. The stone's energy melded with his. The Stone of Faith heated and then lit a bright blue. Ewan added energy, and Lorelei added hers. Their magic merged and lifted the stone into the center of the chapel.

Ewan's gaze went to the window for faith, and as his focus traveled past her, he grinned, and she returned it. His power pushed the stone toward the window and the box beneath. The gem drifted and sat in the box, its energy releasing from Ewan.

Lorelei sighed and lowered her hand. "That's it?"

Ewan glanced at her and back at the box beneath the window as the container faded. "Aye, love. That's it. Another step toward our future together. Just the two of us." He took her hand in his and turned to the chapel door.

When he turned, Lorelei pulled back, stopping him. "Just the two of us?" She smiled, and her cheeks turned a delightful shade of pink. "What if there were three of us?" her hand moved to her belly.

Ewan gasped as her question hit him. "Ye are...ye mean..." he scooped her in his arms, "A baby?"

As he lowered her in his arms, he kissed her again and again. She beamed at him. "Yes, you, me, and baby make three."

Hearing *you, me, and baby* warmed his heart. Cast all doubt and have faith. Happily ever after, it was a perfect fit.

****

A few months later, Kat sat in the Chapel in the woods. She had to escape there after Ewan's wedding. They held a beautiful ceremony on the vessel he'd recently purchased and outfitted as a pirate ship, with Lorelei's family and friends in attendance.

The wedding was a grand affair, all meticulously arranged by Ewan's mother, but nothing could have prepared Kat for when Lorelei's sisters emerged from the loch. One blink—just one—and they stepped onto the shore, unnoticed by the gathering crowd. The water shimmered around them, their sea-slicked forms shifting into human beauty as easily as breathing. Merfolk made flesh—Fae royalty in satin.

Kat froze, breath caught in her throat, as the eleven sisters—Lorelei's sisters—glided forward like a painted dream. Each had long, flowing hair that shimmered with light and moved like silk underwater. Their smooth and porcelain-pale skin looked untouched by the sun or time. As they gathered around Lorelei, they looked like stars circling the moon.

She should have felt honored. She stood among them, after all—one of twelve bridesmaids. And she *was* proud. But that pride coiled uncomfortably inside her chest.

She glanced down at herself. Her pale blue dress—long and lovely—was one she had chosen and cherished. But it suddenly felt ordinary beside the Fae gowns of pastel organza satin. She reached up as if to smooth her hair, then let her hand fall. The freckles she usually liked about herself now felt like specks of dirt against the clean canvas of their skin. Her blonde hair, dull compared to their shimmering waves, seemed to have lost its shine just by standing near them. Still, she lifted her chin. She wouldn't shrink.

Ewan had laughed with delight when Lorelei squealed and threw her arms around her sisters. That joy was real. And Kat reminded herself—she had a place here, too. Not by blood. Not by sea or spell. But by choice. And she would stand tall, even if she was the only one who didn't glow. When Ewan glanced at her before Lorelei walked down the aisle, he'd winked at her, sending a mind message. *Thank ye, sister, for being here.*

Sister. The word sent her down memory lane and into her melancholy mood. The wedding made her think of her brother Doug again, back in the past. She always thought of him as alive now in the past and not as someone from the past who'd died. The image helped, but sometimes she missed him something awful.

Lorelei's family and friends had to depart before the reception was over. Something about returning home before a deadline—Kat took the chance to escape.

Energy filled the room, like before a Fae appeared. Kat stood and turned to the door when a gust of wind blew through the chapel, even though the door was closed.

She approached the wooden doors as a familiar voice spoke from behind her. "Nice dress, Kit Kat, but ye didn't have to dress up for my arrival."

Kat spun, and leaning on the altar was Ceallach, Aodhán's cousin from the Tuatha Dé Danann. His fit body filled out his incandescent shirt, and his pants hugged his well-muscled legs. His jet-black hair matched his mother's, Morrigan's—the MacArthur Fae shone in the light. He strode forward with a confidence and sensuality Kat had not forgotten from the first time she'd met him in the Fae realm at Evie's and Aodhán's wedding. The man still took her breath away with one look. He arrived before her with a smile on his face. When he glanced over her face, he frowned. Ceallach reached up and lifted a tear from her cheek with his finger.

He gripped his fist hard, and when he opened it, a small clear teardrop-shaped gemstone sat in his palm. "Dry ye tears, sweet Kat. Yer face is much prettier without them." He took her hand and placed the gemstone in her palm with his other hand. "When ye hold the gem, yer tears will fade, and happy thoughts shall fill yer head." When the stone touched her skin, her mind cleared, and a sense of goodness washed over her. Ceallach released her hand and moved past her to the doors.

Kat called after him. "Wait, why are ye here?"

Ceallach stopped and turned. "Dagda sent me. I've come to meet with the guardian of the stones. All the gems have returned. The gathering and battle of good vs evil is upon us. The gods have called, and we must answer."

A word about the author…

Margaret Izard is a multi-award-winning author of historical fantasy and paranormal romance novels. She spent her early years through college to adulthood dedicated to dance, theater, and performing. Over the years, she developed a love for great storytelling in different mediums. She does not waste a good story, be it movement, the spoken, or the written word. She discovered historical romance novels in middle school, which combined her passion for romance, drama, and fantasy. She writes exciting plot lines, steamy love scenes and always falls for a strong male with a soft heart. She lives in Houston, Texas, with her husband and adult triplets and loves to hear from readers.

You can email me at
info@margaretizardauthor.com
www.margaretizardauthor.com

Thank you for purchasing
this publication of The Wild Rose Press, Inc.

For questions or more information
contact us at
info@thewildrosepress.com.

The Wild Rose Press, Inc.
www.thewildrosepress.com